For Bob Burnett,
who could have been a '49er

WAYFARING STRANGERS

Tim Champlin

GUNSMOKE

First published in the US by Five Star

This hardback edition 2013
by AudioGO Ltd
by arrangement with
Golden West Literary Agency

ISBN 978 1 471 32107 8

British Library Cataloguing in Publication Data available.

Printed and bound in Great Britain by
MPG Books Group Limited

Acknowledgments

A salute to Joshua Slocum, Richard Henry Dana, Jr., Alan Villiers, Jack London, Herman Melville, and John Masefield, all of whom transformed personal experiences in sailing ships to enduring works of art.

And an admiring tip of the hat to the courage and tenacity of those '49ers who experienced this continent in all its rugged beauty before it was paved and malled. Thank you for leaving behind such graphic and literary accounts of your journeys.

Me-lun-geon, n. [?<Fr.*melange,* mixed; see 'melange'], a member of a dark-skinned people of mixed Caucasian and Indian stock, inhabiting the Tennessee mountains.

WEBSTER'S NEW WORLD DICTIONARY
of the American Language

Chapter One

East Tennessee Mountains

March 2, 1849

"Pull up, there!" Rob Merriman held up a hand and slitted his eyes against the blowing snow.

The buckboard driver drew his mule to a halt and swung up the twin barrels of a shotgun. "Who are *you*, mister? And what do you want?"

"You Deputy Sheriff Cyrus Hobgood?" Merriman called, raising his voice above the gusting wind. He kneed his horse closer to the wagon. His mount, along with a pack mule he was trailing on a long tether, effectively blocked the narrow road that was lined on both sides with heavy timber.

"Yeah, I'm Hobgood." The shotgun didn't waver.

"I'm Robert Merriman, deputy United States marshal from North Carolina, come to take charge of your prisoner," he lied, pointing at the other figure hunched over on the buckboard seat.

"Nobody told *me* about any marshal," the whip-thin lawman rasped. As if to emphasize his words, he shot a brown stream of tobacco juice to one side into the snow and wiped the white stubble around his mouth with a gloved hand.

"I was sent to escort one Clayburn Collins down to Asheville for trial on federal charges of counterfeiting,"

9

Merriman continued, tugging down his hat brim to further shield his face.

"That's where *I* was taking him," Hobgood said.

"Tried to get there before you left Sneedville, but the weather slowed me up," Merriman said apologetically. "Sheriff Fowler said I could probably catch up to you on the road." Merriman held his breath, praying his impersonation was convincing enough.

The animals' steaming breath was all that could be heard in the several long seconds of silence that followed.

"Lemme see your badge and papers," Hobgood finally said, lowering the scatter-gun.

Merriman's heart was pounding as he dismounted, reaching inside his coat. He'd heard from two Sneedville natives in the hotel dining room the night before that Hobgood, a cousin of the sheriff, could barely read his own name. Merriman stepped up to the driver's side and handed over an official-looking document he hoped would dupe the illiterate man. As Hobgood took the paper—actually a bill of sale for Merriman's mule—Merriman slid his other hand inside his coat to the butt of his Patterson Colt, just in case the ruse failed.

The lawman appeared to study the paper for a few seconds. Before he could speak, Merriman said: "Here, I need to sign the bottom of that as a receipt, showing I accepted custody." He pulled out a short pencil and put the paper on the footboard of the wagon to scrawl an illegible signature. He handed the damp document back to Hobgood, who carefully folded and tucked it into his coat pocket without further inspection.

"Here's my badge," Merriman continued smoothly, pulling out a silver star with the words "Deputy United States Marshal" stamped in a circle around its outer rim.

The badge was the only authentic thing about this whole charade, Merriman thought. It had been made in the Nashville silversmithing shop of Chad Merriman, Rob's father, as a keepsake for a retired marshal, but the man died before the star could be redeemed.

Hobgood looked at the badge and grunted, apparently satisfied.

"Get off that wagon, Collins, and climb up on that pack mule," Merriman ordered, hoping his friend would have the sense to keep silent. The man addressed, whose hands were bound in front of him, awkwardly jumped down off the opposite side of the buckboard into the four-inch deep snow.

"I guess you'll be wanting to get on back home, have a slug of hot coffee, and thaw out," Merriman remarked over his shoulder as he helped Collins mount the mule.

"Hell, I'm too far along to make it back up the mountain afore dark," Hobgood said. "I'll just head on down to the Sizemore Inn to spend the night."

Merriman's heart sank at this, since the two of them would have to travel the same road. But he affected a casual attitude. "We'll likely travel faster, but we might see you there," he said with a wave as he mounted up, took the mule's lead, and pulled his horse's head around. "Hang on!" he called to his prisoner as he kicked the horse into a gallop.

He kept up this pace for a half mile, then slowed to a fast trot for another mile, then to a walk. They had rounded several curves on the downslope of the heavily wooded mountainside and, Merriman hoped, had far outdistanced the buckboard. He turned and brought his mount alongside the pack mule. "Damned good to see you, Clay," he said, reaching out and slicing the rawhide thongs that bound Collins's hands.

"That goes double for me," the smaller, dark-skinned man said, rubbing his cold-stiffened hands and wrists. He removed his hat and wiped a sleeve across his face. The thick, black hair had not been cut for weeks, Merriman noted, but the green eyes still glowed with intensity, even in the shadowless, subdued light of the snowy day. "But what are you doing here?" Collins asked.

"I heard there was an ugly Melungeon up here in jail without any friends," he grinned.

Collins shook his head in appreciative wonder.

"You had anything to eat today?"

"Some coffee before daylight."

"I've got some grub in my pack there, but not much. We'd better save it for later. How far is this Sizemore Inn?"

"Near the base of Short Mountain. Not far from the Holston River."

Not being familiar with this part of Tennessee, Merriman had no idea how far that was. "We'll get some food there and carry it with us. I don't much relish spending the night under the same roof with that deputy. He's liable to get wise to me. Do you know any short cuts to save time?"

Collins shook his head. "Not really. In this snow, we'd best stay on the road."

"Let's go, then. You lead the way, since you know the road."

They shifted the pack on the mule so Collins would have a more comfortable seat, then started off again at a fast trot. Merriman had trouble keeping up with him and felt his horse's hoofs slip several times in the deepening snow on the steeper slopes. It was just after midday, but a false twilight seemed to settle over the wooded mountains.

Collins, in the lead, finally slowed his mule to a walk,

and mile after mile passed under their animals' hoofs as the gray day wore on and the snow continued to swirl down from the leaden sky. Except for rising and falling in elevation, the road never varied and the thick forest of bare oaks, maples, elms speckled with stunted cedars unwound in endless panorama alongside them. At one stretch the road began to rise in a series of switchbacks, always trending up, and still up, as the animals labored through the dry snow that was at least a foot deep on the higher slopes.

Now that the rescue of Collins was accomplished, Merriman began to realize that he had run afoul of the law for the first time in his life. Was his six-year friendship with Clayburn Collins really worth the risk? After all, Collins *was* guilty of engraving the dies for counterfeit Spanish pieces-of-eight. The letter from Collins's sister, Laura, had said as much. But Merriman knew of no other way to rescue his artistic friend from a long prison term at hard labor that would probably kill him. A terse note from Collins, smuggled out of his cell and included with the letter, indicated that just before his arrest he'd discovered a small vein of gold in a remote mountain valley. Merriman didn't want to think that a desire to share in the gold had been the deciding factor in him resigning his boring job at a Nashville bank to rush to Collins's aid.

Just as Merriman was on the verge of yelling to Collins to stop for a few minutes, the road leveled out and then began a steep descent. After about two miles of this, Collins reined up at the bottom of the grade, and the two of them dismounted to stretch their stiffened limbs and let the animals drink from a small stream they had to ford. The clear water gurgled over the rocks, and the animals' hoofs crunched the rim of ice that had formed along the quieter edges of the swift stream.

"I believe this is Poor Valley Creek," Collins said. "Been over this way a couple of times, but all this snow makes everything look different."

Merriman squinted at his surroundings, trying to picture this place about three months hence—mountain laurel, splashes of white and pink dogwood against a background of scattered cedar and leafy hardwoods, the earthy smells of rotting logs and fresh pine resin. But now winter had locked all that away. Even the sun was hiding, giving no clue as to directions.

"I'm completely turned around. Hardly know which way is up."

"That way," Collins said, pointing at the gray sky and grinning, white teeth flashing briefly in the dark face. The sight cheered Merriman. It was a smile he suspected no one had seen for some while.

They took a long drink from the canteen Merriman carried on his saddle horn. Then Merriman stepped upstream a few feet, rinsed the canteen, and filled it with cold, clear water. The drink had stimulated his gastric juices and sharp pangs of hunger began gnawing at him. But he said nothing. He suspected Collins was feeling it, too. He stood for a minute or so, listening to the enveloping silence of the winter woods. Other than the quiet shuffling of his animals, the only sound was the whisper of grainy snow sifting down through the dry leaves that still clung stubbornly to a few of the trees around them.

"How much farther?"

"Maybe another couple of hours. We should be there by dark."

The thought of only grabbing a quick bite of food and then riding off to camp somewhere in the snow began to seem like a bad idea. As tired as he was, he could imagine how Collins must feel. The Melungeon's face was pinched and drawn, and he was much leaner than Merriman remembered him.

He made a quick decision to stop at the inn and get a few hours of sleep in a warm, sheltered place. He'd just have to take his chances with Hobgood.

After Merriman's hands and toes began to pain with returning circulation, and the animals had rested, they climbed up and started again.

It seemed a long afternoon, and Merriman began to wonder if Collins's estimate of the distance had been faulty. By the time the short March day was fading into darkness, they were plowing through unbroken snow at least eighteen inches deep, and Merriman was glad they'd gotten over the ridge earlier. He wondered again where Deputy Hobgood might be. Just then they rounded a bend in the road, and he caught the welcome sight of yellow lamplight pouring from the windows of a stout log house a hundred yards ahead through the swirling snow.

Chapter Two

Collins knew he hadn't been asleep nearly long enough, when he was awakened by several loud thumps. His eyes flew open in the blackness, and he heard Merriman rolling softly out of the other narrow bed. The banging sounded again, and Collins turned over in the soft, downy tick to see a sliver of light as Merriman opened their bedroom door a crack. By the dim light of the coal-oil lamp in the hallway, he saw his rescuer crouched in his long johns, pistol in hand, looking out. The pounding came again, louder and more persistent from the front of the building.

"I'm coming! I'm coming! Don't break the door down!" Madeline Sizemore called. Collins saw the buxom innkeeper sweep past their partially open door in her long robe, lighted lamp in hand.

"Who's pounding on my door at this time o' night?" Mrs. Sizemore cried.

Collins heard a muffled reply from without, then the sound of the bar being slid back, and the door opening. He sprang out of bed into the cold room and looked past Merriman's shoulder. In the light of the landlady's lamp, he saw a haggard-looking Cyrus Hobgood stamping snow off his boots on a mat just inside the front door. Collins shivered at the sight of the lawman.

"I need hot food and a room for the night," the deputy demanded in a strained voice.

"That may be what you need, but there's no food served at this hour," Madeline Sizemore retorted sharply. "Breakfast will start at six . . . five hours from now. The coffee pot's still warm on the cookstove. Help yourself to a cup, then take your things to room number four . . . second door on your right down the hall."

"Where can I get . . . ?" Hobgood began in a tired voice.

"I'm not standing here freezin' in m' nightgown at this hour to be quizzed," Mrs. Sizemore cut him off, sliding the bar back in place across the door. "I'm going back to bed."

"Lady, I'm a deputy sheriff from Sneedville and you *will* answer my questions."

"Be glad to at breakfast time," she replied, unflustered, walking away with the lamp and leaving him standing in the dark. "Put your animal up in the barn," she said over her shoulder.

Merriman quietly closed the door of their room and turned the key in the lock. Collins heard him chuckle in the blackness. "Get some sleep," he whispered. "He won't bother us till morning. I think he's more tuckered out than we are, but I'll sleep with my gun under my pillow just in case."

When Collins woke again, he had slept so soundly it took several seconds for his memory to reconnect him to time and place. Then the pieces came together, and he recalled he was safe and warm and dry in a small room of the Sizemore Inn. He cracked his eyelids. Pale light filtered through a muslin curtain covering a nearby window pane and illuminating the whitewashed chinking between red cedar logs. It was very quiet, and he felt lethargic. The silence and the subdued light made him wonder if it might still be snowing. He heard a stirring and looked across at Merriman sitting up on the edge of his bunk, reaching for his pants.

" 'Morning."

"Ready to face Hobgood?" Merriman asked.

"Not really."

Merriman grinned. "The horse and mule are in the stable, and I paid extra for some grain. As soon as we get a good breakfast, we'll be on the road south and east, out of these mountains." He pulled on his boots and stood up. "We better go out there together, so he'll be convinced you're my prisoner."

Collins stretched and groaned wearily at his aching shoulder and back muscles. He knew, from the way he felt, it would take much more than one good meal and one good night's rest to restore his strength and stamina. Three weeks in the county jail with little food and no exercise had taken their toll, along with his flight in the intense cold. Yet he knew he'd been given a respite. He'd received, like manna, only what he needed to go on for another day. No use wishing for the perfect situation, he thought as he stepped to the window and pulled aside the curtain. The sky was still overcast, but the day was lighter and it had stopped snowing. Wind whirled powdery snow off the roof, and a white blanket lay at least two feet deep on the level, deeper where it had drifted against the building. The window framed a picture he wished he had the opportunity to paint. But no—there was too much white—no contrast except the dark line of trees at the far end of the open field. A winter scene needed a focal point, such as this log inn set in the snow-covered hills and trees.

He ran his fingers through his thick hair and shivered at the thought of going out into that winter weather again. Brought up in the Appalachian Mountains, he'd always hated snow and ice. But this storm seemed to compare to the great blizzards on the plains that travelers talked about. At least, it would lock away the tiny vein of quartz gold he'd stumbled upon. It was in such a remote area of the mountains, he hoped he'd be able to find it again once the weather broke. It probably wasn't extensive, but he'd had no time to probe it further before his arrest when he'd returned to town for supplies.

He turned away from the window and finished buttoning his shirt. "I'm ready. By the way," he added as Merriman started to open the door, "Missus Sizemore and her daughter are Melungeons, like me, but don't let them in on this. I'd rather they not think I'm a prisoner."

Merriman nodded his agreement. "Unless Hobgood blows it."

Collins knew that the middle-aged wife of the innkeeper had recognized him as one of their own people. Probably because of this, she and her grown daughter, Lisa, had been very talkative, questioning the two men about the weather, road conditions, happenings around Sneedville and Newman's Ridge. Over steaming bowls of venison stew and mulled cider the night before, the two men had easily answered most of their questions, while leaving the impression of being two friends traveling to North Carolina on business. Madeline Sizemore had indicated that her husband, Vincent, was on a trip to Knoxville, and had likely become snowbound.

They opened the door and went down the hallway to the main dining room. Pans rattled in the adjacent kitchen, and a delicious smell of frying bacon drifted into the warm room. Someone had been up early, and the fire on the hearth was blazing.

Luckily the dining room was empty. "Our friend, Hobgood, is sleeping late," Merriman muttered under his breath. They sat at the table, facing the hearth and the hallway, so they could see him as soon as he came out of his room. Collins felt he needed some coffee and food to stimulate his sluggish thought processes. He still wasn't fully back from his deep sleep.

"Ah, Mister Collins, I hope you slept well," Lisa Sizemore remarked airily as she swept into the room with a platter of flapjacks and a pitcher of syrup.

"The name is Clay," he said absently, completely distracted by her youthful freshness.

She flashed him a smile as she set the food on the table. "Clay it is, then."

"Yes, thanks. I slept like a hunk of stove wood," he said, his artist's eye marveling at the clear, olive skin, the black eyelashes and arching brows, and the hair the color of a crow's wing, swept back and hanging from a single braid. She'd been only a skinny girl of about fourteen when he'd last stopped at this inn some seven or eight years before. She didn't remember him, and he felt it better not to enlighten her.

Madeline Sizemore came out with a huge platter of fried ham, bacon, and grits. She didn't appear as bright as her daughter, Collins noted. Dark circles under her eyes hinted at a sleepless night.

He dug into the food with gusto, washing it down with black coffee, sweetened with honey.

Just as they were finishing up, about a half hour later, Hobgood emerged from the hallway. He stopped short as he spied the two men at the table. "Didn't know you were spending the night here, too," he said, pulling out a chair and sitting down. His eyes were puffy from heavy sleep. Hobgood looked at Collins who was finishing a cup of coffee. "Hell, you don't even have any manacles on him. He could run off in a second."

"No, he won't," Merriman replied, sliding his Colt

Patterson out and laying it on the table next to his plate.

Collins was thankful that neither Mrs. Sizemore nor her daughter was in the room to hear this exchange. Several minutes later, he got up from the table and wandered over to the hearth where he picked up a small piece of charcoal from the bricks. "Lisa, have you got a sheet of paper I could use?" he inquired courteously of the young woman who had entered the room.

She set the coffee pot down and smiled at him. "I think I can find one for you," she said.

"I'd like to sketch you."

"What?" She paused.

"I'm an artist. I'll draw your likeness, if you want me to."

She thought for a moment. "Just a minute." She swept off down the hall. She reappeared shortly and handed him a white sheet of paper about nine by twelve inches. "I cut a page from my diary," she said in a low voice.

Collins turned to her. "Stand over there near the doorway where the light can fall on you." He took the paper and charcoal and sat down at the table.

Lisa flushed self-consciously and glanced at her mother who was washing dishes in a small tub in the kitchen. But then she slipped the apron off over her head and stood up proudly by the doorway, posing in the tight-bodiced dress that pinched in at the waist and then flared out in full pleats to the floor.

She needn't have bothered, Collins thought, since he was only doing a bust. He was at the end of the long table, and, sketching and shading deftly with the charred wood and his fingertips, he had a flattering likeness rendered in black and white in less than ten minutes. "That's about it," he said, giving it a final touch.

"Oh, let me see!"

He handed her the sketch.

"Oh, it's beautiful! You are so talented."

It was his turn to look flustered. "It's yours, if you want it."

"Thank you. Oh, look at this, Momma!" She hurried into the kitchen.

Collins could tell that Merriman didn't want to give the appearance of being in a hurry as he lingered over an extra biscuit and more coffee, before he sent Collins to the room to collect the saddlebags. Then Merriman went into the kitchen, and Collins could hear him talking in a low voice to Madeline Sizemore for several minutes.

"Get your coat," Merriman said, coming back into the dining room, carrying a bulging cotton sack.

"Here, I think you might need this," Lisa Sizemore said, coming up to Collins and holding out a maroon wool scarf and a black felt hat with a low crown and a wide brim. "These are Daddy's, but he never wears them any more."

"Thank you." On a sudden impulse, he leaned forward, put an arm around her shoulders, and kissed her on the cheek. Her olive skin flushed darker as a look of confused pleasure overcame her.

"Will I ever see you again?" she asked in a low voice, her dark eyes giving him a look of intense interest.

"I doubt we'll pass this way again," Collins said with a tone of regret. "Under the circumstances."

They wrapped up against the weather and started out the door as Hobgood sat, eating and staring at them. Surely that look of suspicion Collins thought he noticed was only in his own imagination.

With a regretful backward glance at the lovely Lisa, Collins closed the door and followed Merriman to the stable where they hurriedly saddled the horse and the mule.

22

"Just a minute," Collins said, and began looking around until he found the harness for Hobgood's mule hanging on a peg. He hooked it over his shoulder and climbed the ladder to the hayloft where he buried it out of sight under a pile of hay.

"That might slow him down some, in case he catches on," he said, climbing down and brushing himself off. "Better than busting some spokes out of a wheel. He might make the Sizemore women pay for that."

"He may have to ride that mule bareback," Merriman said.

"Not a happy prospect for either of them," Collins added.

They looked at each other and burst out laughing as they mounted up and rode out into the blinding white world.

Merriman's horse was having a tough time breaking trail in the deep, unmarked snow of the road, and Merriman didn't push him. "I bought a tow sack of food from Madeline Sizemore," Merriman said. "A loaf of bread, a few slices of ham, some cornmeal, salt, a skillet, and some other stuff. But, even better than all that, she drew me a map of where this road leads and how to get on down out of the mountains." He paused. "Sure wish we were holed up by your gold vein while we wait for the snow to melt."

"Me, too. It's miles from anywhere and heavily wooded. I doubt anybody would find us there. But for now, where're we headed?" Collins asked, suddenly realizing they had no destination in mind.

"Well, whenever the law gets the alarm, I'm guessing they'll figure we'll head for Nashville since that's familiar territory." He looked across at Collins. "Thought I might try to confuse them and cut down toward Charleston on the coast."

"Charleston?"

"Yeah. Unless you've got some other ideas."

"No, that's as good as any, I guess. Easier to lose myself in a good-size town until all this blows over and they quit looking for us. We can always come back this summer and find that vein again. The way you flummoxed Hobgood will sting his pride good. And only pride would make him or the sheriff come after us in this kind of weather."

"That's why I figure to get at least a couple days' head start. But we've got a powerful lot of mountains and valleys to cross before we get down into the lowlands of South Carolina. It's not going to be easy."

As Collins glanced at the deep snow and the silent, wooded hills that stretched away in all directions, he thought that Merriman probably spoke more of the truth than he really knew.

Chapter Three

Collins thought the next three weeks were as difficult as any
he'd ever endured. He'd been through some hard times in the
mountains, and in his first days in Nashville, and then after his
arrest. If he had known what was coming, he seriously wondered if a term in prison might have been easier. They camped
out in the snow, using a couple of blankets bought from the
inn. They shivered by windbreaks in front of campfires in the
deep woods—Merriman's loaded Colt handy in case of surprise visitors—slept on pine boughs to keep them out of the
wet snow when it began to thaw. They avoided the small ham-
lets the road passed through, swinging wide through the
woods. Only twice did they accidentally encounter farmers in
wagons on the roads, and once a man out hunting. But, even
though they were strangers in the area, and drew some curious
stares, they were not accosted as they passed by.

The weather broke after four days, and a pale sun combined with a south wind began melting the snow. But the
slush and mire this produced was probably worse than
dealing with the deep snow, Collins thought ruefully.

"Man's present situation is always the worst that's ever
been," Collins remarked philosophically, when Merriman
began grousing about it as they sat around a small campfire
one night, feeling wet and miserable.

"I guess you're right," Merriman said. "We've got a
whole heap to be thankful for."

"Right you are." Then Collins grinned. "After I got over
the shock of actually seeing you appear on the road, I could

hardly keep from laughing when you signed that bill of sale. It's probably the only time in my life I'll ever be traded for the paperwork on a mule."

"I don't know what I would have done if that bluff hadn't worked."

A twig snapped in the darkness beyond their firelight. Merriman reached for his holstered pistol that lay nearby.

"Keep your hands where they are!" a sharp voice commanded.

Collins heard some crunching steps in the undergrowth, and Cyrus Hobgood stepped into view, holding his double-barreled shotgun at waist level. The lean lawman was haggard and unshaven, a short white beard covering his flat cheeks. The trail had obviously been hard on him as well. His black eyes looked like obsidian in the firelight.

"Thought you'd pull one over on me, did ya?" Hobgood grated. "Laughing behind my back, huh? Well, we'll see who laughs now. Don't *nobody* knows these mountains like I do. I ain't had much book learnin', but Cyrus Hobgood ain't nobody's fool. Thought you could sucker me, did ya, you damn' city dude! I'll show you!" His face contorted with fury, and he swung the shotgun toward the coffee pot on the small fire. A blast of flame and smoke spurted from one barrel, and the coffee pot exploded in a steaming spray. But the tiny fire was also blown into a shower of sparks, throwing the campsite into sudden darkness.

Instantly reacting, Collins dove for the deputy, tackling him up under both arms and driving him backward. Collins heard the rush of air go out of him as they landed hard on the ground. But Hobgood still tried to club him on the back of the head with the butt of the shotgun. Collins felt the stock hit him in the back, and the second barrel discharged with a roar that nearly deafened him.

"Hold it right there, Hobgood!" Merriman's voice snapped, close by, and Collins heard the double click of the Patterson Colt as it was cocked next to the lawman's head. "Get that fire stirred up again," Merriman said.

Collins jumped up and fumbled in the dark for the small pile of dry sticks they'd stacked near their fire ring. Blowing on the remaining coals, he soon had a blaze going again.

"You couldn't have caught up with us on foot," Merriman said. "Where's your mule and buckboard?"

Hobgood said nothing as he rubbed his ribs and glared at them.

"Never mind. We'll find it."

Using the deputy's suspenders, they tied him to a small tree and threw a blanket over him to ward off the damp chill. For the rest of the night, they took turns standing guard. "I don't think he can get himself loose," Merriman said quietly, "but we've got to be sure he came alone. Can't take a chance on being surprised again."

The rest of the night passed uneventfully. With the coming of dawn, Merriman, who had the last watch, went searching, swinging in wide circles around their wooded camp. He found Hobgood's mule picketed in a draw about a quarter mile away, and brought him into camp.

The two men moved off to one side and conferred on how to deal with the lawman. To keep from adding the crimes of horse-stealing or kidnapping to the charge of jail-break and impersonating a U.S. marshal, they decided to lead the mule down the road and hobble him where there was decent grass and water.

"Hobgood," Collins said, as he and Merriman mounted up, "we're leaving that mule's saddle here with you. I guess you got that from the Sizemore place. You can play a game of 'find the mule.' He'll be a few miles from here, waiting for you. Sorry we can't leave you any food, but we need it, and there's plenty of melted snow around here to drink. Come to think of it, you weren't real generous with the grub when I was in your jail, so I can't worry too much about your belly growling."

"Let's hope this is the last time we meet," Merriman added. "The shotgun will be near the mule if, or when, you catch up with him."

They rode out through the woods, angling roughly downhill toward the rising sun, leading the mule. After leaving the mule picketed in a meadow about six miles away, they continued traveling as fast as they could.

For the next several days, Collins found himself continually watching their back trail. If Hobgood had done nothing else, he had let them know they could not yet consider themselves safe from pursuit. They went without bathing and shaving, and their meager supply of food dwindled rapidly. Their dialogue became snappish, with longer intervals between comments. Eventually conversation faltered and ceased altogether, each man sinking into his own misery to deal with the cold and wet and an aching belly as best he could. Day after day they followed first one road and then another, sometimes having to detour several miles out of their way to follow a long ridge top, but always trending toward the south and east. Now and then they would spot the snug log cabin of a farmstead at the head of some remote cove, smoke curling invitingly from its chimney. But they took pains to avoid such places. The longer they could stay away from human contact, Merriman said, the harder they would be to follow.

Then cold rain began, and several nights were spent in the woods with no fire, each of them sleeping on a saturated bed of leaf mold. Collins developed a bad case of catarrh, and his breathing was so impaired by swollen nasal passages he couldn't sleep. When he finally did pass out from exhaustion, he woke two hours later with his mouth ajar and his throat dry as parchment. Part of the time he felt feverish.

It was during these times, when he was feeling mentally and physically drained, when he had no reserves left, that he often pondered his reasons for leaving Nashville to return to the mountains six months ago. His pay had been good, and he'd found satisfaction in his work, and in the painting and drawing he'd done on his own time. So, why had he left Chadwick Merriman's established silversmithing business? Was it the loneliness of being a stranger among people who shunned him as a half-breed curiosity? The pull of blood was strong, he had discovered; the desire to mingle once again with his own kind could not be resisted. Yet, in spite of all the reasons he'd given himself, deep inside Collins understood that the human animal could endure only so much of a good thing. Then a person had to squirm out of his comfortable situation—just *had* to make some change that would cause pain or turmoil or bring some calamity down on his own head. It was the nature of the beast. God certainly knew what He was doing when He never let things go on too good for too long. Collins had always wondered how man could be content with heaven if he were ever to reach it.

As they passed slowly down out of the mountains, they encountered roads nearly impassable with mud in the valleys and coves. Then they were forced to take to the trees and wind their way along, parallel to the trace, to avoid sinking into the black quagmire. At each of the swollen streams, Merriman stopped to wash off the legs and flanks of the glossy black horse and the mule to prevent what he called "mud fever."

"If the animals get too caked up with mud, their pores get clogged, and they can't sweat. If they can't sweat and cool down that way, their temperature shoots up and they'll die," Merriman told Collins.

The food they'd brought from Sizemore's Inn had been rationed, but the time came all too soon when they chewed the last moldy crust of bread and, for the next two days, had nothing but cold creek water to sustain them. The animals foraged on sheltered patches of grass, mostly brown, that still retained some nourishment, but they, too, grew lean. Merriman took the chance of slipping into a farmer's barn before daylight one morning and appropriated two buckets of oats, leaving a silver dollar in payment.

"I think we're finally out of the mountains," Collins said, more than a week later, as they rode along, their mounts' hoofs sucking at the soft muck of the road. "See how the soil here is kind of a sandy loam? It's like this all the way to the sea, only sandier."

"How do *you* know *that?*" Merriman asked, sounding more than a little irritated. Neither of them had spoken for the last ten miles.

"My parents took me to Savannah once, when I was a boy. They didn't like it and came back to the mountains and our own people," Collins replied, with the dullness of fatigue that didn't even recognize his friend's rancor.

They were passing a thick stand of straight, tall pines, and suddenly Merriman reined up, looking intently at a spot about forty yards away along the edge of the trees.

"What's wrong?"

"Shhh!" Merriman unholstered his Patterson and checked to be sure it was capped.

Collins followed his gaze and saw two deer standing perfectly still, nearly blending with the dull-brown tree trunks.

Merriman dismounted quietly and carefully, sliding around the side of the Morgan. One of the deer, sporting spike antlers, had its head turned in their direction, and the other presented a side to them, apparently watching with its left eye. Merriman crept forward, holding the pistol in front of him, hammer back to full cock.

Collins admired the beautiful picture they made, perfectly formed, wild and trembling on the verge of flight, liquid brown eyes unblinking.

Merriman very deliberately raised the Colt to take aim.

Collins flinched involuntarily, and the mule started forward with a couple of quick steps. He heard the explosion of the shot. When he looked, two tails were up and flashing white as the animals bounded away among the trees to safety.

"Damn!" Merriman snapped. "What d'ya think you're doing?" He jammed the long-barreled pistol into its holster with a look of disgust.

"The mule jumped," Collins said.

"I'd think you would make an effort to stay still for a few seconds. We could sure use some fresh meat," he said, walking back and slipping his foot into the stirrup. "Hell, we haven't eaten anything but a couple bites of corn meal mush in two days."

"We'll find something else," Collins said in a dull voice. "They were too innocent and beautiful to kill, anyway."

"If I remember right, you ate three bowls of venison stew back at Sizemore's place."

"I didn't have to see that one killed."

"Well, some wildcat or wolves will probably drag 'em down, or they'll die of disease. It's the way nature works. I could have given them a quick, merciful death."

"Not with that Thirty-Six caliber, unless you're a mighty

31

good pistol shot. He would've just run off and died in the woods of a festering wound."

Merriman shook his head and didn't reply.

The landscape began to take on a somber look with tall trees festooned with Spanish moss. A chill dampness clung to everything. They rode mostly in silence for the next four hours, conversing only to share a drink of water from the canteen. Collins knew Merriman was probably beginning to question his own actions for breaking him away from the law. *Probably thinks he rescued a totally unreasonable man who deserved whatever the court would have given him,* he reflected. "You think I had it coming?" he asked aloud.

"What?"

"Prison."

Merriman glanced sideways at him. "Maybe . . . according to the letter of the law," he replied slowly. "But a man has to decide for himself what's right and what's fair."

Collins let that ride for a minute in silence. "Before we go any farther, I just want to thank you for what you did."

"I'd do it again in a minute," Merriman replied quickly and firmly.

Collins took comfort in the answer. "Even if you'd known I was guilty?" he persisted.

"Laura told me in her letter."

"Sometimes my sister is a little loose with family secrets."

"If she hadn't written, I wouldn't be here," Merriman said simply. "But she didn't give much detail."

Collins was silent for several seconds, recalling the pain. "When I came back to the mountains after six years, I thought I was coming home," he said. "Except for my mother and sister, most Melungeons treated me like an outsider. I was different . . . the way I dressed, my way of talking, the fact that I could now read and write. I'd betrayed them and gone to the big city." He shrugged. "I couldn't get a job to help support my mother. I was chopping firewood for food money, when a cousin, Jeremiah Gibson, gave me a chance to make some money. He was refining some silver from a pretty good deposit back in the mountains and wanted to make some Spanish dollars. But he needed someone to carve the dies for him. He knew I was an engraver, so. . . ." He paused. "I knew it was illegal, but I was desperate for money. And I was proud of my skill. But only a month later I was arrested, just after I stumbled on that little gold deposit. Gibson got away into the back country. I had a feeling one of my own kin turned us in." He smiled. "You know, it was ironic, but some of our coins the law tested contained more silver than the real pieces-of-eight."

"Well, we both know there's never enough coinage in circulation. That's one reason those Spanish dollars are so popular in this country," Merriman said. "As far as I'm concerned, you and your cousin were doing everyone a favor."

"Yeah. Just like the Bechtler family. They've been minting gold coins of their own design over in North Carolina for twenty years."

"The only difference is, they're doing it with the approval of the United States Treasury." Merriman grinned.

"I've found out, just lately, that there is really no law against an individual minting coins of his own design," Collins said. "Wish I'd known that earlier. I could have come up with something more artistic than that Spanish coin."

"But you probably couldn't have pushed them as easily," Merriman said.

They were just coming up to a white board fence that stretched a half mile ahead of them along the road. It enclosed a large farm or ranch of some kind. Off in the level distance were scattered groves of tall pines that gave way to thicker brush and what was probably swampy lowland. In the open pasture nearer the buildings, horses grazed peacefully on some clumps and patches of grass. Several minutes later, a white house and some outbuildings came into view.

As they approached, the house materialized into a large, white frame structure, one story in height with a peaked roof and chestnut shingles. Enclosing the house on all four sides was a deep porch, its slanted roof supported by wooden posts.

Merriman reined up and gazed at the layout. "I think it's time we stopped and asked directions," he said. "And buy a little food."

"I'll be your half-breed lackey," Collins grinned, pulling the mule in behind as Merriman kneed his horse through the arched gateway.

Chapter Four

Rob Merriman looked across at Collins as they rode, side by side, down a hard-packed road under a canopy of trees. Another seventy miles to Charleston, the rancher had told them. He doubted Collins had the stamina to make it without pausing for a day or two of food and rest. The rancher had refused their request to buy food, saying he had none to spare. Collins's dirty wool coat hung on his shoulders, and he slumped in the saddle. He had already endured three weeks of jail with little food when they'd started on this arduous flight. But then Merriman had underestimated the smaller man in the past.

"That rancher said there was an inn up ahead about ten more miles. Why don't we stop for the night and get cleaned up?" he suggested casually. "I don't know about you, but I'm tired."

Collins straightened up and glanced at him. "You think it's safe? I keep wanting to look behind to see who's on our trail. I don't mean Hobgood, but somebody they might've gotten word to. Hate to think we've twisted and turned all this way just to have the law come down on us as soon as we let our guard down."

"Just your nerves," Merriman said lightly. "We must've traveled a couple hundred miles on a route even a bloodhound couldn't follow. I need a bath and some place to sleep that's warm and dry. Don't worry about money. I've still got most of what I brought from Nashville, even after buying a couple of feedbags and some oats back there." He was secretly glad Collins was riding the pack mule that was more stolid and sure-footed than his stallion. Collins was never a good horseman, even when he'd lived in Nashville. He had grown up too poor to own a horse, and most of his boyhood had been spent afoot in the mountains.

"I'd like nothing better than to sleep without one eye open."

"Good . . . then, it's settled. We'll stop at the next inn," Merriman said.

They rode in silence for several minutes. Then Collins said: "When do you have to be back to your job at the bank?"

"Never. I quit."

"What?" This news seemed to shock Collins out of his lethargy. "Why?"

Merriman chuckled at the stunned look on his face. "Been looking for an excuse to get away from there. And I think they were as glad to see me go. I was never cut out to be a banker, anyway. Not my kind of people. Too stuffy and conservative."

"What will you do now?"

"Try to make sure the law doesn't lay its clutches on the both of us."

"You know what I mean."

"Haven't given it a thought," Merriman replied. "Something will turn up. I didn't know what I'd run into when I started east, so I emptied my bank account, just in case. Now I'm glad I did. If I'm careful, I've got enough to see us through for a few months." He looked at Collins who was again slumped in his saddle. "Don't worry. Just focus on that gold vein." He spread his hands. "Can't you see it hiding under all that underbrush, just a bit of it peeking out of the rock strata with a nice warm glow, waiting for you to come back and rescue it?"

"You've seen it, have you?" Collins grinned at him.

"I can imagine it, just from what you told me. Something to dream about while we lie low for a few weeks in Charleston or maybe down in Savannah . . . someplace like that. You didn't do anything so terrible that the law will move heaven and earth to track you down."

"No, but *you* did. Impersonating a federal agent and stealing a prisoner."

"Let me worry about that."

The day continued chill and dreary, and by late afternoon they reined in at the Stanhope Inn, stabled their animals, and put up for the night. There were eight other travelers eating in the dining room that evening. But nobody looked twice at two road-weary, dirty travelers. Even Collins's darker skin went unremarked, apparently because most of his face was covered by a short, black beard, and what could be seen of his skin was grimy. His green eyes gave him the appearance of a very dirty, dark-complexioned white man.

Merriman had caught sight of himself and Collins in a mirror behind the front desk when they registered. He was startled by the weathered image that stared back at him. He didn't recognize his own reflection. It was no wonder the owner of the horse ranch had looked at them suspiciously when they'd stopped for directions. Slouch hats, unkempt hair and beards, smelling of woodsmoke and old sweat, they could have easily passed for highwaymen.

After a good supper of grilled steak, potatoes, stewed tomatoes, and bread, washed down with locally made Blackwater Ale, Merriman ordered a metal tub brought to their room. They took turns soaking in hot water carried from the kitchen by Negro slaves. They didn't attempt to wash their clothes, fearing the ragged garments wouldn't be dry by morning.

Despite the reckless attitude he displayed to Collins—

and to himself—Merriman realized he'd been a lot more wary and tense than he knew. The hot bath, along with the feeling that they were probably in a safe haven for the night, caused him to relax, and a great weariness overtook him. He slid between clean sheets for the first time in weeks, and slept a solid ten hours.

The next morning, after another filling meal of flapjacks, corn mush, and sidemeat, they set off for Charleston, making the last forty miles by evening without incident. The food and rest, along with a relatively warm sun, cheered them on the last leg of their journey. Merriman, sensing that it was going to take several more days of food and rest to bring Collins back to his old self, suggested checking into a hotel in the heart of the town under assumed names, then buying some new clothes, eating another good meal, and going to bed.

"I'm agreeable to the first two, but not the last." Collins grinned at Merriman's proposals. "As soon as we get cleaned up, I'm for a few drinks," he continued. "Let's celebrate. If they were after us, I'm sure they've given up by now. If anything, they'll just put out some flyers describing two wanted men. Even if some of those handbills turn up here, there're hundreds of those things posted around, for outlaws and escaped slaves. Nobody pays any attention to them."

Merriman looked at Collins as they dismounted and went into a hotel near the Charleston waterfront. Perhaps Merriman had done too good a job of convincing his companion that they were safe from pursuit. But he had to admit that Collins was probably right.

As soon as they stashed their saddlebags in the small room, they went back out, found a barber shop, got three weeks of beards shaved, and their hair cut. Then they located a general store that was about to close and purchased new clothing, including boots, tan canvas pants, white cotton shirts. Merriman bought a lightweight wool, navy blue waistcoat, and Collins a shorter black one. Their dirty outer woolen coats they deposited with a pair of down-and-outers who were slouched in a doorway, sharing a bottle. The men gave them bleary-eyed looks, but said nothing.

"Hell, I feel like a new man!" Collins said as they walked off down the sidewalk.

Merriman couldn't believe the change in demeanor from the day before. If he didn't know Collins better, he'd swear he was drunk. But he'd long since come to expect and accept his friend's ups and downs, just crediting them to a mercurial artistic temperament.

They retrieved the horse and mule from the hotel stable, mounted, and rode off down the streets of Charleston, admiring the stately old homes with lamplight glowing through the curtained windows. Light from the street lamps reflected from the wet cobblestones after an early evening shower. Carriage and foot traffic began to thin somewhat as they gradually left behind the large residences of the wealthy. The clopping of their horses' hoofs rang hollow on the stone pavement. The clouds that had been hanging low for two days had at last begun to shred and blow away out to sea, and the two men reined up to admire a sudden vision through the trees at the end of the street. Bright moonlight was shimmering on the dark waters of the harbor. Merriman inhaled deeply, smelling the earthy scents of the surrounding marsh land on the warming wind. It was only the last of March, but already he was beginning to sense the stirrings of spring.

His attention was gradually arrested by the happy chatter of female voices, and he pulled his gaze away from the moonlit water to see three young women on the nearby sidewalk. They paused at the corner to cross the street toward a well-lighted dance hall and saloon. Two of them wore hooded capes against the chill, while the third was bare-headed. Light from the street lamp caught the sheen of yellow silk as she lifted the hem of her dress to step over a puddle in the gutter.

The sharp clatter of a trotting team and the heavy grinding of iron-rimmed wheels suddenly sounded loud in Merriman's ears. A delivery wagon rounded a corner, and the snorting draft horses bore down at a fast trot.

The next few seconds were a blur. Merriman's athletic reflexes took control as he leapt from the saddle. In one smooth bound, he snatched the woman around the waist and flung her backward. Both of them landed in the muddy water of the gutter as the team and wagon thundered by without slowing.

"Aagghh!" She gave a strangled cry of surprise and pain.

Merriman got to his feet, and helped her up. "Are you hurt?"

"I . . . don't think so . . . ," she stammered, stepping back up onto the sidewalk as the other two women crowded around her, both talking at once. "No thanks to you, though," she added, giving him a hard look, her dark eyes snapping. She smoothed down the back of her long dress, and her hand came away wet and muddy. "Oh, no! Look at me. My dress! It's ruined."

Merriman stepped away from her, wiping his hands on his britches. He suddenly realized how dirty he was himself.

Collins had dismounted and was holding both of their horses.

"Sshh! April, he saved your life," one of the women cautioned in a stage whisper.

The one addressed as April dropped the handful of spattered yellow silk and looked at Merriman for the first time. "Yes . . . yes. Thank you, sir. Never mind the dress. You did what you had to do." She held out her hand, and Merriman took it with a slight bow. Her shoulder-length black hair gave off a glossy sheen in the dull light of a nearby street lamp. She had dropped the shawl she'd been wearing over her bare shoulders, and, if he wasn't mistaken, her skin was a light *café-au-lait* color. A beautiful, sloe-eyed octoroon was Merriman's quick assessment.

"Ah, April, my dear, are you injured?" The owner of the voice with the soft dialect brushed past Merriman. "I saw it all from the door of the club," he continued without waiting for her reply. "I believe I owe this gentleman a great debt of gratitude." He turned to Merriman, looking him up and down. The newcomer was slender, of medium height, dressed in striped gray pants, black vest, white shirt, and cravat. His dark hair was combed, pompadour style. A neatly trimmed mustache decorated a thin upper lip. "I am Alexander Sloan," he announced without offering his hand. "And who might I have the pleasure of addressing, sir?" he asked in the overly formal manner of one slightly inebriated and trying to remain steady and articulate.

"Rob Merriman," he replied, giving his real name without thinking. He started to extend his hand, but changed his mind. Instead, he pulled out a handkerchief, began wiping his hands and futilely brushing at his soiled canvas trousers.

"What can I offer you, sir, as a reward for saving my April from being run down by that damned madman? A hundred in gold?"

Now that the rush of the moment had passed, Merriman was feeling very awkward to be the center of attention, especially with several pedestrians stopping to gawk.

41

"Nothing, nothing, Mister Sloan," he muttered, trying to sidle out of the ring of people and reach his mount that Collins was holding.

"Surely, sir, there is *something* I can do for you," Sloan persisted, pressing forward. "A selfless act such as yours cannot go unrewarded."

Merriman took the reins from Collins. "I really want nothing," he demurred. "I happened to see the lady in trouble, and reacted instinctively. That was all. Anyone would have done the same."

"Honor requires that I, at least, invite you to refresh yourself in my club across the street," Sloan insisted, in a tone that told Merriman he would be gravely insulted if the offer were refused.

"Let's go have a drink with him, so we can get off the street," Merriman whispered to Collins. At all costs, he wanted to keep from drawing any more attention to themselves.

"You can bring your man servant," Sloan added, apparently realizing Collins was with him.

"Thank you," Merriman said in his most gracious tone. "I'd be delighted." He stepped out of the way as Alexander Sloan, the beautiful April on his arm and the other two women on either side, led the way across the street with Merriman and Collins following, leading their horses.

Swinging on a wooden sign board over the sidewalk was the name **Shearwater** in fancy indigo script. The plain-looking brick façade of the building was lent an air of elegance by a uniformed Negro doorman of massive proportions.

"Good evening, ladies and gennemans," the blue-coated Negro said in a bass voice, sweeping off his beaver-hat and swinging the door open for them with the other hand. His teeth gleamed in a shiny black face.

"Percy, see to their horses!" Sloan ordered as he entered.

The Negro dutifully took the reins from Collins and Merriman. As Merriman stepped inside, he looked back to see the Negro tying their mounts to a four-foot high iron hitching post set along the curb.

Merriman silently cursed his luck, but then took a deep breath and decided to make the best of it. If Collins was bent on celebrating with a few drinks, then what better way than to have them paid for by this obviously wealthy young dandy? But Merriman was uneasy. He wanted to remain anonymous, which meant not having anything to do with strangers. And there was something about the oily manner of this Sloan that put him on edge.

The exterior of the building gave no hint as to the plush furnishings of Alexander Sloan's "club." Sloan kissed April who then went off to a back room, apparently to clean up, while her two companions joined other men and women they obviously knew in the card room. The three men went through a colonnade into a haze of cigar smoke that lingered over the barroom.

Sloan joined them for a drink at the long, ornate bar.

"Two beers and a brandy, Cecil," Sloan yelled over the din of talk and laughter after asking Merriman and Collins what they wanted.

The drinks came, and Sloan sipped at his brandy, obviously not his first of the evening. After a couple of minutes, Merriman noticed their host eyeing the card room, and shifting from one foot to the other. Finally Sloan slipped a ten dollar gold piece out of his vest pocket and placed it on the bar. "You gentlemen have yourselves a few more drinks on me. I see a couple of men at the tables that I want to talk to." He started to move away. "By the way, sir, if you wish to clean some of that dirt off before you leave, there are ample bathing facilities down that hallway, the last door on the right. The niggers in there will take care of cleaning your clothes, if you wish." With that, he took his glass and started toward the card room.

After Sloan left, Merriman relaxed only slightly, determined to keep his wits about him, especially in a strange environment. He leaned on the polished mahogany, sipping his beer and studying the crowd by way of the ornate back-bar mirror. Mostly well-dressed males, portly, bewhiskered, with a few bald pates and gold watch chains shining in the light of the chandeliers. Wealthy planters, businessmen, and slave-owners, Merriman guessed. The majority of the younger men were gambling in the next room. A scattering of bejeweled women moved among them, a few serving drinks from trays, others stimulating the luck of the players by sitting on their laps or leaning on their shoulders.

Mingling with the odors of tobacco smoke was the aroma of fried meat, and Merriman saw food being brought to some of the patrons. There were no tables open, so he and Collins ordered two steaks with potatoes and onions to be served where they stood, near the end of the long bar.

After eating, Merriman felt better, and was more confident that Collins, with some food in his stomach, would not be as affected by the alcohol. A wise precaution, he thought, as Collins switched from beer to some kind of red wine.

They spent the $10 Sloan had left, and considerably more as the hours wore on. Merriman forgot all about the dirty water staining his clothes as it dried on his pants.

Now and then a loud burst of laughter or a curse came from the card room as Dame Fortune distributed her favors unevenly. Talking beneath the hum of noise in the room, Collins reminisced about their time in Nashville and his life in the mountains. As the wine loosened his tongue, it also softened the tense, frowning expression, and Merriman saw a more youthful face emerge—a face he remembered from their first meeting six years earlier. Merriman mainly listened, nodding and commenting, one foamy glass of stout blending with the next.

It didn't seem as if they had been there more than two hours, but time had taken on a pace of its own because they were now seated at a table and at least half the barroom was empty.

"I'm going to use the privy," Collins said, getting up. He disappeared down the hallway toward the back of the building.

Merriman sat back and relaxed, thinking he'd had more to drink than he intended, and resolved to leave as soon as Collins returned. Sometime later he felt that Collins had been gone far longer than necessary, even if he'd gotten lost finding the outhouse. He got up to go look for him. Halfway down the hall he was startled by a shouted curse, followed by a crash of glass. A door just ahead on the right was flung open and slammed back against the wall. Merriman caught Collins as he stumbled out, blood running from his nose.

In the space of a second, two images in the lamplit room were seared into Merriman's suddenly alert mind: the octoroon, April, snatching up her clothes in a vain attempt to cover her nakedness, and Alexander Sloan, pulling a Derringer from his vest pocket. Merriman saw the seeming slow movement of every detail. As if with infinite deliberation, Sloan brought up the pocket pistol, thumbing back the hammer. Before he could level the black bore at Collins, Merriman's fist impacted against Sloan's cheek bone, snapping his head sideways. The Derringer exploded, the slug splintering a floorboard.

There was a pounding of feet somewhere, and Merriman sensed men crowding the doorway behind him. Out of the corner of his eye, Merriman saw April shrug into a shift to cover her voluptuous body and then silently slip out of the room by an open back door.

Sloan was steadying himself against a sofa and slowly shaking his head. Merriman had put all his weight behind the blow, and was surprised the slender dandy hadn't gone down. Sloan straightened, his stunned expression evolving into a look of sneering malevolence. "*That*, my friend, was a grave personal insult to my hospitality," he said, putting a hand to his face. "I was going to put a bullet into your half-breed for touching my April, but, since you've dealt yourself into this, I'll assume you are a gentleman, so we can settle this as gentlemen."

Merriman was poised, fists ready, for the follow-up, but there was none. He backed off, hearing the rush of more footsteps at the door.

"What's going on?"

"You all right, Alex?" came voices from behind him.

Six or seven men pushed into the room from the hallway.

"I'm fine," Sloan said, slipping his empty Derringer back into his pocket. "I am challenging this man for interfering in this matter and striking me."

There was a murmur of interest among the men.

"I demand satisfaction for your insulting churlishness, sir!"

"What are you talking about?" Merriman demanded, a sinking feeling in the pit of his stomach.

"I'm calling you out. A duel, sir," Sloan replied, fixing slightly bloodshot eyes on him.

"You're drunk! As far as I'm concerned, this little misunderstanding is over," Merriman said. "Thank you for your hospitality," he continued, turning to leave. "I think every-thing's about squared up now."

Three men crowded close to block his way. Others had Collins by the arms.

"Pistols at twenty paces," Sloan continued in a deadly even tone. A purpling bruise was swelling his left eye.

"It's only about an hour till daylight," one of the men said.

"Well, we certainly can't just let this *gentleman* walk away from here and expect him to show up at the proper place and time, now can we?" Sloan continued, a note of devilish glee in his voice. "We'll just have to escort him to the du-eling ground since he probably doesn't know the way."

"The usual place by the Ashley River?" someone asked.

"That will do nicely," Sloan nodded. "Fetch the club's matched set of weapons from the library," he added. "Cosworth, will you agree to serve as my second?"

A tall man with side-whiskers and the sad look of a bloodhound nodded. "With pleasure."

"I presume, sir . . . Merriman was it? . . . you will want your lackey to act on your behalf."

"This is damned foolishness!" Merriman said, trying to fight down the panic. He looked at Collins, who appeared befuddled by it all. Probably just drunk, Merriman thought. "Wait a minute. I'm not fighting any duel! Let's talk about this like men," Merriman shouted over the noise as he and Collins were borne down the hall on a tide of humanity, and out the front door to where their horses were still tied to the hitching post. They mounted, while about a dozen other men climbed aboard their own horses.

Merriman fervently wished he had left after his first drink and dragged Collins with him. But it was too late to bolt now. Merriman was still armed with his Colt, but dared not start anything while the two of them were surrounded by so many hostile strangers. His mind was working furiously as he watched Sloan and Cosworth and two other men lead the procession through the deserted streets. Other horsemen followed behind, all of the iron-shod hoofs ringing a clattering tattoo on the bricks and cobblestones.

There seemed no way out, unless he could talk some sense into Alexander Sloan. Not a promising prospect. If he went through with this and shot Sloan, he would certainly be killed by the seconds who would swear he had violated one or another of the rules of the *code duello*. But, much more likely, Sloan would shoot him dead. Since Sloan was so eager for this, he was likely an experienced duelist, and no doubt was familiar with this particular set of dueling pistols that his second carried suspended in a sack from his saddle horn. He wondered how many men Sloan had sent into eternity with them. Merriman had run into men like this before, men whose all-consuming pride and arrogance, stoked with a few successes and considerable brandy, drove them to live on the sharp edge of danger. Apparently it gave them a thrill that couldn't be entirely satisfied by gambling.

Merriman resolved not be this man's next victim. Yet he could see no obvious way out. His mind was racing ahead, sorting the possibilities. The mist and fog could dampen the powder and cause a misfire, but he couldn't bet his life on that long chance. Or, he and Collins could make a break for it on horseback. If they weren't shot before they got out of range, they would be running blind in the fog, and these men knew Charleston and all its byways. There would be little hope of escape. Sloan was probably a good shot, unless the fog, his swollen eye, the sleepless night, or the amount of brandy in his system might adversely affect his aim.

They wound through the streets fronted with shuttered

houses and, after two or three miles, left Charleston behind.

"What the hell did you do to that woman?" Merriman asked in a low voice, leaning across toward Collins.

"I thought that door led out back to the privy. She must have been getting undressed for Sloan. But she invited me in." He shook his head as if trying to clear the image of what had taken place. "We were just getting cozy, when that damned Sloan came busting in the other door. He got a good punch in before I could get off the couch."

Merriman was disgusted, but knew the same thing could have happened to him. He knew Collins probably would have used better judgment had he been sober.

A murky dawn was beginning to light up their surroundings as they rode out onto a flat, grassy stretch of an acre or more. A heavy, clammy river mist softened the outlines of tall trees, trailing beards of Spanish moss. Merriman reined up with the others and watched the dark figures begin to dismount and tie their horses to the slender pines bordering the open area. It suddenly occurred to him that he was having a nightmare. That was it. He knew the secret now. He would wake up shortly in a cold sweat, these fearful images evaporating with his restless sleep. But . . . this was certainly a realistic dream. He took a deep breath of the damp air and watched the gray dawn grow lighter through the fog. He shivered in the chill of early morning, felt the heaviness of his legs as he dismounted, heard the horses snort and the low voices of the men a few rods away. This was a nightmare, all right, but a horrible, *living* nightmare.

He focused on the details of everything around him. He wanted to savor these moments and these sensations because, thanks to some irrational, outmoded code of chivalry, this might be the last dawn he would ever see.

Chapter Five

Merriman and Collins tied their animals to some bushes and moved out of earshot, but under the watchful eyes of several of the other men. Merriman tried to remember everything he knew about dueling, which wasn't much. Maybe he would aim for Sloan's leg, so as only to wound his opponent, because he did know that any blood drawn ended the affair honorably. It didn't have to be fatal. But what if he aimed to wound, and Sloan aimed to kill?

It wasn't as if Sloan had only pretended to have his honor sullied in order to save face in front of his friends, because none of his friends, except the octoroon, was in the room when Merriman hit him. So it appeared Sloan was one of those arrogant rich bastards who went around looking for a fight. And the more he drank, the more belligerent he got. It really had nothing to do with avenging his aggrieved honor, but everything to do with building his reputation.

Cosworth, a spectral figure in tall hat and cape, was helping Sloan out of his coat. The dandy, now in shirtsleeves and vest, did a few bends at the waist and then flexed his arms, as if limbering up for a fencing match. Merriman was at least thankful that they weren't dueling with foils or rapiers. Cosworth produced the boxed set of dueling pistols, and approached Collins. Merriman saw them speak briefly. Then Collins shook his head and withdrew. Cosworth set the gun case on the ground and began to load and prime the weapons.

Merriman pulled Collins to one side. "Clay, what'd he say to you?"

"Offered to let me load one of the pistols, but I'm not familiar with those guns."

"Don't suppose it'll make any difference, since I can pick the one I want." He paused. "Clay, we've got to figure some way out of this." He wondered if perhaps an apology would suffice. At this stage, he doubted it. "Maybe I can use their own rules against them," he said finally. He tried to put aside his apprehension and focus his memory. "Ah, I think I've got it. . . ." He stepped toward the cluster of men on the other side of the clearing. "Sloan, a word with you in private, if you please."

They stopped talking and looked up.

"Anything you've got to say to me, you can say in front of my friends," the dandy snarled.

"Very well. Before we commence this affair, I want to tell you that I, as the challenged party, have the choice of weapons, time, and place. And I've got some different ideas."

"What the hell are you talking about?"

"I thought, as a gentleman, you would certainly abide by the customary rules of conduct set down in the Irish Code of Honor of Seventeen Seventy-Seven."

The blank look told Merriman all he needed to know. He pressed his advantage. "Since you hustled me into this affair of honor, I insist on my right to, at least, select my own weapons and time. And I choose two-handed battle axes right now. If you can't produce the weapons, we'll just have to postpone this affray until a couple of battle axes can be rounded up."

"You're trying to make a mockery of this," Sloan sneered. "You're no gentleman. I shouldn't have even offered to settle this in an honorable manner."

"Not at all. Those are my choices. Duels have been fought with axes before, and with swords, shotguns, rifles, and knives. Nevertheless, if you can't abide by the rules, I would suggest that you are no gentleman yourself, sir."

A look of cold fury spread over Sloan's countenance. His pale face darkened apoplectically, and there was spittle on his lips as he struggled to get the next words out. "We adhere to a later set of rules you may be familiar with . . . THE CODE OF HONOR OR, RULES FOR THE GOVERNMENT OF PRINCIPALS AND SECONDS IN DUELING. It was compiled and published only ten years ago by our own ex-governor, John Wilson. He says that the challenged party no longer has the exclusive right to choose these things. He wrote that the weapon must be the usual weapon . . . in South Carolina . . . the pistol . . . and the place and time and distance the usual. And that's what I have selected . . . this dueling ground at twenty paces."

"Without the agreement of both seconds," Merriman countered.

"Stand away from me, sir," Sloan gritted through his teeth. "It's obvious you are only stalling. As you know, my second is empowered to shoot you, if you violate the rules."

"My second may do the same," Merriman said softly. "Maybe we should have our seconds fight this out." He allowed an irritating smile to slide across his lips. The truth was he could hardly keep from laughing at Sloan's appearance, since the dandy's left eye, swollen to a slit, almost made him appear to be winking.

But to Sloan this was no laughing matter. He pointed at the birdseye maple box that Cosworth held. "Select one of these pistols, and prepare to defend yourself, or these men will cut you down where you stand," he grated.

"Well, so much for the rules of *gentlemen*," Merriman sneered, picking one of the ornate single-shot weapons from its green velvet couch. He looked at Cosworth. "These are both loaded and capped identically?"

"Of course. I offered to let your second load one of them, but he declined."

Merriman carried the pistol back across the clearing. "It was a good try, but they're having none of it," he remarked to Collins. "Those fine points I brought up about the rules or a code might work in a court of law, but not here. They came for a shoot, and they're determined to have one."

Collins looked sober and scared in the chill light of dawn. "We didn't come all this way just to have you get shot by this arrogant fool, did we?" he asked in a low voice.

"I hope not. But it looks like I'm going to have to go through with it."

"Let me do it," Collins said, holding out his hand for the pistol. "I'm the one who got us into this. It was all my fault."

"Remind me to ask you about that, later," Merriman said with a wry smile.

"I'm the one he wants," Collins insisted.

"Maybe so, but you're the wrong color to fight as a gentleman." He shook his head. "Listen, now. If Sloan should get me, then this affair is over. They won't harm you. There's plenty of money in my pocket. Either get me a doctor, or see to my burial, and let my parents know what happened here."

"Don't talk like that," Collins said.

"If I'm still standing and Sloan is down," Merriman continued as if he hadn't heard, "they should let us walk away from here. But be ready, just in case. We may have to fight our way out." He raised the heavy smoothbore and examined it more closely. It was of archaic design and, from the size of the muzzle, looked to be about a .50 caliber. He carefully drew back the hammer to full cock, impressed with the strength of the spring. It would certainly fall with enough force to set off the charge, he thought. The nipple was capped with a copper primer. Since it was a percussion piece, instead of a flintlock, there was probably less chance of a misfire. He hardly noticed the scrollwork on the inlaid silver. Such niceties could only be appreciated by someone who was not about to face a lead slug from the identical twin of this weapon. He held the handgun out at arm's length, drawing a bead on a slender pine tree, trying to steady himself and hold his breath so the long barrel would not waver. It was a difficult task. He lowered the pistol and eased the hammer down.

"You're not really going through with this, are you?" Collins asked, appearing thoroughly shaken.

Merriman nodded. "You see any other way out?"

"Just say you're not going to fight. Who cares if they call us cowards?"

"They won't stop at ridicule. They'll just shoot us, and then concoct some story about us violating the rules of the code of honor. It's all very legal. Besides, beyond this bunch, who would know what really happened here?"

"I'll hold your coat," Collins said.

"No. I'll leave it on." He didn't know if he was shaking from the chill or from nervousness.

"I can't believe this is happening," Collins groaned.

"I know. And all because of jealousy over some rich drunk's mistress."

"Do you think you really have a chance?"

"Yes. Did you notice that he's left-handed?"

Collins shook his head.

54

"That means he'll have his left side to me when he aims. Some men leave both eyes open when they shoot, and some sight with one and close the other. His left eye is almost swollen shut where I hit him. No matter how he shoots, it's bound to affect his aim a little."

"But he's an experienced duelist."

Merriman shrugged. "Can't be helped. We could figure the odds all day, but when it comes right down to it. . . ."

Cosworth approached, his long, black cape swinging wide around his lean figure. "You about ready?" he asked.

"Any time," Merriman nodded. "My second will have a weapon trained on you," he lied. "If, for any reason, this pistol misfires, he'll cut you down."

Cosworth hesitated, but Merriman couldn't see his expression under the tall hat in the murky light. He moved away without answering, motioning for Merriman to follow.

The two principals met near the center of the open, grassy area, their two seconds by their sides. Merriman tried not to look at the handsome, sneering face of his opponent while Cosworth intoned the ritual.

"You will stand back to back. I will count to ten as each man steps off ten paces. Then, at my signal, you will turn and fire. Is that understood? Any questions?"

Neither Sloan nor Merriman spoke. Merriman kept his eyes down, trying to concentrate on what he had to do.

"Commence."

Collins walked off several yards as the two principals faced away from each other, their backs barely touching.

Merriman thumbed back the hammer to full cock, leaving his forefinger outside the trigger guard, the gun at his side.

"One . . . Two . . . Three . . . Four . . . ," Cosworth called out in a slow cadence as the two men began stepping off the distance, their footfalls nearly silent in the soft, wet grass. "Seven . . . Eight . . . Nine . . . Ten. Turn."

Merriman faced about, raising the gun, his heart hammering in his chest so hard he couldn't hold his arm steady.

"Fire!"

He fought the urge to fire quickly at the slim, black silhouette in the fog twenty yards away. He sighted down the barrel, held his breath for an extra second, then pulled the trigger.

The pistol roared and jumped in his hand, a cloud of white smoke obscuring everything in front of him. He slowly lowered his shaking arm as the smoke began to clear. He was still standing—and so was Sloan. *Oh, God, I missed! Now Sloan's got a clear shot at me. If I duck or run, the others will cut me down.*

Cosworth stepped forward. "Is either man hit?"

So Sloan had fired, too! A rush of warm relief flooded over Merriman.

"If not, then we will reload and try again," Cosworth continued. "But, before we do, I must ask if this is not sufficient to satisfy honor? Each of you has adequately demonstrated courage."

"Reload," Sloan snapped. "That craven bastard will shed his blood before I'll be satisfied."

It was with apparent reluctance that Cosworth collected the weapons from the two men and proceeded to pour a measure of powder down each barrel from a brass flask.

Merriman figured that all the men here were now thoroughly chilled and sober. Most of them had seen about enough of this farce, and he heard several of Sloan's friends trying to dissuade him from continuing.

"A bad sign, you missing like that," he heard one man say in a low voice. "Maybe it's an omen that you should let it go and go home." Because of some quirk in the swirling fog, the voice came as distinctly to Merriman's ears as if the man had been standing beside him. He looked around and saw Collins approach.

"You have to do this *again?*" he asked in an almost tremulous voice.

"Appears so," Merriman said. "At least I know he's as bad a shot as I am. And now I know how this weapon feels. That's more than I knew before." He didn't want to admit that a reaction was setting in and his knees felt so weak they could hardly hold him up.

Merriman watched Cosworth recharge the two pistols, noting that he did them exactly alike. He had an instinctive feeling that Cosworth, regardless of his personal feelings in the matter, was taking his duties as second very seriously and was being as neutral as possible.

Merriman walked a few steps away with Collins to settle his nerves, regulate his breathing, and return some strength to his knees.

"Ready again!" Cosworth called.

The two men accepted the weapons and took their places, back to back. Once again, Cosworth boomed off the count, like the ponderous strokes of doom. This time Merriman was much more in control of himself and paced with his elbow bent, the cocked pistol pointing upward.

"Turn and fire!"

He whirled about, standing sideways, brought the pistol down in one smooth motion, lined up the dark figure, held his breath, and fired. As the pistol bucked in his hand, pain seared the left side of his neck like the sting of an angry hornet. Through the swirling gunsmoke and fog he saw Sloan stagger and fall. He stood, transfixed, for several heartbeats, unable to grasp the fact that his bullet had found its mark. He was hardly aware of warm blood trickling down the side of his neck as he dropped the dueling pistol in the grass and, on wobbly legs, started toward the fallen Sloan. Cosworth and three other men were already crouching by him. Merriman pushed in beside them, uttering a silent prayer that Sloan was still alive. The men were crowding out much of the dim light, but Merriman could see a growing stain darkening the front of the dandy's white shirt. He heard the harsh, ragged breathing of the unconscious man and knew it for what it was—a prelude to death. He had heard that sound before from a man who'd collapsed with a fit of apoplexy.

"Let's get him to Doc Petigrew," someone said.

Hands were ripping open his vest and shirt to find the wound.

"No need," Cosworth said, removing his tall hat and setting it beside him where he knelt on the grass. "Prayer is the only thing that might do him some good now."

They all paused and looked to the older Cosworth.

Merriman rocked back on his heels and stood up, knowing that he had to get away before they recovered from their shock.

"Damn' shame," another voice said. "Alexander Sloan was from one of the finest families in Charleston."

"So young. . . ."

"They don't come any better than him. A sporting man of the highest. . . ."

Merriman took a few quiet steps backward. He was suddenly aware that the hoarse, stentorian breathing had stopped.

"He's dead," Cosworth said, genuine sadness in his voice.

Merriman had Collins by the arm, and they were halfway

to their horses when he heard a man behind him say: "That damned outlander started all this row."

"That sum-bitch will pay for this," a short, red-faced man growled.

"Hold on now," another man cried. "It was a fair fight all the way. Sloan had a chance to call it off."

But the voice of reason might have been crying in the wilderness for all the influence it had. A rumble of discontent began to drown it out.

"Mount up and follow me," Merriman whispered urgently. He and Collins made a dash for their mounts, jerking the reins loose from the bushes.

"Hold up there, you two!" a man behind them yelled.

The pair leapt into the saddles and kicked their startled animals away among the tall, straight pines. More yells and a scattering of gunshots followed them. Merriman instinctively hunched over the horse's neck and glanced back. Several muzzle flashes lit up the mist. Just before the men were lost to sight, he saw several of them already mounted and starting in pursuit.

He turned his attention to riding, urging his mount forward, dodging among the trees, with no idea where he was going. It was full daylight now, but the lowland fog still wrapped the whole area in a cottony mist, confusing even his general sense of direction.

Collins was sticking close behind, apparently trusting Merriman to lead him to safety.

After several minutes of this, Merriman saw the faint figures of several horsemen cutting across his line of sight from the left, angling to head them off. Swearing under his breath, he jerked his horse to the left, nearly bumping Collins, who was on his left flank. "This way!" he yelled, his mount plunging blindly away toward . . . what? He didn't know, except that it was away from the pursuing horsemen who had somehow known of a short cut and headed them.

They rode, flat-out, for several more minutes. But Collins's mule was no racehorse and quickly began dropping back. Merriman was forced to slow down and wait for him. He heard a yell from behind. A quick glance showed the pursuit closing. Merriman reached under his coat and pulled his Colt Patterson. He had five shots, and he fired all of them in quick succession over his shoulder. He couldn't tell if he'd hit anything, but the chase never slackened.

"We've got 'em now!" a voice whooped. "They're pinned against the river."

Merriman shoved the pistol back into its holster and galloped through a line of trees and bushes. The flat water of the Ashley River was before him so suddenly, he yanked his horse back on its haunches to keep from plunging over the low bank. They leapt off, and Merriman, without hesitation, led the way down the slippery mud bank into the water. The horse and mule, relieved of their burdens, went trotting off.

"Swim toward the middle as fast as you can!" Merriman gasped, the cold water taking his breath. He struck off in a sidestroke. "The fog will hide us."

The mist was, indeed, even thicker over the water. They swam desperately, kicking and splashing, heedless of the noise. They were hardly twenty yards out, when the pursuit reined up on the bank and began shooting, the bullets spurting up small jets of water around them. They struggled onward, their water-soaked clothes and boots dragging at them. Another ten yards and the trees and horsemen were completely swallowed up in the fog behind them.

"OK, slow down and stay quiet," Merriman gasped in a whisper, treading water. Collins was apparently too busy getting his breath and staying afloat to answer.

The shots had stopped, but they could hear the men's voices for several more minutes until they finally faded away.

"How . . . wide is this river?" Collins asked breathlessly.

"Don't know. We're near the mouth. Probably too wide to swim across. If you can hold up a little longer, we'll swim back to the bank. They'll probably be gone by then, figuring we got away."

"Or d . . . drowned," Collins stammered, his face a ghastly gray in the dim light.

Merriman didn't answer. His attention had been diverted by a tree trunk drifting into view a few yards off. It was floating higher out of the water than they were and was moving a little faster. Apparently the current, swollen by spring rains and aided by a falling tide, was flowing swiftly toward the harbor. Merriman had no sense of motion in the smooth river with the fog all around. But the log gave him a point of reference, and showed they were being rapidly swept out to sea. In their weakened condition, he doubted they could break the grip of the current and return to shore.

Fear knotted his stomach even harder than it had on the dueling ground. Here was an impersonal force from which they could expect no mercy.

Chapter Six

Collins wanted to kick toward the unseen shore, but wasn't sure he had the strength to make it. It required all he had just to tread water and stay afloat. He could feel his energy draining out as if someone had pulled the plug.

"The log," Merriman said, rolling over into an overhand stroke and thrusting his body toward it. The log was within reach; the riverbank might not be.

Merriman's decision had come almost too late, Collins realized as he measured the angle with his eye and saw how quickly the driftwood was moving. He held his breath and forgot himself for several long seconds until he saw Merriman, with one last lunge, get a hand on the partially submerged roots of the trunk as it floated past.

"Here! Grab on!" Merriman yelled.

Collins struggled toward him with a combination sidestroke and dog paddle. His water-soaked clothing and boots dragged at him like quicksand. He fought with all his fading strength to cover the several yards that separated them, knowing Merriman was helping by pushing the end of the log sideways toward him. Just as he was beginning to feel he'd never make it, he stretched out one arm and his fingers gripped the stub of a projecting limb. Merriman moved around to his side, and the two of them held on, gasping. Collins knew that he would never have reached the riverbank if it had been two yards farther than this log.

Neither of them spoke for what seemed a long time. Collins had no sensation of motion, until the sun and breeze began to shred the fog, and he caught glimpses of shoreline that looked to be more than a mile away. Apparently Merriman saw the same thing because he finally commented: "Looks like we've drifted out past Charleston into the harbor. That's the far shore to the north, I believe."

As if to verify his guess, an onshore wind began to blow counter to the tidal current, kicking up a chop on the wide expanse of water. Collins detected a slight salty taste in the waves that were lapping into his face.

"From the frying pan to the fire," Collins groaned, at the same time thinking how silly the comment sounded. He wished he had a fire right now. He was so cold and stiff, his arm felt as if it were permanently crooked through the fork of the log. The massive roots of the tree had been torn from the ground. They acted as a stabilizer to keep the trunk from rolling.

"As soon as it lifts enough to see, we can start kicking toward the nearest shore," Merriman said.

They would have to push this heavy tree trunk with them, Collins thought, because they needed it to keep themselves afloat. It seemed an almost impossible task. He was chilled to the core and began to feel lethargic. He wanted just to let his head droop and sleep while his body hung suspended in the water. Several times his face fell forward, but each time the cold water brought him, strangling, upright and alert. He became aware of Merriman's talking to him, then suddenly Merriman was at his side, supporting him against the log as he was coughing out water again.

"Hold on just a little longer. Don't let go now."

Collins shifted his position, moved his arms, kicked with his legs to get some circulation back. "I'm OK." He focused his eyes on Merriman. "You haven't got a shot of brandy on you, by any chance?"

"You won't do," Merriman grinned at him.

"One thing about it," Collins said, a fit of shivering shaking his body, "when . . . a man travels . . . with you, he sure as hell doesn't get bored."

Collins began to think, with regret, of getting drunk the night before and starting a chain of events that had put himself and Merriman in danger of their lives. By the grace of God they had escaped, but it now appeared as if they were doomed to die by exposure or drowning. He had only a vague recollection of stumbling down the hallway of the Shearwater Club, opening doors, looking for the way out the back to the privy. The last door he'd yanked open revealed the startling, but delectable, sight of the woman, April, half-naked, in the process of changing clothes. She not only was not embarrassed by his unexpected entrance, but had invited him in. One thing had led to another, and, through an alcoholic haze, he recalled having her stark naked on a couch and telling her he was an artist and wanted to capture her beauty on canvas. Even now, the thought of her made his heart beat faster, warming him slightly. But apparently April had been getting herself ready to receive Alexander Sloan, because the next thing Collins remembered was Sloan yanking him up and the blinding pain of a fist slamming into his nose. Then Merriman had shown up, and everything had begun to spiral downhill.

The memory of his actions embarrassed him, yet he could not roll back time and undo them. But, if they never got to shore, he was determined at least to apologize for his weakness that had brought them to this sorry fate.

"Rob, I. . . ."

"Look!"

He swiveled around in the water to follow Merriman's gaze. The dark bulk of a ship's hull loomed up a few yards away out of the thinning fog.

"Our best chance," Collins said. "Let's go for it."

"When we get close, grab for the anchor chain," Merriman added.

The drifting log had slowed.

"Ready? Now!"

They let go in unison and swam the last several yards, reaching the anchor chain, slightly out of breath. The running tide was pulling back the ship, taut on her chain, pointing her proud, bare-breasted figurehead and bowsprit toward the city.

"Ahoy, the deck!" Collins shouted.

"Anybody up there?" Merriman yelled.

The fog was quickly thinning now, and bright water stretched away in all directions. Collins looked up at the towering masts, whose trucks seemed gently to rake the blue sky as the ship rocked at her mooring.

They yelled again and waited, but there was no response. The ship seemed deserted.

"They either didn't set an anchor watch, or he's asleep on the job," Merriman said.

Suddenly a startled face appeared over the bulwarks at the bow.

"Hey! Give us a hand. We're freezing!" Collins yelled.

The face disappeared, and Collins heard running footsteps on the deck. A minute or two later, the face reappeared. "Swim around to the port side," the sailor said. "There's a ladder."

Collins and Merriman followed instructions, and soon were struggling up the rope ladder on cold-stiffened legs to the main deck, five feet above the water line. A sailor pulled up the ladder behind them and swung the gate shut, dropping the cap rail into place on top of it.

Two other sailors were there to greet them, looking more curious than concerned as Collins and Merriman dripped water onto the deck and shivered in the morning breeze.

"Well, what's this flotsam that's washed off the beach?" one of the sailors growled. Collins almost cringed at the sound of the voice. The spokesman was a bear of a man, probably six foot, one, with massive shoulders and arms that stretched the faded blue denim coat. He was not fat, just big-boned and heavily muscled. Collins sensed the animal presence of the man, and shivered even more violently as he approached like some hulking grizzly.

"We got washed out of the river and couldn't get back," Merriman said.

"Taking a swim for your health, now were ya?" the giant said. "This time o' year, and in your clothes at that." He obviously didn't believe the answer.

"I'll pay you for something hot to drink and to row us ashore," Merriman said, in an effort to get to the heart of the matter with no further delay.

Collins didn't know why, but he was glad Merriman's holstered Colt was out of sight. He was grateful to be alive with something solid under his feet, but he'd learned to trust the fluttering premonition in the pit of his stomach.

"I'm Abel Stark, first mate of this vessel," the big man said, ignoring the request, and eyeing them with large gray eyes from under heavy brows. "And who might you be?" He was hatless and his brown hair was liberally salted with silver. He was not as youthful as Collins first had supposed, noting the seamed, wind-burned face and the slight stoop of the shoulders.

"Clayburn Collins, and Rob Merriman," Collins answered for both of them.

"What vessel is this?" Merriman inquired through clenched teeth as he hugged both arms around his sopping coat.

"The *Inverness* out of Nova Scotia," he replied.

"Where bound?"

"To Boston with a load of Cuban molasses." He turned suddenly on the man nearest him. "Johnson, what the hell you standing there for?" he snarled. "Get down to the galley and fetch up some hot coffee!"

The sailor jumped like he'd been stung, and ran off to obey.

"Come with me. I believe Captain Blackwell will want to talk with you," Stark said, turning abruptly and walking away aft.

The two men followed the mate to the break of the poop and through a doorway. At the end of a short passageway, he rapped discreetly on a door.

"Come in."

They entered.

"Captain, the watch just fished these two out of the water. Thought you'd want to see them."

Captain Blackwell shoved the tray of breakfast dishes aside on the small table where he sat. "Thank you, Mister Stark," he said in a calm voice. The first mate nodded and withdrew, closing the door quietly.

"I'm Captain Amos Blackwell," he said, standing up. His head nearly touched the overhead gimbaled lamp.

"Collins and Merriman," Collins said by way of introduction.

"Well . . . ?" the captain asked, fixing them with clear, gray eyes. He was a tall, ascetic-looking man, clean-shaven and past middle age.

"We got swept out of the Ashley River before we could

swim ashore," Merriman said. "We'd be obliged if you'd take us to Charleston."

"If you don't want to tell me what happened, I suppose that's your own business." He paused and looked at them critically. "I see you have a fresh gash across the side of your neck there," he observed to Merriman. "And you seem to be having some difficulty breathing through that swollen nose," he said to Collins. "But, actually, I can't spare the time or the manpower to row you ashore. I'm waiting for my second mate and two men to return in the longboat right now with the last of our supplies. We should have caught this strong ebb tide an hour ago."

Collins began to feel uneasy under the regal stare.

"Have either of you ever been to sea?" Captain Blackwell was asking.

Collins anticipated where the question was leading, but wasn't quick enough to head off Merriman's answer.

"I shipped before the mast on a brigantine carrying soldiers down to Vera Cruz during the war," Merriman answered.

Someone rapped sharply at the cabin door.

"Enter."

"Hot coffee for the castaways, sir," a sailor said, entering with two large pewter tankards. He set them down on the table, glancing curiously at Merriman and Collins, then ducked out.

"Help yourself."

The two men proceeded to warm their hands and their insides with the molasses-sweetened brew.

Collins had a sudden idea. He caught Merriman's eye over the lip of his cup and gave a slight nod. Turning to Blackwell, he said: "Captain, do you take paying passengers?"

The tall man looked down at Collins and replied: "Not as a rule. Especially when I have a strong hunch they're running from the law."

Merriman took up the cause. "Captain, I assure you, it's nothing like that. I can't give you the reasons for our being in the water, but it was a personal affair. An affair of honor, if you get my meaning."

"Ah . . . ," the captain nodded. "Very well. And what might you be using for passage money?" he asked, dubiously eyeing their sodden appearance.

"Would fifty dollars, gold, for the both of us be sufficient?" Merriman asked, digging into his wet trousers pocket.

"Make it sixty and the Boston owners needn't know about it," Blackwell said with Yankee thrift.

"Better yet, make it forty and I'll lend a hand as able seaman," Merriman said.

"No, I've got hands enough to work the ship, even though I'm paying off the carpenter here in Charleston. Sixty it is . . . and you'll bunk aft as supercargo." He paused. "Except for your servant, here, who'll sleep in the midship house."

Collins had heard this too often to be offended.

"He's like my right hand, Captain. Waits on me hand and foot. I need him at my side," Merriman said hastily.

Captain Blackwell compressed his thin lips and considered this. "There's never been a colored man in the afterguard on this ship. But, as long as you're paying for him, and he's a personal servant, and you're going only as far as Boston, I'll allow it," he said. "As long as he's some sort of half-breed and not an African blue gums, that will do. We just delivered a cargo of them to Havana."

Collins felt a sudden chill in the cabin that wasn't due to

his wet clothes. They were aboard a slaver! He would have preferred they take their chances back in Charleston. Captain Blackwell had begun talking about him as if he weren't even there. But, before Collins could interrupt to say they'd changed their minds and would pay to be put ashore, Blackwell was ushering them out of his cabin. "I don't want any morale problems on this vessel. I'll call the crew and show them the two passengers who've come aboard. Mister Stark, call all hands aft! Then prepare to get under way."

An unnamed dread dragged like lead weights at Collins's feet as he followed the two men up the stairway to the quarterdeck.

Chapter Seven

Lone Oak Mansion

Charleston, South Carolina

With a low rumble, one of the big oak double doors slid open on its oiled rollers, and Trevor Sloan entered the front parlor. With lagging steps, he approached the open coffin and looked down at the body of his only son. The scene had an unreal quality, like a distorted nightmare from which he would shortly be roused by his valet. He felt dull, detached, unable to grasp the fact that Alexander was dead. Many friends and business associates would be gathering within the hour to begin the wake, a traditional all-night vigil of food and drink and conversation. Maybe by morning, or at the funeral tomorrow, his stunned mind would begin to accept the fact that Alex was gone, never to return.

How could it be? From all appearances, Alex had only stretched out to take a nap in his best black suit, his hands folded comfortably across his chest. He was very pale, true enough, but his son always had had a pale complexion since he rarely went out in the sun. The undertaker had done a fair job of covering up the swollen bruise under his left eye.

The burning candles at the head and foot of the coffin gave off a faint scent of beeswax. Their flickering flames seemed to suck the oxygen out of the air. The room felt close, his high collar too tight. Yet, even as he stood with his hands resting on the edge of the polished cypress coffin, rage was bubbling just beneath the crusted surface of shock and grief.

Trevor Sloan glanced through the open door at a sideboard in the back parlor. His gaze rested on the amber liquid in a cut-glass decanter. He wanted a drink badly to dull the anguish and help him get through the rest of this day. But he dared not start this early. He had to stay in control in front of the people who would be arriving shortly. His wife, to distract herself, was in the kitchen, supervising the preparation of the food. He'd hold off drinking anything until the guests were beginning to leave later this evening, and the small core of watchers who were to sit up with the body were settling in for the night. Then he'd have a couple of brandies before he retired, to help him sleep. He longed for oblivion. A man's children should not die before he did. It was against the natural order of things. He almost wished he were there in that box instead of Alexander. But he couldn't lie down to his eternal sleep until his son was avenged. He could not rest until everything was again in balance, as he felt all of life and death should be. It was a principle arrived at by instinct, rather than reason.

He took a deep breath and turned away from the casket. He had to get some fresh air. He walked into the entrance hall and then out the big front door to the columned porch. Pulling a flat metal case from an inside coat pocket, he selected a slim cigar and lit it. As he drew in the aromatic smoke, he welcomed the chill air of evening. The sun was going down in streaks of purple and gold beyond the trees. He leaned against a pillar, feeling very weary. It had been a long day. He could hardly realize that he'd just been sitting down to breakfast this morning when the terrible news was brought to him. His wife, Emily, had gone into immediate shock and spent most of the day in her bed with a personal maid attending her. He and Emily had gone through many personal hardships during their married life, including the loss of an infant child to fever. But tragedies seemed harder to deal with the older one got. It was as if age robbed a person of the flexibility to bend with the storms.

He wondered if Jason Biggers, overseer of his sea island cotton plantation, had been able to discover any further news of the whereabouts of the man who'd murdered Alex. The men who'd witnessed the duel, it was reported, had run the man and his half-breed friend into the Ashley River where they'd presumably drowned. But he would not be satisfied until their bodies were found. He would never let it go until he could personally blast a .45 caliber slug between the eyes of the man who'd killed Alex, even if the head of that man was forever beyond earthly pain. Yet he knew, from experience, that the bodies of men drowned in the tidal rivers were seldom found, especially when the rivers were nearly at flood. He gritted his teeth in frustration, biting off the end of his cigar. Dropping the cigar to the porch floor, he ground it out under his polished boot.

The clopping of horses in the street invaded his consciousness as a black carriage pulled up in front. With a sigh, he brushed a trace of white ash from his lapel and prepared to receive his first guests.

Trevor Sloan had broken his resolve. It was barely midnight, and he'd been sipping at a large brandy for almost an hour. There was a low murmur in the room from the dark-suited men, conversing in twos and threes, drinks in hand. Several of them had attempted, early in the evening, to discuss the details of the duel with him. He'd politely, but firmly, changed the painful subject, not trusting himself to speak of this matter now. He could only keep up his stoic façade if the topic were something neutral, such as speculation about the weather for spring planting, or the news of a slave who'd run off or been taken by swamp fever.

Their ladies were gathered in the back parlor, everyone sampling the sweet meats, fresh bread, sliced beef, and beverages. Emily was among them, dressed in black silk, apparently holding up well, the dark circles under her eyes hardly noticeable in the subdued lighting. Sloan had taken the edge off his sobriety, and his pain was endurable for the moment. But he was still relieved when the first few mourners began to collect their cloaks and hats, mutter their final condolences, and head for the door.

A house slave was arranging the upholstered, straight-backed chairs for the all-night watchers, and all but two or three of the other guests had departed when Jason Biggers, dressed in riding boots and a dark coat with the collar turned up, was ushered into the front hallway.

"Mistah Biggers to see you, suh," the elderly bald slave intoned quietly to Sloan.

With a glance over his shoulder at his wife, who was talking with another woman, Trevor Sloan stepped into the entrance hall. "What is it, Jason?"

The tall overseer stood uneasily in his boss's presence, turning the broad hat in raw-boned hands. "Mister Sloan, I think I've got some news about those two men."

"You *think?*"

"I'm not sure it's the same two, sir."

"What is it? Are they dead? Where are the bodies?"

"A friend of mine was having a bite to eat in the Red Rooster Tavern this evening. He told me he met up with a carpenter who'd been paid off from a ship, here, earlier in the day. They got to talking, as drinking men will do, sir. . . ."

"Get on with it, man!" Sloan snapped.

"Yes, sir. Well, this carpenter was telling him about two men who were picked up by the crew of his ship this morning, just after the fog lifted. A look-out discovered 'em hanging onto the anchor chain, looking like a couple o' drowning wharf rats. Of course, the crew took 'em aboard."

"What names did they give? Was it Merriman and Collins? Those were the two, according to the men who brought my son back to me this morning."

"That was it . . . the very names, all right! He heard the captain introduce them to the crew as new passengers, just before the carpenter was paid off and came ashore. Said one was about six feet tall, mostly lean muscle, and the other a smaller fella with black hair and dark skin, like an Indian or a half-breed. But he had green eyes."

Sloan pursed his lips and tried not to show the excitement he felt. "The name of the ship?"

"The *Inverness* . . . a bark. . . ."

"Saddle my horse! I'll meet you out back in ten minutes as soon as I load my Colt. . . ."

"Sir. . . ."

"Don't try to talk me out of this, Jason! This has to be done, and the quicker the better."

"But, Mister Sloan, it's. . . ."

"Don't interrupt. How did you get over from the island? In the skiff?"

"Yes, sir."

"Good. Don't let on where we're going. I'll just tell Emily I'm . . . uh, going out for a walk to clear my head before I go to bed."

"The ship's gone."

"What?"

"The carpenter said the *Inverness* hove up anchor and stood out to sea while the tide was still running this morning."

Trevor Sloan took a step backward as if someone had struck him a blow in the solar plexus. He stared at the weathered, worried face of his overseer in the soft overhead light of the hall chandelier. "Where's it bound?"

"Boston."

"Is the ship hauling passengers or cargo?"

"Molasses from Cuba."

"So, I'll wager it has no scheduled stops until it gets to New England. Unless they pay dearly to be put ashore somewhere along the coast, those two won't get off that ship until it hits Boston harbor." He smiled grimly. "I've shipped enough cotton in Yankee ships to know that most of those captains aren't going out of their way for a couple of passengers. I think I can get a letter by courier to a good friend of mine in time to have him greet that ship. Then we shall see. . . ."

"Mister Sloan, if I may be so bold, sir . . . the gossip on the street is that young Alex had had a bit too much to drink and was spoiling for a fight. They're saying it was a fair and equal fight . . . that young Alex could've stopped it after they both shot and missed with no loss of honor. But he insisted the duel continue and. . . ."

Sloan held up his hand, and the overseer's voice trailed off.

"You're telling me that my boy was at fault?" he said with carefully controlled fury. "Well, coming from one in your station, I can understand that. But, this man, Merriman, struck Alex with his fist. Alex *had* to challenge him, and *had* to draw blood to satisfy honor. As I got the story, Alex even gave this man the benefit of the doubt that he was a gentleman in allowing him to fight the duel. He could have shot this Merriman down where he stood. Jason, you will never understand that men like me exist in our own world. We could not go on, if we did not adhere to a strict code of conduct. Our way of life would crumble, if we did not uphold the honor of our class."

"Yes, sir." The overseer was showing signs of nervous embarrassment for having transgressed beyond his limit.

"Go on, now. I'll see that you get extra pay for this information. Be sure to keep your eyes and ears open for anything further."

"Yes, sir." Jason Biggers thrust his hat back on as he was shown to the door.

Trevor Sloan returned to the wake in a much lighter mood than when he'd left it.

Chapter Eight

Aboard the Bark, Inverness

Charleston Harbor

"Here we are, gentlemen." Gilbert Malloy, the second mate heaved back the trap door to the lazarette and hooked it securely. Holding his lantern up, he led the way down the ladder into the cramped space below the after cabin that held the ship's stores. There was hardly room for the three of them to stand and move between the racks and bins lined with kegs of salt horse, sacks of dried beans, coffee and meal, boxes of tobacco and kegs of rum, stacks of spare clothing, including sea boots, southwesters, and dozens of other items. The place smelled faintly of onions, and Merriman realized dried onions weren't there just to make the cook's job easier. In place of perishable lemons, limes, or fresh vegetables, sacks of onions were carried on voyages as an ascorbic to prevent scurvy, the crippling curse of earlier seafarers. If they began to sprout before being eaten, all the better.

"There's not much selection, but take your pick," Malloy said, indicating a stack of coarse canvas pants and cotton shirts.

Merriman and Collins shuffled through the pile, holding up the items to themselves until they approximated a fit.

"When you've changed, bring your clothes, and I'll have them strung on deck to dry," Malloy said, locking the trap door back in place as they departed.

The second mate was a short, compact man, balding and, Merriman guessed from his slight dialect, a native Virginian. Like the mate, Malloy was no youngster. He looked to be every bit of fifty, probably a good ten years younger than Abel Stark. Outwardly civil and courteous, even courtly, Malloy nevertheless gave Merriman the impression that something sinister was lurking behind the façade. Maybe it was the eyes, Merriman thought as they followed the second mate through the passageway toward their own adjoining cabins on the port side. Windows of the soul, the eyes seemed to allow glimpses of the true self beneath. Normally not sensitive to such things, Merriman had the oddest feeling that he was talking to two people when he talked to Malloy—one the outer, gracious ship's officer, and the other . . . who? Or maybe Merriman was talking to one person and being watched by another. He'd always been dubious about the veracity of Biblical stories concerning demonic possession. But the skin-crawling sensation he experienced around Malloy made him almost believe he was in the presence of the Evil One. And he had only just met the man. He silently resolved to ask Collins his impression as soon as they were alone.

Merriman was amazed at how much better he felt by just having dry cloth next to his skin. If nothing else, the swim in the river and harbor had washed all the mud out of his clothes he noted as he and Collins carried their sodden garments up the ladder to the quarterdeck. Malloy took a piece of sizing and tied it between a backstay and the taffrail. Merriman wrung out their clothes and tied them by the arms and legs to the line.

While they were at this, Merriman could hear Mr. Stark snarling orders at the sailors on the foredeck who had fitted

79

wooden bars to the windlass and were breaking out the anchor. Or, they were attempting to break out the anchor.

"You couldn't be hungover 'cause you didn't go ashore!" he yelled at them. "Put some muscle into it!"

Merriman paused to watch as five men appeared to be leaning against the projecting handles.

"Come on, heave and pawl! You bunch of weaklings! God-damned wharf scum! You move faster than that going to the head."

Stark glanced aft, and Merriman noted he was looking at Captain Blackwell who had come on deck and was silently observing the operation. Merriman got the feeling the mate would have waded in among them, cuffing heads right and left had not the captain been present. Stark seemed to hold himself in check, but the frustration was apparent in his voice as he thundered: "Start a song! Get some snap into your step! If you can't break the hook out of a sandy bottom, how the hell you gonna reef a topsail off Hatteras?" He watched their feeble efforts for another moment or two, then jumped in alongside one of them, lending his power, and raising his deep baritone voice in song: "Oh, Shenandoah, I long to see you. Far awa-ay, you rolling river. . . ."

With the mate's added strength, the windlass began to turn, slowly at first as the ship was pulled toward her anchor. Catching the lift of the melodious chantey that seemed to put strength in their legs, the men tramped around the capstan at a steady pace, picking up the chorus: "Awa-ay, we're bound away, across the wide Missouri!"

Before the anchor was up and down, Malloy had a man at the wheel while the rest of his port watch was scrambling to set the outer jib and brace the foremast yards around.

Merriman watched in pleased fascination at the orderly

maneuver, remembering his few months before the mast some four years earlier.

The south wind filled the jib and began to swing the bow. The helmsman put the wheel over to starboard, and the head of the vessel began to pay off, swinging away from the land with the tide giving her a strong push. No pilot came aboard. Apparently Captain Blackwell knew this shallow harbor well enough, and, with the *Inverness* drawing only a few feet of water fully loaded, he had no worry of running aground.

"Set your course south by east to give that island a good berth," Malloy instructed the sailor at the wheel, nodding toward Fort Sumter.

"Loose the fore tops'l!" Mr. Stark shouted, and four men sprang into the rigging to go aloft on the foremast, their former lethargy apparently gone. *Probably realize they're on the last leg of their voyage home,* Merriman thought. He noted the *Inverness* was a three-masted bark, carrying five square sails on each of her fore and main masts, and a fore-and-aft sail, or spanker, on her mizzen mast. When fully dressed, he guessed the ship probably had four jibs on the bowsprit and several triangular staysails hoisted between the masts. This vessel could oppose the wind with an impressive spread of canvas. Standing on the poop, he ran his gaze over the clean lines of the ship. It was no clipper, but, unlike the tubbier and shorter whaling ships, this bark was probably a hundred seventy feet long he estimated, and could carry a cargo with good speed over long distances.

As he watched both the port and starboard watches at work, taking the ship to sea, something was tickling the back of his mind. He struggled to capture the thought, whatever it was that was needling his unconscious. Then it came to him. Including the two mates, he counted a total of only fifteen men. The carpenter had been paid off, and the cook and the steward were below. Thirteen sailors to drive a ship of this size seemed only about a third the number needed. But, with more countries outlawing slave-trading, maybe it was harder to recruit sailors for this sort of business. He had not been into the hold where the barrels of molasses were stored, but guessed it had been thoroughly scrubbed before the cargo was loaded in Cuba. The filth and stench of a slaver in the middle passage was notorious, given the total lack of sanitation when the captured slaves were hauled like animals.

Should he communicate his apprehensions to Collins about the shortage of crew? No. If approximately the same number had sailed this ship from New England to Africa and back to Cuba, surely they would have no trouble getting her back up the coast to Boston. His own limited experience at sea was just enough to cause him to worry about things that were really no problem. He was here as a paying passenger, and he resolved to enjoy his cruise.

"What do you think of the crew?" he asked Collins as the they stood near the rail on the port side of the poop.

Collins shrugged. "Just a bunch of sailors doing their work."

"Take a closer look. I'd bet about half of them aren't out of their teens yet, and the rest don't look like proper sailing men to me. More like the dregs of some big city who went to sea one jump ahead of the police."

"Could be," Collins agreed. "But, as long as they can sail this ship, it's no problem of mine. As you remember, you and I have just been granted a short reprieve ourselves."

Merriman smiled. "It was mighty quick thinking for you to propose we pay our passage out of here. What better way to put some distance between ourselves and Sneedville . . . and Charleston."

"We may not have anybody looking for us in Charleston," Collins said. "I'm sure they think we drowned."

"I hope so, but it never hurts to be gone from there. When you don't show up in court in Asheville, a federal warrant will be issued for your arrest. This is better than hiding out in Charleston or Savannah. Boston is a larger city, and nobody will come looking for us there. We'll take a few weeks to decide when it's safe to go back and hunt up your gold discovery."

"Maybe I can get a job as an artist," Collins said.

"Better stay away from engraving for a while."

Collins nodded. "Sure wish I had some paint and canvases right now. I'd love to capture that." He was gazing aloft at the swell of ivory-colored sails and the men on the yards who were loosing the main topgallant.

It *was* a beautiful sight, Merriman thought, his eyes following the intricate tracery of lines, stays, and braces running up the masts that towered a hundred and twenty feet above the deck. The yellow spars swaying gently against the blue sky and the white clouds created a beauty he had not appreciated at first, being more concerned with the practical side of things. As they cleared the harbor and more sail was set, he could feel the ship lift and heel slightly to port as it caught the full force of a south wind and the long swell of the open ocean.

He looked back, and the buildings of Charleston were only a smudge across the low horizon of the inner harbor. Taking a deep breath, he relaxed, letting his mind think of only good things for the future.

Watching the magnificent ship work her way into the South Atlantic was such an enjoyable experience for Merriman, that it seemed only a few minutes before the two of them were called to dinner. As the only two paying passengers, they were to dine at the captain's table in his cabin, along with the first mate, Abel Stark. Given his uneasy feelings about Gilbert Malloy, Merriman was grateful the second mate ate his meals in the midship house, usually with the carpenter and sail-maker, when such were aboard.

The Oriental cook, whom Merriman had glimpsed in passing, was excellent. He and Collins, Captain Blackwell and Mr. Stark were served by a Chinese steward who went about his job with a whispery efficiency that Merriman guessed had been cultivated over many years of being a domestic. The man, who was called Louis, was probably past fifty years of age, had a completely smooth, bald head and round face, with slanted eyes couched in small pouches of fat. His only facial hair was a thin, black mustache that drooped on either side of his mouth.

Abel Stark, who sat opposite the captain, had combed his thick, graying hair and donned a dark suit coat for the occasion. The sack coat with no shoulder padding for shape was plenty large enough on him, but his was not the type of build that was enhanced by civilized clothing, Merriman thought. Bulging arm and shoulder muscles stretched the material as Stark moved. Merriman knew that he himself was not a small man, but that's just what he appeared to be alongside the mate.

Merriman and Collins sat opposite each other at the small table, with Captain Blackwell on Merriman's right. The meal consisted of creamed potatoes and peas, fresh-baked bread and—wonder of wonders—fried chicken.

"Marvelous food," Merriman enthused, thinking that maybe hunger made it even tastier.

"A rare treat," Captain Blackwell answered. "Although we sometimes carry live chickens and pigs aboard on longer voyages, they don't always survive. Mister Malloy brought these from Charleston just this morning."

Merriman couldn't help wondering what the men in the forecastle were eating. A sure bet it wasn't fried chicken. When he himself had served before the mast, he'd been acutely aware that the unbridgeable gulf separating heaven from hell could hardly be wider than the hundred feet separating the aftercabin from the forecastle, the masters from the slaves. All in all, although he empathized with their situation, he much preferred sitting at the captain's table, being served well-prepared food by a steward, and having a berth in a private cabin with no watches to stand. Except for the democratic crews of Norsemen in their open longboats, it had always been thus since man first built ships and went voyaging.

Collins ate mostly in silence, possibly because he was just hungry, Merriman thought. Or perhaps the Melungeon felt out of place here because of his dark bronze complexion.

On the other hand, Merriman wanted to know everything he could about this ship and his surroundings. He realized that he actually missed his days as a seaman along the coastal waters and the Gulf of Mexico. He'd not been a deep-water sailor, but had found he loved the sea and ships, in spite of the hard work and low pay of a seaman's life.

"What was the matter with the men at the capstan this morning, Mister Stark?" he asked, hoping to strike up a conversation.

Stark glanced at the captain before answering: "Nothing. Just hadn't got their sea legs back yet. We'd been in port a few days."

"I have a feeling you'd have knocked their heads together, if they'd shirked much longer," Merriman grinned.

Mr. Stark kept his eyes on his plate and didn't reply.

"If both watches were on deck earlier, we seem to be considerably short-handed," Merriman continued, trying again to generate some conversation.

But he was met by an uneasy silence until Captain Blackwell said: "There is one rule I have on this ship, Mister Merriman. And that is, the crew is never discussed at table. My two mates, Mister Stark and Mister Malloy, are able men who take care of the operation of this vessel."

And that was that. The talk turned to neutral subjects, such as food, ports visited, and life ashore, none of the men volunteering anything about himself or his background.

Merriman noted that the captain was a slender man, quite aristocratic in his bearing and manners. He was probably in his late sixties, getting on in years for command. But Abel Stark, of the great, scarred hands, big-bones, and heavy muscles, while not many years younger, seemed to have been hardened, rather than tempered, by the passing years. From what little Merriman had seen, he sensed the mate possessed a temperament that, when unleashed in earlier, wilder days, had probably accounted for the death of many a poor wretch who'd dared cross him. In spite of the physical and temperamental inequality between the two men, Merriman was amazed at the deference, or respectful awe, in which Stark held the captain. The mate could have broken him in two with one blow of that mighty fist. Yet he didn't so much as speak to the captain during the meal. Nor did Captain Blackwell deign to address him directly, although they sat facing each other less than three feet apart.

When the meal ended, the mate excused himself and departed, the captain retired to his cabin while the steward cleared the table.

Merriman and Collins retrieved their dry clothes from

the line on the poop deck and went below to their tiny adjoining cabins.

"I'm for a nap," Collins said, stretching out on his bunk fully clothed in the seaman's work clothes, and talking to Merriman through the open door.

"Same here. After what we've been through for the past two days, with no sleep, and now a good meal, I don't think I can hold my eyes open another ten minutes," Merriman said. "By the way, did you notice anything strange about the second mate?"

"Mister Malloy? Now that you mention it, yes. But I can't really place what it is."

"There's something about the man that makes me not want to turn my back on him."

Their cabins were on the lee side of the ship, and a sudden gust of wind heeled the vessel farther over. Merriman could hear the water rushing alongside the hull only a few inches from his head. He removed his hand from the brass handle of the porthole he'd started to open for some air as blue-green water churned past the thick glass. "Wind's freshening," he remarked, bracing himself in his bunk. "If this fair breeze keeps up, we should be in Boston in a few days."

His only answer was silence. Glancing through the doorway, he saw Collins already asleep, on his back, moving gently to the roll of the ship.

Chapter Nine

Sizemore Inn

East Tennessee Mountains

My heart is aching, aching, but I hear them, sleeping, waking;
It's the Lure of Little Voices, it's the mandate of the Wild.

Robert Service

Lisa Sizemore was in a quandary. There were so many things she wanted to take, but her father had made it very plain they all must keep their personal possessions to a bare minimum.

She sat on the floor in her room at the family inn, looking around at all the things she'd accumulated—cherished items she'd have to sell, give away, or just leave behind. The open cedar chest spilled forth handmade quilts, bed linens, embroidered towels, a white silk wedding dress—most of the things that made up the trousseau she'd assembled, with her mother's help, toward her eventual wedding day.

There in the corner sat the spinning wheel inherited from her grandmother. On the shelves were her beloved books—much too heavy to carry. And there was her doll collection she had started as a little girl—rag dolls, china dolls, spool dolls. There was her cherrywood jewelry box, holding not so much valuable gold or gems, but such things as cameos, a tortoise shell comb, gold rings and trinkets, fake pearls, and keepsakes of all kinds. Framed and hanging on the wall was the intricate geometric design woven from her mother's hair. Individual long black strands had been collected painstakingly from her hairbrush until she had enough to weave this delicate pattern—the type of artwork that was presently so much in vogue.

So many things, so little room. She would have to leave most of it behind, concentrating on practical clothing and shoes, a small sewing kit. Most of the weight and space on their journey would be taken up by food and blankets and other necessary, usable items. No room for sentiment or nostalgia. Not least of which was this very log building she had lived in since before she could remember. This inn had been the only home she'd ever known. Now she, her father, and mother were selling it, and using the money to outfit themselves with a wagon and team and all the necessaries to travel across the continent to the gold fields in California.

When her father had come back from Knoxville two weeks ago with the news, she'd been thrilled. She was more than past due for a change. At an age when most of her female friends were already married and starting their own families, the last thing she wanted to do was stay here, helping her parents run this inn, growing older and less eligible with each passing month. True, she had met a few young men who'd been passing through and stopped here for the night. But most of them were married or not anyone she might be interested in. There'd been that handsome young artist, a Melungeon named Collins, who'd stayed overnight a month ago, during that awful snow storm. She'd like to get to know him. But he and his friend had seemed in a hurry to get to the Carolinas on some kind of business. If only he would come back. . . . But she couldn't spend her life sitting around, wishing and waiting for something that would likely never happen. Better to take things into her own hands. And this trip with a wagon train to California might just be what she needed. Even if she decided to stay here, get a job and live on her own, what were her prospects? As a Melungeon, she was restricted to those dances, parties, and social events that were for her people only. She thought, with distaste, of the young men she'd met there, some of them distant kin, and most of them illiterate. She groaned at the thought of marrying one of them, bearing seven to ten children, and trying to hold body and soul together while her husband grubbed for a living from a poor hill farm, or worked somewhere in the lowlands for wages, coming home every other week-end, and then maybe getting drunk with his friends. What little joy there might be in family life would certainly be offset by the grinding poverty of such an existence where she'd grow old before her time. She'd seen it happen all too often.

She had been lucky. As an only child of parents who could read and write, she'd led an insulated existence here. Vincent Sizemore had inherited enough money from his parents to buy the land on which this inn was later built. But her father was aware of the restrictions that hemmed them in here. He'd told her that California had all kinds and colors of people and was quickly attracting more—Mexicans, Indians, Spaniards, whites. No one would think anything of their racially mixed background.

"What are you doing? Wool-gathering again?" Madeline Sizemore interrupted as she stood in the doorway, hands on hips.

"Oh, Momma, I can't decide!" she sulked.

Her mother came into the room and lowered herself onto the red velvet seat of an old walnut rocking chair. "I know," she replied with gentleness. "I'm having the same problem with my things, even to what pots and pans to take." She cast a glance around at the array spread out on the oval hooked rug that padded most of the pine floor. She smiled wistfully. "Men are lucky. They don't seem to form attachments to such things. They can just pick up and go without looking back." She paused as if thinking about what she'd just said. "At least your father can. If gold hadn't been discovered in California, I believe he would have found some other reason to leave. I've noticed him getting very restless these past few months."

Although they shared many confidences, Lisa was surprised at her mother's candor. Seeing Vincent from the totally different perspectives of husband and father, they seldom discussed his vicissitudes.

They were silent with their own thoughts for a few moments. The realization suddenly came to Lisa that every choice a person makes automatically eliminates many other choices. There was no going back. It was something she'd never stopped to reflect on before.

"Why don't you pick out some small, personal items you just can't do without, and then give the rest to Jennifer and Faith."

Lisa grimaced at the thought of these two addle-headed cousins taking possession of her treasured keepsakes. "Can I at least take my trousseau? Surely there's room in the wagon for that," she said.

Madeline Sizemore shook her head. "The three of us will have to live in that wagon day and night for months," she said.

Lisa pictured the green, solidly built Studebaker wagon her father had purchased in Knoxville along with a pair of stout mules used to the harness. Empty, the wagon looked as big as this room, but she nodded sadly at the truth of her mother's words.

"I'll help you wrap your wedding dress, but all the rest will have to be left here. Some of these things, like my shelf clock and your spinning wheel, we can leave with my sister. If we don't return, at least they'll remain in the family." Then she smiled. "It'll all work out. You'll see." She heaved herself wearily out of the rocker. "Well, let's get busy. A man and his wife are coming this afternoon with an eye to buying the place. I have to cook supper for them. Vincent thinks they're good prospects."

In spite of herself, Lisa's eyes filled with tears. "I don't want to leave here," she admitted, trying to keep her voice from trembling. It felt as if someone were ripping her life up by the roots. Then she felt her mother's hand on her shoulder.

"Just think of it as a beginning, not an ending . . . like opening a new book you got and can't wait to get lost in." Madeline Sizemore paused. "If you stay, you'll look back when you're my age and be bitter about the opportunity you missed."

Lisa nodded, swallowing hard. "When do we go?"

"If we can sell the place quickly, your father wants to be on the road within a week. Says we should be in Saint Joseph, on the far side of Missouri, by mid-May, just over a month from now. That's where we're to meet up with the wagon train. The grass on the plains will be greening up by then."

Chapter Ten

Aboard the Inverness

South Atlantic

Clayburn Collins was so thoroughly and miserably seasick that he had ceased to be embarrassed about it. In fact, as his stomach contorted and he gagged up its last liquid contents into a bucket, he began to wonder if he would even survive this ordeal. He almost wished he would just go ahead and die and have done with it. No sense prolonging the agony.

As his rigid abdominal muscles relaxed from their spasm, he lay carefully back on his bunk, staring at the beams that formed the ceiling support of his cabin. At the very least, he was becoming very dehydrated. He groaned as the ship rolled, paused, heaved herself upright, then rolled the other way. The *Inverness* had been performing this same dance for the past four hours, and there was no end in sight. And the motion was accompanied by the nerve-straining crashing and banging of all the running rigging overhead as it was whipped back and forth.

Merriman had told him the fair wind they'd enjoyed had been the tail end of a circular weather system that had moved off to the east, leaving behind huge, smooth swells on the disturbed ocean, with no wind to steady the ship. The calm had persisted since just before daylight, and, if the captain had any idea how long it would last, he wasn't saying. Merriman had looked a little green himself after the first hour, but a turn around the deck in the fresh air had set him right.

"Come topside." Merriman's voice was irritatingly cheerful as he appeared in the doorway. "You'll feel better."

"I don't dare move," Collins replied.

"There's one sure cure for seasickness," Merriman said, moving toward the bunk. "If you can fix your eyes on something that doesn't appear to be moving . . . like a cloud, or the horizon, you can stop your inner ear from getting off balance. A little trick I learned when I was at sea a few years ago. That's why *mal de mer* is worse at night because there's nothing visible that's not in motion." He reached out a hand. "Come on. I'll help you."

With only one stop at the bucket the steward had thoughtfully provided, Collins made it out the door and up the swaying steps to the poop. A whiff of something cooking in the galley almost made him gag again.

"If it's any consolation, Mister Stark told me the captain has been confined to his cabin for the last hour," Merriman said as they emerged into the bright sunlight. "Says the old man's subject to a touch of seasickness every time he leaves the land. We're right in the middle of the Gulf Stream and that's making it even worse."

They held onto the rail, and Collins stared off at a cloud for several minutes, breathing deeply of the clean air and trying to ignore the slanting rise and fall of the deck under his feet.

Sure enough, in less than ten minutes, he felt almost normal again, although very weak. And his stomach muscles were sore to the touch. He tried to act as if nothing were wrong, especially when the sailor at the nearby wheel glanced in his direction. He could have sworn the man had a smirk on his face. Or maybe that was only the man's normal look. The sailor was one of the older ones, a villainous-looking individual, lean and wiry, with a thin nose crooked to one side. Long, stringy hair was fashioned into one ratty pigtail behind, reaching past his collar.

"His name's Jacobus," Merriman said under his breath, nodding at the helmsman. "They call him the ferret."

"It fits," Collins said, observing the amused look the helmsman slanted in his direction. He resented a sailor like Jacobus who judged landsmen by his own occupation. Except as a man could hand, reef, and steer, Jacobus probably had no way of knowing a fool.

The helmsman was paying little attention to his job of steering since the vessel had no headway. Easily accommodating himself to the ship's motion, Jacobus slouched on the grate behind the wheel and every few seconds turned the big, brass-studded spokes this way and that. But with absolutely no headway in the dead calm, the heavily laden bark was at the mercy of the swells, her time bell tolling as she rolled her scuppers under.

Mister Malloy stood near them on the poop, observing a half-dozen men in his watch aloft furling the sails.

"This is very hard on the gear," he remarked to them. "I'd rather have a good, stiff blow any day than this."

Collins could see the truth of his words. The sails that were still set boomed a hollow thunder as they filled and emptied with every roll. Besides this noise, they were treated to a constant slatting and banging of blocks and downhauls as the booms and yards were jerked back and forth. "I'm surprised it doesn't whip the masts out of her," Collins said, turning away to look at the horizon again to steady his stomach.

"Mister Stark told me the *Inverness* is only eight years

old and stoutly built," Merriman said. "The best Nova Scotia spruce, pine, and white oak. Teak decks. She was designed to stand a lot worse than this."

At dinner time, Merriman went below to the captain's cabin, while Collins excused himself to remain on deck. "Make my apologies to Captain Blackwell. But I can't stand even the thought of food just now."

"I'm sure he'll understand. I'll save you a greasy hunk of salt pork," Merriman grinned as he disappeared behind the charthouse.

"Ugh."

The calm lasted the remainder of the day, and most of the night. During that time, Collins never fully recovered. He divided his time between his bunk near the open porthole, and pacing the poop deck. Hard crackers and water were his only fare. He felt his stomach grow flatter, but, at least, the vomiting had ceased.

He awoke sometime in the blackness of the following night. Unable to go back to sleep immediately, he slipped out of his bunk, felt for his shoes and jacket, and, balancing against the roll of the darkened room, made his way out the door and up the steps to the deck. By the tiny light sheltered in the binnacle, he could see the face of the man at the wheel. It was one of the youthful sailors he didn't recognize. Most of the men he had seen only from a distance as they worked on deck or aloft. The only time any of them came aft onto the poop deck was to stand a wheel watch or to handle the sheets of the big spanker sail that was hoisted on the mizzen mast. Collins avoided speaking to the sleepy-looking helmsman and went around to the rail on the starboard side where he detected a slight movement of air. The night was chilly and there was no moon, he noticed as he looked up at the uncountable spangle of stars. Although he couldn't actually see them, three sails blotted out the stars as the masts arced gently across the sky. By their positions he identified them as the main topgallant, the fore topsail, and the flying jib. He smiled to himself as he realized that, with no conscious effort, he'd actually absorbed the names of these sails in only a couple of days.

There was a slight movement of air against his cheek, and the sails of the *Inverness* detected it and were no longer slatting. The ship was barely moving through a sea that had dropped down to gentle swells. He wondered why an efficient mate didn't have more sail set to take advantage of whatever breeze there was. Besides the man at the wheel and a look-out who was always stationed in the bow, the rest of the watch was probably standing by somewhere on the main deck, in case they were needed.

Just then he heard voices several feet away and below him on the main deck. He attuned his ears to catch the sounds and recognized the Virginia dialect of the second mate. If Gilbert Malloy had the watch, then it had to be sometime before midnight, given the four hours on, four off rotation. Who was he talking to? Abel Stark was probably sound asleep in his bunk below. From the conversational tone of the voices, this had nothing to do with ship's business. His curiosity was aroused. Moving silently closer to the break of the poop, he looked down into the blackness. All he could see was the glow of a pipe bowl, and he caught a faint whiff of tobacco smoke.

He felt sneaky, eavesdropping like this, but, from what he had seen and heard, it was a serious breach of discipline for a mate to fraternize with the sailors under his command. Unprofessional at the least, dangerous at the worst.

"It's all settled, then," Collins heard one of the men say.

"What about Mister Stark?"

"Never you mind. I'll deal with him," Malloy's suave tones came out of the darkness. Collins felt a chill go over him.

"That's what I'm afraid of," another voice said, and there was a general chuckle.

Just then eight bells was struck from just forward of the midship house, and the conversation ceased. There was a parting word among them, and Collins heard footsteps shuffling away to change the watch. He slid back along the rail to the stern, intent on not being noticed by anyone. He waited several more minutes until the man at the wheel was relieved, and he heard the deep voice of Abel Stark, ordering men aloft to set more sail. Then, shivering and thoroughly chilled, he slipped into the charthouse, down the stairs to the dimly lighted passageway, and into his cabin.

He felt he had been privy to something sinister, but couldn't make out what. It could wait until morning; he was too tired to worry his head about it now. As he settled into his warm bunk, he could feel the ship beginning to move.

At six the next morning he awoke to a fine cold spray coming in the open port. He hastily closed it and pulled on his clothes. The *Inverness* had picked up a wind at last and was dashing through the water under an overcast sky. Collins's seasickness was also a thing of the past, and his appetite had returned with a vengeance.

He went into the adjoining cabin and woke Merriman who sat up, stretching. "Whew! I was dead to the world last night. I believe I'm beginning to like this seafaring as a passenger," he grinned. "Good food and all night in." He yawned as he pulled on his own clothes. "You look glum. Still seasick?" He rolled up the work shirt and pants and laid them aside.

"No. I was on deck last night just before midnight," Collins began, then related what he'd overheard.

Merriman's expression never changed. "Malloy should have known better than that. He's no tyro."

"You think it's anything to worry about or report to the captain?"

Merriman shook his head. "I think we should let well enough alone and not get involved. That may be Malloy's style of supervision. Some men can be familiar with their subordinates and still command respect. Although I've never heard of that being the case aboard ship."

"What about his remark that he would *deal with* Mister Stark?"

"Could be most anything . . . some kind of anchor pool, or a request from the men that will be presented to Stark by Mister Malloy. Malloy is certainly much more civil and approachable than the mate."

Collins nodded. "You're right. I'm seeing ghosts where there are none. Let's go to breakfast."

At the morning meal, Captain Blackwell was his usual quiet self, but took note of Collins's return with a cool nod and the comment: "You're looking much better." In view of the fact that the captain had looked upon him as a colored servant when he first came aboard and had been reluctant to allow him to bunk aft, Collins considered this comment as almost a friendly embrace.

"Thank you, sir. Think I've finally got my sea legs under me."

Abel Stark was more morose than usual, and, at first, Collins set it down to the gray weather. But then he thought that a seafarer like Abel Stark should be jubilant that the ship had picked up a good wind and was reeling off the miles.

As Stark reached for a biscuit, Collins noticed fresh abrasions on the mate's massive knuckles. There was no telling what had taken place in the wee hours of the mid-watch. Doubtless a couple of insubordinate sailors were nursing black eyes or swollen jaws. Collins couldn't help but think of the contrast to the easy-going atmosphere during Malloy's watch. Collins was certain Captain Blackwell was aware of many of the things that went on with the mates and the crew but, for some reason, chose to ignore them, as long as the ship's work got done and discipline was maintained. Captain Blackwell was like a king, his mates were the nobles who did his bidding, and the sailors the serfs who tilled the land and held up the whole structure. This may have been the mid-19th Century, Collins thought, but the system was closer to medieval.

Stark quickly excused himself after eating and returned topside.

Twenty minutes later, Collins and Merriman emerged by way of the hall door directly onto the main deck. Collins caught his breath at the sight of the tall ship dressed in her ball gown. Every piece of canvas, including the staysails, was set and drawing. The yards were braced around at an angle to catch the force of a westerly gale blowing over the port beam. The *Inverness* was plunging her bow through a gray, lumpy sea, throwing spray high over the forecastle The heavily laden ship had little freeboard and, at every roll, a thousand tons of Atlantic poured across her main deck.

A few seconds later a rogue wave, larger and from a different direction than the rest, curled above the rail. The two men saw it coming and jumped for the ladder. They'd barely cleared the top of the ladder to the poop, when the sea exploded against the after cabin, shattering into a sheet of spray that was caught and dissipated by the wind.

Collins clung to the port rail as the fury and the splendor of the spectacle literally took his breath. Every straining sail was as rigid as carved ivory. From his higher vantage point, he could see the full length of the ship as she staggered and rolled, pressed over and down with every gust. Gray-green seawater spilled over her rail at the waist, rushed across the deck, and spilled outboard with the opposite roll. And all the while the vessel was plunging ahead at a good twelve knots. Mr. Stark was driving the ship hard, apparently to make up for the day or more they had been becalmed, Collins reflected. The burdened ship was like a log awash, as much under the water as above it. Her scuppers spouted streams of water in a continuous effort to rid the decks of the weight of ocean that swamped her amidships.

And the noise! Besides the crashing of the sea, Collins was struck dumb by the roaring of wind through the rigging. All the stays and shrouds and braces—every rope and line thrummed or howled or shrieked a different note that blended into the elemental chorus. King Neptune in full voice, Collins thought.

Conversation was out of the question. Merriman turned his face away from the blast and grinned at him. As much as his senses were stunned by the concussion of noise and wind and movement, Collins couldn't help but admire the two mates below them, struggling with the men of both watches as they tried to secure some wreckage. A pinrail had been torn loose along with the top of the rail in the waist of the ship. A tangle of belaying pins and lines and splintered pieces of wood were washing about on the deck near the main hatch. Between bursting waves, six men were attempting to capture the tangled mass of gear. But each time the force of the sea swept them off their feet and rolled them into the scuppers. Finally Abel Stark and Gilbert

Malloy let go of the rail and sprang into the fray, getting hold of the tangle of ropes and blocks. As the next wave burst, they not only kept their legs under them, but managed to keep hold of the raffle with one hand and one of the sailors with the other. Each of the mates was as good as any two of the men they commanded, Collins could see. Once the tangle of lines was temporarily secured again to the rail, they attacked the splintered hatch cover. Even a landsman like Collins could see that this was potentially a much more dangerous situation. If the main hatch cover was completely breached, the hold would flood and the ship founder. There was no carpenter aboard, but the two mates and three of the men were able to fasten a stout piece of wood across the broken cover as a strongback and lash it in place, wedging in pieces of canvas around it to keep most of the water out. Again, the two mates did most of the work on the makeshift repair, while the three sailors were tumbled off their feet with each breaking wave, or jumped for the lifelines that had been strung across the deck, and hung on as the cold, creamy flood stretched them full length.

As Collins clung to the taffrail and watched this drama for several minutes, he began to sense a rhythm to the waves and the movement of the ship. Because of that he was suddenly aware of a larger sea curling its foam-streaked lip above the port rail amidships. "Ferret" Jacobus saw the giant green sea first as it loomed fully fifteen feet above the rail and made a jump for the shrouds. The rest of the men and the two mates never had a chance as the full weight of the huge wave fell on them. The men disappeared. The longboat atop the midship house was splintered as the wave impacted against it, spouting spray as high as the lower yardarms. The ship trembled and settled down, water filling her main deck from rail to rail. The next moment the ship plunged down by the head, and all this mass of water surged forward. Collins saw arms and legs and heads, a tangle of rope, and jagged pieces of wood emerge here and there from the creaming surface as everything was tumbled over and over until the whole mass fetched up against the wall of the forecastle. Collins cringed at the mauling the men were receiving. Again it was the mates who emerged first and strongest, waist deep in the flood, gripping a sailor in each fist, dragging them to the relative safety of the rail as the ship rolled to port, spilling most of her burden outboard.

Captain Blackwell had come up from below and stood nearby on the poop, his oilskins and southwester gleaming black with the flying spray. He scanned the clouds and ran his gaze over the reeling skysails, his feet planted wide as he accommodated himself to the antics of the ship. If Collins hadn't known better, he would have mistaken him for a well-to-do passenger. After several minutes he turned to the second mate who had come up the ladder onto the poop. He didn't shout, but his voice came to Collins's ears as clearly as the tones of a brass bell. "Take the spanker and the staysails off her, Mister Malloy."

"Aye, sir." Malloy turned and relayed the order at the top of his voice.

The captain watched for several more minutes, pacing up and down. Finally, with a last look at the sky, he disappeared into the charthouse to go below.

Merriman put his mouth close to Collins's ear and shouted: "We'll draw some oilskins today."

Collins nodded. He couldn't stand much more of this without some kind of protection. He was freezing and moved around the taffrail, preparing to make a dash for the charthouse door and the stairway.

Two muscular young men were at the wheel, one on either side, trying to keep the ship on course. Collins saw they had all they could handle as the heavy wheel kicked each time a roller passed under the counter and struck the rudder.

Just before he ducked into the charthouse, Collins took one last glance down at the deck and saw two men carrying away one of their own. Blood smeared his forehead.

Collins was soaked by spray, thoroughly chilled, and out of breath as he descended the stairs to his cabin. The sudden cessation of the tumult on deck made the below-deck spaces seem almost dead quiet. He went into his cabin and wedged himself into a corner to strip off his sodden shirt and pants and don his own clothes, reflecting that he had experienced only the merest taste of what the mates and the crew were going through.

That afternoon the captain opened the lazarette for them to purchase sea boots, oilskins, and southwesters so they could go on deck in foul weather in some degree of comfort. To Collins's delight, he was even able to buy a couple of pencils and a large, leather-bound book with unlined pages to do some sketching.

"That's actually an extra logbook," Captain Blackwell said. "But we won't need it this trip. I'll get another one in Boston."

Collins began by rendering an excellent likeness of the captain and presented it to him just before supper.

Smoked ham, boiled beans, and onions was the main course at table that evening, and things were becoming so pleasant Collins thought idly of a possible career at sea for himself. Without a lot of money, one couldn't continue to cruise as a pampered passenger, but maybe he could hire out as a portrait artist on a passenger packet, and also fill in as a steward. It wasn't likely to happen, he knew, but it was nice to dream, and he had to keep his options open. Plenty of food, plenty of rest, and his beloved art work. A life at sea would provide endless possibilities to exercise his artistic talents, especially if he got some oils, brushes, and canvases.

When he came on deck after breakfast with his sketchbook the next morning, only a moderate sea was running, and a pale sun was trying to break through some ragged clouds.

"Good day, sir," the man at the wheel greeted him.

"Ah, yes, it is," Collins answered. He took a closer look at the helmsman. He was a man of average size, but mature years if the gray, curly hair was any indication. He had clear, intelligent blue eyes in a face that was seamed and creased. A fresh bandage circled the top of his head, and he seemed to be favoring his left arm or shoulder. Collins thought at first the man might have been the object of Mr. Stark's wrath, but this sailor was in Malloy's starboard watch.

"What happened?" Collins asked.

"Had a wild time of it on deck yesterday," he replied. "Got rolled into a stanchion and split my head open."

Collins cringed.

"It's all right now. Mister Stark stitched it up. It's this shoulder that's bothering me more. Wrenched it pretty good."

Collins nodded, thinking that Abel Stark was probably a pretty rough surgeon. But one never knew. The mate might have the touch of a woman when it came to something delicate. He'd probably stitched many a sail and not a few sailors in his day.

Collins had dragged a small chair with him and sat himself down nearby to sketch the three tall masts that were carrying just over half their canvas at the moment. As he worked, he noticed the helmsman eyeing him.

"Whatcha doing?"

Collins held out the book for him to see.

"Nice. Didn't know you were an artist."

"That's about all I can do well."

The man nodded. "I'm just the other way around. I can do lots of different things, but none of them very well."

"What's your name?" Collins asked.

"Will Fjelde."

"How do you spell that?"

"F-j-e-l-d-e. Pronounced, Fee-yell-dee." He lowered his voice. "It's Finnish, but I was born in Canada."

"I'm. . . ."

"I know. Clayburn Collins. I remember the captain introduced you when you came aboard."

Collins guessed the man would not have been so friendly and familiar with a member of the afterguard if Collins had been a white man.

"Truth of the matter is, I'm a better sailor than most anything else," Fjelde continued, checking the compass rose in the binnacle and pulling down a few spokes to correct his course. "But, by and large, sailors are a superstitious lot. And Finns are supposed to be like warlocks, and have power over the weather. We're generally considered bad luck. That bit of wind we had yesterday was blamed on me, along with all the damage and injuries it brought . . . even to me." He gave Collins a look as if he expected him to know what prejudice was like. "I had nothing to do with it . . . spring storms are common in this latitude."

"Why don't you change your name?" Collins asked.

"I've thought of that," Fjelde said, studying the draw of the sails, "but that would be like saying I'm ashamed of who I am."

"I know what you mean," Collins nodded, thinking that changing his own name would mean nothing, since it was so common. Changing his dark bronze skin was another matter. He wondered if he would do it, even if he somehow had that capability.

Gilbert Malloy, who had the watch, came strolling toward them from the port side.

"Mind your helm," he said to Fjelde in a pleasant tone, but with a quick glance at Collins.

Fjelde turned his full attention back to his job, while Collins continued his sketching.

The wind continued to fall off during the day, and by sunset the ship was slipping through a confused sea at about three knots, with all sails set.

"Being swept out of that river may turn out to be the best thing that's happened to us since Sneedville," Collins remarked as he and Merriman retired to their cabins, pleasantly stuffed, after supper.

"Don't get too relaxed," Merriman said, admiring the sketch Collins held out to him. "Remember, you're on a slaver. I'll breathe a lot easier when we get ashore and on our own again." He reached under his bunk and pulled out his gun belt. "I borrowed a little oil from the mate to clean my gun," he said, wiping it off with a rag.

"You think you're going to need it?"

Merriman shook his head. "Hope not. Won't matter if I do. It's empty, and all my extra powder, caps, and balls were left behind in my saddlebags when we went into the river."

"I think maybe I'll get a small pocket pistol when we get to Boston. It never hurts to be armed, just in case."

Merriman shoved his gun belt back under the bed. "Think I'll take a turn around the deck before I go to sleep."

After Merriman left, Collins undressed and crawled into his bunk, his eyes heavy. The gentle motion of the ship soon had him oblivious to his surroundings as he fell into a deep slumber, with no premonition of what was to come.

Chapter Eleven

The next morning the ship was a-buzz with rumors that something had happened to Mr. Stark.

Merriman had his first inkling of it when he came out onto the main deck just at daylight and saw two young sailors, talking quietly near the base of the mainmast. The breeze brought snatches of their conversation to his ears. ". . . split his skull, I hear. Jack says he's laid up in his bunk." ". . . hell to pay now, you can bet. . . ."

The heavy door slammed behind him, and Merriman saw two startled faces looking in his direction. They abruptly quit talking and shuffled forward toward the second mate who was yelling for the watch to tighten up some slack rigging.

Merriman's curiosity was piqued as he went into the main cabin and sat down to breakfast. Before he could say anything to Collins, who was there ahead of him, Captain Blackwell and Abel Stark came in.

The mate was even quieter than usual as he took his place across from the captain while Louis, the Oriental steward, began serving them. During the meal, Merriman watched Stark fumble his fork a time or two, almost as if his co-ordination were off. Once, when he looked up to have a bowl passed to him, Stark looked directly at him, and Merriman thought the eyes seemed glazed. He wondered if the mate was only feeling the effects of lack of sleep since the watch rotation kept the mates from getting more than three and a half hours of sleep at any one stretch. But this notion was soon dispelled when Merriman got up to shut the door that had failed to latch behind the departing steward. As he passed behind the mate, he noted a prodigious lump on the back of his head and remnants of what appeared to be clotted blood in the grizzled hair.

The mate ate little and, mumbling an excuse, left the table early. If the captain had even taken note of the mate's strange behavior, he gave no indication of it.

"Well, I confirmed what you suspected about Stark," Collins said when the two men were alone in their cabins an hour later.

Merriman arched his eyebrows in silent query.

"Louis, the Chinese steward, told me one of the sailors tried to bash Stark's skull with a belaying pin during one of the night watches."

"How did Louis know?"

"He bunks near the galley and talks a lot with the cook, who's also Chinese. The cook is friendly with the two Cubans in the forecastle. They knew about it, but they wouldn't tell him who did it."

"How come Louis told *you?*" Merriman was still dubious as to the accuracy of the information.

"Louis is friendly to me. Gives the impression that those of us who aren't white have to stick together. And I'm the only one in the afterguard who isn't white. He told me he wanted me to know since I was a passenger and not part of all this."

"All of what?"

"He wouldn't say. Just warned that things weren't as they should be, and to be on my guard."

"Guessing from the way those two sailors were acting, I guess Louis has got the straight of it."

"That old man must have a head harder than oak."

"He's probably toughed out worse things in his day."

"Somebody resents the way he rides the men," Collins said.

"Hard discipline is usually the rule, not the exception," Merriman mused.

"But on this ship there's a world of difference in the way the two mates operate."

"That could be the reason, right enough, since Malloy is so all-fired cozy with the crew," Merriman said.

"It could have been Malloy himself," Collins went on. "I did hear him say he was going to take care of Stark."

Merriman nodded soberly. "If there's some kind of grudge between those two, I hope they wait till we're ashore before they settle it."

"If Stark knows who hit him, that man may vanish over the side come dark."

"Wish I had some ammunition for my Colt," Merriman muttered. "I'd feel a lot safer."

Collins took his sketchbook up on deck, and Merriman stretched out on his bunk to read a book on ancient Rome he'd borrowed from the captain's scanty library.

The two men met again at the midday meal, but the mate was absent. Late that afternoon, Merriman came topside to watch the sailors pulling and hauling on various lines and ropes. Judging from the thudding of feet and the shouted commands he'd heard all day from below, Merriman knew the men had been busy changing sail as the wind puffed up and died in addition to boxing the compass. An exasperating weather day for all concerned.

Merriman stood near Collins's chair and watched him sketch several men who were laid out along the royal yard, fisting a sail. Against the background of a light gray sky, Merriman thought the dark figures looked like a row of blackbirds on a rail fence.

Suddenly he heard a shout and the figure nearest the end of the yardarm was cartwheeling through the air. Merriman caught his breath as the man bounced off the starboard shrouds and was propelled out over the rail into the sea.

"Man overboard!" the mate boomed. "Belay that line and get a boat over the side!" he shouted at the half dozen men who were hauling on clewlines from the deck. For a few seconds they looked at him, dumbfounded, without moving. "Quick!" the mate shouted, heaving a wooden bucket over the side in the direction of the fallen man. "You dim-witted spawn of whores! Get the lead out of your legs and move!"

The men charged for the starboard longboat. Merriman and Collins joined the rush. By the time they descended the ladder to the main deck and reached the midship bulwark, the sailors had the boat rigged to the falls and were swinging it outboard on its davits. Four sailors and the mate, along with Collins and Merriman, clambered into the twenty-foot boat as two men on deck lowered away.

Merriman didn't know if Collins had ever rowed a boat before, but they each grabbed an oar, sitting side by side on a thwart, while Stark took the tiller in the stern. "OK, men, together now . . . stroke!" The six rowers pulled in unison. Merriman glanced sideways and felt a surge of pride at the way Collins was handling his oar.

As they glided away from the side of the ship, Merriman realized the sea was not nearly as calm as it had appeared from the poop deck. A long swell was running. They pulled strongly for almost a minute.

"Hold!"

The six men rested on their oars. For the first time from a distance, Merriman was able to admire the graceful lines of the tall, white-hulled ship. Built for commercial hauling and heavily loaded, it was still a thing of beauty as it rested on the smooth swells.

Stark was scanning the surface for the man in the water. Merriman looked over his shoulder. The sea had apparently swallowed the unfortunate sailor. There was no sign of a head bobbing among the watery hills and valleys around them. He might have been knocked unconscious when he hit the sloping shrouds and already be drowned. The mate's face was grim.

"There!" Stark boomed. "Pull! And put your backs into it!" He pushed the tiller away from him, and the men bent to their work as the boat surged ahead, sliding down the back of a long, foam-streaked swell. Merriman couldn't see where they were going, but he felt the power they generated as the boat knifed through the water. He was glad the sea wasn't choppy. He cast one hurried glance over his shoulder without losing his rhythm and saw a head in the water, some fifty yards away. Then it quickly disappeared in a valley. He concentrated on pulling strongly with the others.

Suddenly Stark gave the order to belay, and he stopped rowing, breathing heavily. A few seconds later, eager hands were dragging the man over the side of the boat. It was Fjelde, the Finnish sailor Collins had told him about. He fell heavily onto the floorboards, his sodden sweater streaming and water pouring from his sea boots. Stark reached over the side and snagged the wooden bucket, which had apparently kept the man afloat.

After a quick look at the rescued seaman, Stark yelled: "Oars in the water! Pull!"

Fjelde slumped in the bottom of the boat, groaning, and Stark gave him only a cursory glance, not bothering to see how badly he was injured. *Typical,* Merriman thought. Stark apparently assumed that, if he could shrug off injuries, then everyone else could do the same.

But they had other problems at the moment, Merriman realized as he noticed the sky growing darker and then felt several raindrops on his face. The ship was nowhere in sight, and a rain squall was sweeping down on them, blotting out everything in a gray veil. As he turned back to his rowing, he had an uneasy feeling in his stomach. But Stark didn't seem worried. He wore his usual grim expression as he squinted into the slanting rain that was beginning to drench them, the droplets stinging the exposed flesh of their face and hands. The downpour increased, hissing into the sea, and limiting their view to a few yards in any direction.

The squall passed over in about ten minutes, and Merriman stole another look downwind. He was shocked at how far away the *Inverness* had drifted. The mainsail had been backed, but the larger vessel was drifting downwind much faster than the men could row the longboat.

"C'mon, put your backs into it!" Stark growled, wet hair plastered across his forehead. The mate demonstrated his seamanship by maneuvering the boat to take advantage of the push of the long swells.

For the next twenty minutes or more, they rowed as if their very survival was at stake.

"More damned bad luck!" Collins gasped as he struggled with his oar.

"What?" Merriman slanted a quick look at him.

"Fjelde," Collins added, jerking his head toward the groaning figure at their feet.

"Huh!" Merriman snorted. "It didn't take you long to adopt *that* superstition." His grin belied the sting of his words.

If Gilbert Malloy hadn't ordered the remaining crew to sail upwind to meet them, Merriman doubted if they would have ever reached the ship. He'd heard of this happening before—usually in worse weather when the men and the small boat were never seen again. He guessed the nearest land was more than a hundred miles away. At least the longboat carried a mast and furled sail, lying lengthwise across the thwarts.

Suddenly the boat rose up on a swell, and there was the *Inverness*, looming closer. Stark steered the boat expertly alongside as the men shipped their oars. The men on deck had backed the sails and threw over some thick rope fenders to prevent the two vessels from banging together in the uneven surge. With the help of reaching hands, the six oarsmen leapt nimbly aboard. Stark attached the hooks to the eyes and, gauging the moment when the boat rose almost even with the deck, sprang to the rail. Then he lent a hand as the men began to haul the boat up with the injured Fjelde in the bottom.

Just as the boat was swung inboard and lowered into its cradle on deck, Malloy pulled a pistol from under his coat and aimed it at Stark. "This ship has been taken over, and Captain Blackwell is no longer in command."

Merriman caught his breath and looked at Abel Stark. He thought the old mate's eyes were going to bug out of his head. Three of the men who had been rowing the boat moved quickly to stand behind Malloy.

"Mutiny, by God!" the mate finally breathed. Merriman looked to Stark to react violently. But the formidable old man only stared at Malloy and at the pistol in his hand, his face darkening like the weather.

It didn't appear this development came as any surprise to most of the crew who stood facing Stark, Collins, Merriman, and the young sailor Fjelde was leaning on.

"What the hell is all this about?" Stark finally asked, his

deep voice grating with ridicule.

"The boys and I have taken a vote and. . . ."

"You and the boys is right," Stark interrupted. "You should be in the fo'castle . . . not an officer of a sailing vessel."

"Be that as it may," Malloy continued, unruffled, "we've decided we're going to the gold fields. We've talked it over among ourselves, and most of us feel that, if we wait much longer, all the good places will be staked, and a lot of the nuggets picked clean."

"You're a damn' fool!" was Stark's quick assessment. "Where's the captain?"

"In his cabin with Stenson, preparing to go ashore."

"Ashore, is it?" Stark sneered.

"We offered him a chance to join us, but he called us a few names and said he wanted no part of it. Of course, as a captain, he's drawing a princely salary while the rest of us will likely leave our bones on some lee shore after spinning out our days as wage slaves of rich ship owners."

"You're free to leave the sea if you want to," Stark retorted.

"Right you are, Mister Stark, and that's just what we're doing now," Malloy replied, his blue eyes snapping. "After one last voyage. I'm now in command of the *Inverness*, and we're taking her around the Horn to San Francisco."

Merriman's heart sank at this. Just when they were so close to Boston and freedom!

"And what about me?" Stark inquired.

"You will stay aboard as first mate to help navigate."

Before Merriman could open his mouth, Malloy said: "I know one of our two passengers has been to sea before, but we can't let either of them go ashore because we'll need all the hands we can get. We're short-handed as it is."

Merriman and Collins exchanged glances. The Melungeon showed no fear. Maybe he was just used to dealing with adversity, or, more likely, he had no inkling what hardships lay ahead of him as a working member of this crew on at least a four-month voyage. Merriman thought that maybe they could beg to go in the boat with the captain. Collins was apparently thinking along the same line, as he burst out: "You might as well let me go with the captain. I'm no sailor. Never been on the ocean before now."

"You're not the first man, or the last, who'll learn the ropes because he has to. You look young and healthy enough. We'll make a sailor out of you," Malloy replied.

Collins looked at Merriman, who added: "The two of us are wanted by the law. We'll leave and be out of your hair. One less reason the law will be looking for you."

Malloy gave a chuckle. "The law is looking for half this crew. You're staying aboard with us."

Merriman ground his teeth in silent frustration. "I'm a paying passenger. If you choose to take this ship somewhere besides Boston, I can't stop you, but I don't have to help you."

"You're saying you won't work?"

"That's about the size of it."

A slow snarl twisted Malloy's bland face, and Merriman cringed at the demon that almost showed its fangs from under the bushy brows.

"We'll take care of that," Malloy grated through clenched teeth. "See if you sing the same tune after we trice you up and give you a good flogging. If that doesn't do it, then maybe you'd prefer a few months in irons on bread and water."

Merriman made no reply; he knew he was at the mercy

of Malloy and his mutinous crew.

"If I come along, what's to prevent me from slitting your throat some dark night?" Stark inquired in a matter-of-fact tone, showing absolutely no fear at what was taking place.

"If anything happens to me, you'll be food for the fishes before the next watch is out," Malloy replied evenly. "You know how most of the men feel about you, and it was only by the hardest that I persuaded them to serve under you. As captain, I'll give the orders, but I'll still handle one watch and you can take the other. I've appointed Jacobus as bo'sun."

Merriman expected a sour retort from the mate, but Stark said nothing for several seconds. Merriman realized the mate, like he and Collins, really had no choice. Malloy had the gun. If he said stay, they would stay, or be shot. If charges of mutiny were ever brought in court, what judge would believe they'd been coerced into going along? It looked as if all of them, except Captain Blackwell, were in this for the long haul.

"I'll stick," Stark finally said in a tone that seemed to indicate he was trying to save face and wanted to appear he still had some choice in the matter.

Merriman didn't know whether to be relieved or not. If nothing else, Stark was an opportunist. Somehow Merriman felt the mate could be an ally. He might be their only protection against a hostile crew. Merriman really didn't know any of the crew. As he stared at the resolute faces in front of him, he wondered about their motivations and feelings. How many of them had been forced into joining this mutiny? Of those who joined willingly, Merriman guessed the younger ones were out for the adventure and sudden riches that would make them men of leisure for the rest of their lives. Of the older ones, he surmised they had nothing to lose. Some of them probably had criminal pasts, and the others had toiled for years with nothing to show for it except the diminishing skills of advancing age. The gold fields represented one last chance for them to accomplish something. At least four of the sailors appeared to be under twenty years of age. They were all attempting to grow mustaches or beards, probably to look more mature, he guessed. They needn't have bothered. The faces that stared at him were no longer the faces of youth. Something had aged them—the sea or toil or hard living ashore.

Just then Captain Blackwell came on deck, escorted by a tall, red-haired sailor. The captain was carrying a small leather grip. He looked squarely at Malloy. "If you want to reconsider this rash action, I'd be willing to forget it ever happened. It will not be reported and will not be entered in the log."

Malloy was his usual courteous self, the alien presence having retreated inside his skull for the moment as he replied: "I'm sorry, Captain, but what's done is done, and there's no turning back. All of us are agreed." He turned to look at the men. They said nothing, but several of them nodded their agreement.

The captain was not cowed by the situation. "You men had better think of what you're doing," he urged. "This is a criminal act on the high seas. If you aren't caught and hanged, you'll never work as able seamen again. This will haunt you the rest of your lives. Those of you younger ones who aspire to be mates or captains someday, this one ill-advised decision will end all your hopes and plans."

"Hell, what do we need with that?" one of the men growled. "By September, we'll be picking up gold offen the ground." His slightly slurred speech made Merriman wonder if he'd been drinking.

"Satisfied, Captain?" Malloy smiled. "Now, into the longboat with you." He gestured with the barrel of his pistol.

"May I, at least, have a sextant and a chart?"

"You won't need 'em sir," Stark interposed almost gently. "Just sail west by the sun until you strike the coast somewhere. Have you got plenty of food and water?"

"Right here," the sailor named Stenson replied, setting a wooden box in the bottom of the boat.

Captain Blackwell, who was wearing his oilskins, sea boots, and southwester, stepped into the boat with dignity.

"Haul away, boys," Malloy cried. "And a *bon voyage* to you, Captain. Nothing personal, you understand."

The boat was quickly hauled up, swung out over the bulwark, and lowered once again into the sea.

Merriman admired the way Captain Blackwell held his poise throughout this ordeal. But, as he cast off the falls, the mask slipped for a few seconds, and Merriman saw a look that was a mixture of fear, anger, and humiliation. And, yes—utter defeat. The captain's aristocratic demeanor crumbled, and he looked as gray and worn as a gravestone in a Nantucket churchyard.

Merriman watched him go, wondering if the old man would have trouble stepping the mast by himself. But, as the distance increased between them, he saw Blackwell drag out the short mast and step it with no trouble, fastening the stays. He unfurled the spritsail and let it swing wide. Then, standing up, he turned back and raised a fist over his head.

"Damn you to hell, Gilbert Malloy!" he shouted, his voice coming downwind to them as if he were ten feet away. "May this ship be accursed for what you've done! Not a man-jack of you will ever get around the Horn to see California!"

Merriman shivered, thinking that Moses, breaking the stone tablets of the ten commandments in his rage at the Israelites, must have sounded just like this. Then the lean figure seated himself at the tiller and sailed away from them without looking back.

"Man the braces!" Malloy yelled. "We've wasted enough time. Stenson, take the wheel. Your course is east by south. We're slanting toward the hump of Africa. Then we'll pick up the northeast trades, and we're bound for Cape Horn."

Chapter Twelve

Lone Oak Mansion
Charleston, South Carolina

Trevor Sloan suddenly lost a taste for the remainder of his breakfast. He shoved aside the fresh biscuits with bacon and adjusted his wire-rimmed spectacles to focus on a copy of the *Charleston Courier* before him. A back page item had caught his intense interest. He scanned the short piece quickly, then went back and read it again, slowly. A man identifying himself as Amos Blackwell, captain of the bark, *Inverness*, had landed in a small boat on the coast of Virginia, near the entrance to the Chesapeake Bay. He stated to authorities that he was the victim of a mutiny by his mates and crew. He claimed to have been put adrift in the longboat with enough food and water to reach land. He had been three days making a landfall on a stretch of deserted beach where he'd managed to surf through the breakers without capsizing. Not knowing where he was, he'd hailed two boys digging for shellfish and asked to be taken to the nearest police station.

When questioned by the police, he presented proper credentials and stated that the second mate had instigated a mutiny for the purpose of taking the vessel to the California gold fields. Blackwell stated they had been on their way to Boston with a cargo of molasses, and that their last port of call had been Charleston, South Carolina. A message had been sent to the Boston owners of the vessel, and Captain Blackwell had been assured that other seaports and departing captains would be alerted to be on the look-out for the pirated bark.

Sloan slowly lowered the newspaper and stared out a nearby window with unseeing eyes. He had no interest in this Captain Amos Blackwell, or his ship—except that the killer of his son was aboard the *Inverness*. The courier he had dispatched to Boston to intercept the two fugitives had just about had time to arrive there. But now it was to no avail. It appeared that Merriman was destined to elude his grasp—because of a fluke of fortune, to sail forever beyond his reach. Or was he?

The papers had been filled for the past weeks with advertisements of sailing vessels leaving the East Coast ports for California, and also notices of companies forming to make the trek overland by wagon train. The talk at his club lately had not been about the growing tensions between the Northern and Southern states, or damning the rain for delaying spring planting, or trying to predict the price of cotton on the London market. Nearly everyone wanted to speculate endlessly on the gold that had been discovered a few months earlier on the American River in far-off California. It wasn't just the young bucks, eager to make a quick killing, independent of inherited wealth, or the poor, who longed to escape the drudgery of keeping body and soul together, who were victims of this craze. Men of his acquaintance, who had more gold than they were likely to spend in their remaining years, were suddenly hot to get more. Even staid shopkeepers and clergymen were not immune. Everyone, it seemed, was susceptible to the "yellow fever" that was raging across the country. Judging from the number of people who seemed to be selling out and heading West, California would be bursting at the seams before the year was out.

He sighed, suddenly feeling old. The world was changing too fast for him. Many of his old friends were rushing off and leaving him. His big house, his lands, his slaves, his crops now seemed more of a burden than an asset. It was with a sense of familiar duty that he turned his attention to these things, rather than with the zestful enthusiasm he'd felt earlier for the running of his fiefdom.

One thing, and one thing only, had fueled his inner passion lately. And that was the burning rage at his boy's killer. He had not confided his feelings to his wife for two reasons. First, he knew she would disapprove of his motive for revenge, and, second, because her mind had been deranged since their son's funeral, and he was no longer able to communicate with her. Even as he breakfasted alone, she was upstairs, confined to her bed. Dr. Rudolph Vetter, who'd joined him in the spacious dining room for a cup of coffee before leaving the house hardly an hour before, had not given him a great deal of hope.

A man of about his own age, Dr. Vetter had said, with Teutonic bluntness: "Trevor, we've known each other for many years. I must tell you the truth, no matter how it hurts."

Sloan had nodded, his throat dry.

"Your wife is suffering from shock and grief. When her baby died years ago, she had much the same reaction. But she was a younger woman then, and she had your son and you and her friends to bring her out of it, to distract her mind to other chores.

"Actually, very little is known about the human mind. It has a depth and complexity that medical science has not even begun to explore, even if we had the tools to do so. So

I do not pretend any expertise in this field." He had paused as the stooped, bald Negro filled his coffee cup and silently withdrew. The doctor had added a spoonful of coarse, brown sugar from a silver bowl and stirred it in before continuing. "Emily is a strong woman, but this seems to have hit her very hard. She is now childless and has no grandchildren. Also, she has no worry for her. . . ."—he had gestured, groping for the right word—"financial comfort, if you will. Except for her social circle of friends, she is at loose ends. What I'm trying to say is, she has given in to her grief, precisely because she has nothing urgent that demands her attention. We've found, in cases like this, that very often if the patient must work to survive, or feels a desperate need to be the only protector of a small child or a helpless invalid, it takes the mind off one's own troubles and can bring the grief-stricken person out of herself to serve some external cause."

Sloan had nodded dumbly, feeling as if he were back in school, having a chemical formula explained to him by the headmaster. But he had accepted his old friend's medical opinion without question.

"Continuing to give her laudanum indefinitely to provide surcease of sorrow is not the solution. It's been enough time now since Alexander's funeral that she should have begun to come out of it." He had gestured helplessly. "I have nothing in my medical bag that can cure her."

He had drained his cup and set it down. The *clink* of the China cup on the saucer had sounded like an exclamation point on a prognosis of doom. Sloan had been only vaguely aware of mumbling his gratitude and good bye as Dr. Vetter retrieved his hat and leather bag, and departed.

That had taken place an hour ago, and Sloan had continued his breakfast alone at the end of a long, empty table in a large, empty room. If he sat around this house for many more days, listening to the chiming of the grandfather clock, he would soon be listening to the demons inside his *own* head as well.

The news item in the paper had given him the beginnings of a solution for several problems at once. He could turn over the day-to-day operation of his plantation to his wife, and depart for California himself. The chance he could overtake or find two men he had never seen among thousands of Argonauts over a distance of thousands of miles was very remote. But he had to try. He would just dump the running of his plantation into Emily's lap. It would be sink or swim. If that shock didn't jar her out of her trance, then nothing likely would. He knew he stood a good chance of losing everything he had by this move, if she didn't respond, or if she made some bad business decisions. But, he reasoned, they had both lost nearly everything that made life worthwhile as it was. Deep down, he felt confident she could do it, if given the chance. She had been at his side for many years as he was gradually building his small inheritance into the vast holdings they now possessed. And, unlike other men he knew, he had confided in his wife, had discussed business decisions with her so that she would feel part of the enterprise. Jason Biggers, his overseer, would be a great help to her, and he could be trusted. He made a mental note to increase the overseer's wages as an added incentive.

After turning the idea over in his mind for several minutes, he finally resolved to do it. Once the decision was made, he felt himself growing excited at the prospect. He turned back to the newspaper and folded it open to a page that contained three separate advertisements for steamship lines carrying gold-seekers to Panama. Looking at the three options of travel to California—overland, Cape Horn, or steamer to Panama, a short jaunt across the Isthmus, then a steamer up the coast to California—the third seemed by far the best. It was a short cut to the other side of the continent.

Money was no problem. He would take plenty of cash to reach his destination. Physically, he wasn't quite so sure. A hearty fifty-five, he smoked too many cigars and drank too much brandy. In recent years, he had been less active. There had been fewer hunting trips, fewer horseback rides and walks over his properties to observe operations. And the inactivity had begun to show in the form of some added fat around his middle. But he was confident he could make the trip. Mentally and physically, it would be good for him, he thought. And if he should be lucky enough to find gold, so much the better. At least enough to pay for his trip, and any losses suffered by his plantation while he was away. The possession of gold held no great allure for him. Having already experienced wealth, he'd found it wanting in the more important things of life. Granted, he enjoyed what it could buy and the status it gave him in the community; it had actually conferred on him what amounted to an American royalty. But a man could only ride one horse at a time, could only wear one suit at a time, could only consume so much food and wine at a meal. So what if he had these things in abundance? Was he any better off than a local cobbler he knew who lived in a modest house, and had enough to eat and wear? No. In fact, in his view, the cobbler was infinitely better off because his grown son, sober and industrious, was learning his father's trade at his workbench. And the cobbler was not weighted down with the responsibilities of making his land productive, of entertaining wealthy friends, of being a helpless victim of the prices of a far-off market, of concerning himself with the welfare of slaves and employees, of spending vast sums maintaining a mansion and grounds. Sloan had access to the best medical care, it was true, but what did that amount to when no doctor could have saved his son, and now could not cure his wife?

He wiped his mouth with the linen napkin and tossed it on the table. "Hector!" he called, rising from the table. The stooped Negro slave entered the room. "I'm through here. If anyone comes calling, I'm riding into town, and then over to the island. Be back sometime tonight. I'll look in on Missus Sloan before I leave and give instructions to Clara."

"Yas, suh." The old man began clearing the table.

Trevor Sloan took his coat from the hall tree and shrugged into it, then climbed the stairs toward Emily's bedroom. His first stop would be the bank, he thought, then the office of the steamship line, then a visit to Jason Biggers. He was putting a tremendous load of responsibility on his overseer, he knew, but he judged Biggers to be the type of man who would respond to the challenge. And Biggers could certainly use the extra pay for his growing family. Now, if he could just get Emily to rouse up enough to feel the sting of her duty. . . .

Chapter Thirteen

Overland Trail

Nebraska Territory

With shouts, the cracking of whips, and the creaking of dry wheels that churned up the gray-brown sandy soil, the train of twelve wagons pulled off the main trail to line up six abreast in a grassy swale near the meandering Platte River. After two weeks on the trail, the noon stop had evolved into a kind of organized confusion, Lisa Sizemore thought, as her father hauled the span of mules to a halt. Being much more familiar with mules than oxen, he had chosen the former to pull the Sizemore wagon. They would be sure-footed in the mountains, he'd told Lisa and her mother, would not eat or drink any more than oxen, would probably be easier to harness, and could be driven from the wagon seat with no problem. In a pinch, they could also be eaten just as the oxen could. But he had not counted on the fact that several other wagons were drawn by the lumbering oxen, and the pace of the entire train was the pace of the slowest ox team.

She bounded off the seat of her family's green Studebaker wagon and hurried toward the river to gather a scattering of dry driftwood before those from the other wagons had a chance to grab up all the nearest pieces. From the beginning of their journey, it had been her father's job to handle the animals and grease the wheel hubs, her mother's to do most of the cooking, and hers to gather wood and water, build the fires, and do any other chores that needed doing, including the washing of clothes whenever there was enough water available. So far, this arrangement had worked well. But it was fairly early in the journey and the weather and terrain had been good to them, allowing time to get toughened up to the trail.

As she gathered an armload of dry sticks and branches that had snagged in the bend during the last high water, she saw the ox teams being led just downstream of the wagons to drink. Nooning had become a welcome respite from five or six hours of jolting over the trail. Not only did it provide a little rest for both humans and animals, it provided time enough to cook and eat the first food of the day. No time was wasted on cooking fires early in the morning, the wagon master being of a mind to get under way without delay as soon as it was daylight. But this routine suited her perfectly since she had long been accustomed to rising early to start work at the inn.

Carrying an armload of small dead branches, she dragged a larger limb with the other hand and dropped them on a bare, sandy patch of ground several feet from their wagon. While her mother was slicing bacon into a frying pan on the tailgate of the wagon, Lisa broke up the smaller branches with her hands and laid a cross-hatch pattern on the ground, then took the axe from the wagon bed and chopped the larger limb into usable pieces. Swinging the axe gave her some welcome exercise, and she was breathing heavily when she stuffed several handfuls of dry grass under the smaller twigs to complete the preparations. She brushed off the twigs and dirt, noting how rough and callused her hands were becoming. To save the precious block of matches, she pulled a small magnifying glass from its leather case in her skirt pocket and used the strong rays of the overhead sun to start the blaze. Her father had brought the glass for the purpose of reading the small print in his Bible, but she'd come up with the idea of using it to start fires as well. Once the white smoke curling up from the grass burst into a tiny flame and began to eat its way up through the small twigs into the larger wood, she was finished for the time.

Now she had twenty or thirty minutes before the food was ready—time she coveted to herself each day, time to enjoy the fresh air and sunlight and to write an entry in her diary. She got the cloth-bound book from her trunk, along with a small bottle of ink and a sharpened quill, and hastened off toward the river. The nooning spot the wagon master had picked for them this day was particularly beautiful, she thought. It was in a bend of the sluggish Platte, with grass about shoe-top deep. The river, running fairly full with spring snowmelt, gurgled around the roots of gnarled cotton-woods that were almost fully leafed out with new growth.

She seated herself comfortably on the fork of a weathered gray log, leaning her back against the upper limb of the fork. It was a tranquil spot, sheltered from the constant prairie wind, and she closed her eyes for a moment, feeling the welcome warmth of the midday sun on her hair and face. She breathed deeply of the soft, fragrant air that was tinged with a faint scent of earth and the dampness of the river and some unidentified species of small wildflowers that grew around her feet.

This country was so much different from her own that, for the first ten days out of St. Joe, she had marveled at it. She missed the hills, and felt almost indecently exposed to the sky without the shelter of trees. She was uncovered to the direct gaze of God, Whom she vaguely pictured as living somewhere beyond that great dome that now stretched from horizon to horizon, making their small caravan seem even less significant than it was. Perhaps that was why she naturally gravitated to the nearest trees whenever the wagons halted. And, for the past four days, the only trees were mostly cottonwoods. Twisted into various attitudes by years of wind and water, those rough-coated giants that had managed to put down deep enough roots to survive the winds, floods, blizzards, and droughts almost cried out to be recognized for their hardy beauty. Even though the air was still where she sat, she could hear the quiet soughing as the wind bent the topmost limbs, revealing the pale green undersides of the dancing leaves and sending the downy cotton swirling down around her like some warm weather snow. She got up and walked over to take a closer look at the largest which, even in this empty land, already showed the scars of man's passing. Into the rough bark, about head high, someone had hacked, **R.M. 1846.** As she wandered back to her seat on the log, she noticed the blackened remains of an earlier campfire. From talk she had heard around the camp in the evening, she knew they had gotten a fairly early start in the season, but already more than three dozen trains had gone out ahead of them, and were toiling west along the broad, flat, Platte River Valley. This was why they often found the usual campgrounds churned up by hoofs and wheels and had to go much farther off the trail than this to find enough grass for their animals.

She sat down and opened her diary on her knees, congratulating herself that she'd had the foresight to bring along this journal. In fact, anticipating that she would have many things to record on this journey, she had secured a second book with two hundred blank pages. She scanned her last two entries:

May 25, 1849

Reached the banks of the Platte River and will be camping along it tonight and for many nights to come. Even though we're not even a third of the way, it feels like we are now connected to our goal by this river because, I'm told, it stretches all the way to the Rocky Mountains. So far our journey has been rather unremarkable. More difficult and irksome than exciting. We've not even seen any wild Indians as yet.

I try to stay busy so I don't miss home so much. We have crossed Tennessee and Missouri and are now well out onto the great plains. Always having a plenitude of water in the mountains, I never appreciated what a precious commodity this is. But now the country is leveling out and the forests have thinned. Perhaps this is because of less rain. I am now more accustomed to the rigors of travel on a hard wagon seat than I was at the beginning. I have bounced on that hard wood for so long already that my backside must have as many calluses as my hands. As for my skin, I am probably a shade darker than when we started, but the change is hardly noticeable when I look at the other women, and men too, who are much fairer than I. Even though they wear large hats and sunbonnets, their skin is wind-burned and sunburned to a degree that makes me cringe with pain just to look at them. There is one young couple from Ohio who are both blond and freckled. Their faces are now a rosy color as if they are constantly blushing. They had to rub bacon grease on their faces and hands to relieve the burn. And this just drew flies and gnats. I can see now why the Indians are said to be dark-skinned. They were probably once white before their ancestors came to this country. Have to close now as it's getting too dark to write.

Her entry for yesterday was simply:

May 26, 1849
Nothing much happened today. Traveled twenty easy miles and camped. Two young boys got in a fight after supper.

She uncorked the ink bottle and set it on a flat part of the log. Dipping her quill, she held it poised for a moment.

May 27, 1849. Noon, she began, then paused, thinking. She was far enough from the wagons that the clatter and conversation came only as background noise to the sound of the river and the soft wind.

The grass for the oxen and horses has been good. The weather has been fair and the nights rather chilly, but not so much as in the mountains back home this time of year.

She paused, thinking that she wanted to make this journal much more than just a record of miles traveled and observations about the weather. She took another deep breath of the fragrant air, this time catching a whiff of woodsmoke and the familiar smell of the draft animals. She heard the steady *thunking* of an axe somewhere upstream. She dipped her quill and continued:

My father did his best to select a good company to join up with. But in any group of about 75 people, there will always be a few that one would prefer not to associate with. I guess it's like dealing with travelers at our inn. Many the time I've had to just grit my teeth and go on doing my job. And so it is here. We were hardly one day's travel this side of the Missouri River when I noticed a man in the wagon behind ours, watching me very closely. He's about my own age and is apparently traveling with his cousins or brothers. (By the way, more than two-thirds of our train is made up of men only, who have left their families behind to seek their fortunes in California.) I don't like the way this man, who tells me his name is Zeke, looks at me. Each day he has gotten a little bolder and has taken the opportunity to catch me alone when I'm gathering wood or trying to find a secluded place to bathe in the river. He has made some lewd remarks which I pretend not to hear. It's the same old story. Because I'm dark-skinned, I'm sure he thinks of me as some sort of half-breed trollop who will tumble in the hay with him without a second thought. Actually, even if I were so inclined, he's the last one I'd choose. He's revoltingly dirty, and has bad teeth, crooked and tobacco-stained. There is no telling when he last bathed, or even took a swim in the river.

She paused again, trying to get her wording as exact and descriptive as possible with the thought that she would transcribe part of her diary into a letter to her cousin, Abigail, and leave the letter at Fort Kearney which the train was due to reach in about three more days.

She looked at the sky. White, fluffy summer thunderheads were billowing high in the heavens, blowing up on a steady south wind, filling much of the blue canopy overhead.

She closed her diary, capped the ink bottle, and slid off the log to stretch out in the soft grass. It felt good to rest her back and not to be constantly moving. As she stared upward, the clouds mushroomed higher and higher, puffing out white billows, while lower down, their base turned darker. A slight grumble of far-off thunder hinted at some distant rain. It only made her proximate surroundings seem more peaceful.

"Think it's gonna rain?"

She jumped at the nearness of the nasal voice. A wide hat brim was suddenly blocking out the sun as a man stood over her, looking down. It was Zeke.

Without answering, she sat up hurriedly and snatched up her book and ink bottle.

"Where ya going? I'm not gonna hurt ya," the man said. He caught her by the arm and spun her toward him. She gasped as his hard grip jerked the diary from her hand and it fell to the ground. "Whatcha reading, Lisa?" he asked. "I never learnt to read, myself. Always workin'. Never had time for school. Waste of time, anyway."

"Thank God for that," she muttered to herself, thinking he might snatch up her diary and read it.

"What's that you say? You makin' fun of me?" He pulled her close, his foul breath causing her to turn her face away. His grin turned to a leer. "My, but you're a soft-bodied thing! My name's Zeke . . . that's short for Ezekial . . . Masters. I'm from Pike county, Missouri, and I'm twenty-seven years old. There, now, we've been properly introduced." He ran a hand over her hair. "You oughta take the braid outta

136

your hair. That long, black, shiny hair would look mighty nice down over your shoulders. It'd hang might' near to your butt, if you let it loose."

"Leave me alone." She tried to twist away, but his grip was like iron manacles. "You're hurting me."

"Your name is Lisa Sizemore, and you're from Tennessee. I don't see why we can't get along. We're gonna be together for a long time yet on this trip, and we could make it mighty pleasant for each other."

Not if I can help it, she thought, giving a sudden lunge and breaking free and staggering away. He made no attempt to pursue her.

"You needn't be so high and mighty, missy," he said as she retrieved her book and ran back toward the wagons. "I'm sure a hot-blooded little 'breed like yourself ain't no stranger to men."

His laughter followed her as she rounded the base of a large cottonwood and came in sight of her mother bending over the skillet on a smoky fire. She slowed down and tried to compose herself as she approached.

They were entering wilder country now, out of the United States, where the only civilization was what they brought with them, she thought as she sat on the wagon tongue and ate the hot bacon on leftover cornbread. She had better forget about the old days and the old ways and stiffen herself to face whatever came. And this included men like Zeke Masters.

Her first step in that direction came that evening after dark when they had camped for the night. Following supper, she slipped into their wagon and undid the long braid that hung down her back. The light of the campfires was wavering on the sides of the white canvas top stretched over the wagon bows as she sat on her trunk and thought of what she was about to do. Then with a sigh, but with steely resolve, she took her mother's sewing scissors and snipped off her long hair, a hank at a time, trying to make it as even as possible all around, just below her ears. She couldn't bear to throw away the long, shiny tresses, so she bound them with a piece of ribbon and placed them carefully in her trunk. She shook her head and ran her fingers through her hair. It was a strange sensation, after years of long hair—like wearing someone else's head. But the deed was done, and there was no going back. And it would be much easier to care for. At least that's the reason she'd give her mother.

The next part of her plan would be much harder to explain. She cocked her ears toward the music outside where the fiddles were sawing out a rough rendition of "Turkey in the Straw" to a rhythmic clapping of hands. With a feeling of guilt, she opened her father's trunk and rummaged around until she found an old, worn pair of his overalls. Quickly slipping out of her full skirt and petticoats, she pulled on the pants and fastened the cloth suspenders over her shoulders. She didn't dare cut off the legs to fit her, but just rolled them up. She was about five foot, six and well-fleshed out, so the pants were not excessively large on her. She was glad she had opted to bring along a wide-brimmed hat instead of a sunbonnet that restricted vision like blinders on a horse. She put on the hat and looked at herself in the small mirror her mother had fastened to one of the wooden bows. What she saw by the dim outside firelight was the brown and white checked blouse, the brown hat, the bobbed hair framing her dark face. It all added up to a beardless male Indian wearing white man's clothing. She could hardly believe it was her own image staring back at her. She had turned herself into a boy—a rather handsome boy, she had to admit, but still a boy. On impulse, she stuck out her tongue and then laughed at the ridiculous reflection, her white teeth flashing. She reached into the open trunk and pulled out a stiff paper folder. Inside was the charcoal sketch Clayburn Collins had drawn of her. It was a good likeness, and she compared it to what she now saw in the mirror. The reflection already looked more mature than the recent picture. She wondered what had happened to Clayburn Collins, the handsome Melungeon. She wished he were on this trip now, instead of Zeke Masters and his bunch. She didn't even really know Collins, but she fancied she could come to like him very much. She imagined herself in his arms, kissing him, making love to him. She shook her head. A lot of silly nonsense. She had to deal with what was real.

As she turned aside to take off the pants, she hoped this transformation would put off the attentions of Zeke Masters, although she had no realistic hope of this. But she had to try something. Perhaps she could incite the ridicule of his companions when they saw him chasing—not a skirt, but a rough-looking figure in pants. She only wished she had thought of this ruse before he'd seen her as an attractive woman.

The next hurdle would be somehow to explain her outlandish appearance to her horrified parents. But that could wait until morning.

Chapter Fourteen

Aboard the bark, Inverness

Atlantic Ocean

"Not the clewline, you landsman's spoor!" Stark thundered, yanking the rope from Collins's hands. "This one! The halyard! Watch the men. If nothing else, look aloft and see where the line runs. Gaw-dammit, before I'm through with you, you'll be able to lay your hand on the right line out of several hundred in the blackest night with a masthead sea running. We've got to make a sailor of you in jig time. Old Cape Stiff ain't that far off."

Collins gritted his teeth and ignored the smirks from two of the other sailors as they tailed onto the halyard, and tramped away across the deck with the line over their shoulders. Collins let the rope cut into his shoulder before he noticed the others taking most of the pressure on their hands.

For a fortnight, as the bark, *Inverness*, dashed into the South Atlantic, Collins suffered the tortures of a Roman galley slave. Separated from Merriman and ordered into Abel Stark's watch, he knew only screaming mates and screaming muscles. Fitful sleep punctuated long stretches of humiliation, bewilderment, and many cuffings for blunders committed.

"Belay!" Stark yelled. The line was secured to a pinrail.

"Aloft and shake out the fore royal."

Collins sprang into the shrouds with the first two men and scampered up the ratlines. The men worked with a will now, he thought, knowing they were bound for the gold fields instead of Boston, a drunken spree, then another outbound ship.

Working aloft, at least, had not been a real problem for him, since he had no innate fear of heights. Standing on the swaying footrope, some eighty feet above the deck, he'd quickly learned the sailor's dictum of one hand for the ship and one hand for himself.

Two young Cubans who'd joined the crew in Havana, apparently recognizing his trace of Hispanic blood, had quietly come to his aid when the going got rough.

"Like this, *señor*," Raul Riaz said, showing him the proper way to slip a gasket. Three days before, Juan Verdugo, who now worked alongside him on the yardarm, had shown him the knack of fisting a sail that was rock-hard with wind pressure. The mates seldom went aloft, so Collins felt a little freer up in the rigging. And the view, when he had a few seconds to look, was magnificent. His artist's eye drank in the long, sweeping curve of the ship's hull, the tiny figures on deck, the spider-web tracery of lines that so bewildered him. He clung to the varnished yard as the tall vessel leaned with the wind, and watched the bow cleave a foaming white V in the choppy, leaden sea. It was almost as if he were a detached observer from on high who had no part in the life going on so far below him. The sky-reaching spars with their huge spread of canvas seemed to defy gravity. And the relatively slender shell of a hull was bearing up from the sea bottom hundreds of tons of cargo. It seemed preposterous that mite-sized men could have conceived and built so magnificent a contrivance, then bent it to their will in defying the elements. While they were aloft, Collins heard eight bells struck for the change of watch. The men finished their work quickly and descended.

Collins had not been forced to bunk in the forecastle with the crew since he and Merriman were already ensconced in adjacent aftercabins. Second mate Gilbert Malloy, now the self-proclaimed captain, had moved into Captain Blackwell's cabin in the stern of the ship, and assumed the personal services of the steward and the cook as well. But Collins and Merriman now got their own meals from the galley and carried them to the midship house to eat. Only in the dog watch did the schedule allow them time enough to sit and eat together. Abel Stark retained his same room in the after part of the ship.

"Damned strange arrangement," Merriman observed when they were eating their evening meal in the midship house. "You and I bunking aft like passengers or officers but working as part of the crew, while the two mates, one of 'em now the skipper, are still taking watch-and-watch."

"There's plenty of room for four people to eat at the captain's table," Collins said.

"Appearances," Merriman answered. "We're no longer paying passengers on our way to Boston. We're sailors before the mast now. Besides," he grinned, "would you want to share meals with those two?"

Collins shook his head. "Have you noticed how Mister Malloy has gotten very arrogant? Not playing the part of the Southern gentleman any more."

"Sitting in the captain's chair will do that to some men," Merriman said. He paused, then continued thoughtfully: "The other side of that double personality showing itself."

Collins shivered involuntarily, imagining some evil, unseen force waiting to ambush him from under Malloy's bushy eyebrows. "You know, I was hoping I could get transferred into Malloy's watch so you could teach me the ropes and save me a lot of grief from Stark. But, now that I think about it, Stark is a straight-up bastard I can deal with better than with Malloy."

"They'd never allow you to switch, anyway. Malloy grabbed me because he knew I was experienced."

"I'd like to know what they talk about at meals," Collins snorted, spooning up some hash, "now that they've flip-flopped positions of authority."

Merriman shrugged.

"I can't tell that he's playing any favorites, either . . . especially where I'm concerned." As Collins raised the tin cup of coffee to his lips, he winced at the pain and stiffness in his shoulder.

"Stark's a hard one to read," Merriman acknowledged. "I've got him pegged as a loner. Out for himself first and last."

Collins nodded. "I kind of figured that when he lined up the whole crew the first day and broke the points square off their sheath knives." Sometimes simple solutions were the best, Collins thought. This would leave the cutting edge of their essential tool for everyday use, but would reduce the greater danger of fatal stab wounds. And, more importantly, this move let the men know that Stark, a wiley old-timer, would be alert to any trouble.

"I guess it's best not to trust anybody but ourselves, and see how this thing plays out," Merriman concluded.

"Those two Cubans . . . Riaz and Verdugo . . . have taken pity on me," Collins said. "They're giving me a little help."

"And Fjelde is a good man, too," Merriman added. "Probably the best sailor in my watch when he's at full strength. So that's at least three crewmen who shouldn't give us any trouble."

"How are the Finn's ribs?"

"I think they're healing up. Apparently several of 'em were cracked in that fall. But if he hadn't bounced off the shrouds and been flung overboard, he would have landed on deck and been killed. He could hardly move for a couple o' days. And he's no youngster and can't be expected to recover as quick as one."

"Stark and Malloy expect him to."

"A man could be shaking hands with the grim reaper, and they'd still expect him to stand his watches."

"I wonder if he's responsible for the bad luck of this mutiny?" Collins mused.

"Huh! How do you know this turn of events won't work out to be good luck for us? If Fjelde's caused any ill luck, it's been mostly to himself."

"Maybe you're right," Collins said reluctantly. "What about that curse Captain Blackwell put on the ship?"

"The understandable rage and frustration of an abused old man," Merriman answered shortly.

"So you don't think it'll have any effect on us?"

"No man has supernatural power like that. Whatever will happen, will happen regardless. 'The rain falls on the just and the unjust alike' . . . or some such quote. We're all in this together now. If anyone's of a mind to blame any accidents or bad weather on somebody besides God or the caprices of chance, I guess the captain's as good a target as the Finn or the Cubans or a Melungeon I could name."

Collins grinned ruefully. "Say no more." He wiped his tin plate with a last crust of bread and popped it into his mouth. "It's my watch below. I can hardly keep my eyes open."

"Don't let it get you. Take my word for it. You'll toughen up to this routine before long."

Collins nodded.

"We were headed for Boston, just by chance, to get away from Charleston," Merriman continued. "Now we're headed for California just by chance. Looks like our plans to trek back into the mountains after your gold will have to wait. But maybe we can pick up a little gold in California, like everybody else is trying to do. Might find enough to at least set me up in some kind of business. What do you think?"

"California here we come!" Collins grinned, feeling a sudden surge of inner resolve. He rose from the table, timed the roll of the ship to line up the doorway, and dodged through, carrying his plate and cup.

"What the hell is this stuff, anyway?" Ferret Jacobus grumbled as he crawled along the deck, sweeping a wooden-backed scrub brush in a circular motion. Collins hauled a bucket of sea water from overside and sluiced it across the planks. Three other men were doing the same thing several feet away.

"Blood-red dust from the storms of Africa," Stark said, striding up to stand with hands on hips, watching the wash-down. "The damp night air settled it on the ship."

"Are we that close to Africa?" Jacobus asked, cocking an eye up at Stark.

"Close enough," the mate replied. "Within four-hundred miles."

Collins wondered why they had to go nearly to the hump of the African continent if they were bound for the tip of South America, but had learned not to open his mouth if he didn't have to.

As if by way of answer, Stark gazed up at the cloud-streaked morning sky. "Weather's fairing. We're picking up the Northeast Trades right on schedule," he said with an obvious tone of satisfaction. He rubbed his hands together. "Now for the long slant down to the line." He turned on his heel. "What the hell you standing there, gawkin' for?" he snarled at three sailors behind him. "Get that mainsail set!"

Collins knew as soon as he and the others were finished cleansing the decks, they'd be ordered into the rigging to add more sail. Some of the mates' actions were beginning to make sense to him. They had waited to set all sail until the watches were changing in order to have use of the whole crew without having to call up the watch from below.

An hour later he nodded to Merriman who was at the wheel and ducked through the door at the break of the poop on the way to falling gratefully into his bunk. He was tired and still sore, but he was beginning to think that maybe he would live, after all. He gave thanks to God that he had a small room and bed of his own, instead of being forced to bunk in the forecastle with the rest of the crew. One young sailor, named Rafer McCook, who spoke with a pronounced New York dialect, had referred to him a time or two as "that useless green-eyed nigger." Collins wanted no part of having to sleep with one eye open in the same room with men who were not his friends. Normally, the off watch would be so tired they would be sound asleep and have no time for taunting or trouble. But now, they were entering the Trades, and Merriman had told him they could expect mostly steady winds from the northeast for many days, with few sail changes and light duty. All this added up to leisure for trouble, his cautious mind warned him. He wondered how his new friends, Riaz and Verdugo, were faring amongst the forecastle crowd. Instinct told him these two Cubans would watch each other's backs and would do well, even though they were dark-skinned and spoke Spanish between themselves.

They had worn ship while he was on deck, and now the *Inverness* was before the wind with all sail set, heading south by west. Her motion had smoothed out, and she surged along, rolling gently, pushed by the steady Trades. He lay on his bunk, fully clothed except for his sea boots, and watched a shaft of sunlight move up and down as it slanted through the porthole. *Focus on California,* he thought. *Nothing else. Just grit your teeth and endure whatever comes in between. San Francisco and the gold fields beyond—that's the end of the rainbow.* He took a deep breath and closed his eyes, trying to think of something that would make this voyage a little less painful. An image of Lisa Sizemore came to mind—the lovely blue-eyed, black-haired Lisa from the hills of his Tennessee home. If only she were here now. But picturing her aboard this ship was nearly beyond the stretch of his imagination.

Chapter Fifteen

Aboard the steamer, Lexington

Off the southeastern coast of the U.S.

Trevor Sloan was not a seafaring man, and he'd discovered there was a lot more water between Charleston harbor and the south side of the Gulf of Mexico than it appeared to be on the map. As long as the sidewheel steamer, *Lexington*, stayed barely within sight of land as she worked her way down the coast, he felt reasonably comfortable, like a man with one foot on solid ground. But, once the ship passed the tip of Florida and began bucking the north-flowing Gulf Stream, he became not only violently seasick, but also nearly panic-stricken that he could see nothing but sea and sky in every direction.

When he wasn't in his cabin, lying flat on his back and sweating profusely with the porthole open for fresh air, he was in the main salon, playing poker with several other Panama-bound passengers. This pastime, at which they bet only low table stakes, kept the participants from becoming overwrought as they sought to kill the long hours of their journey. Whenever Sloan felt panic stealing over him with the thought of where he was on the sea, he took another drink of straight whisky. The slow burn this produced on an empty stomach only added to the slow burning anger he felt when he thought of his son's killer. In this state of mind and inebriation he passed several days, hardly aware of how much money he won or lost at the card table. One good thing he did notice as the slow days passed was the slack that developed in his belt from eating very little.

Only when the ship dropped anchor off the mouth of the Chagres River in Panama did he actually begin to feel better. He celebrated the occasion, on a broiling hot noon, by sitting down in the shade of a deck awning to a meal of steak, boiled potatoes, gravy, fresh apple pie, and coffee. As he ate, he could look at the paying passengers, assembling with their luggage near the rail, although the boats to take them ashore would not be loading before one o'clock in the afternoon.

As he cleaned up the last of his meal and pulled a gold toothpick from his vest pocket, he heard some others in the room already grumbling about the tropical heat and humidity. He was perspiring freely himself in his vest and shirtsleeves and frequently mopped his face with a large handkerchief. But this was no worse than his lowland plantation around Charleston in the summer, he reflected. Staring at the jungle, he wondered how much fever was there. He would just have to chance it. He was convinced this was still the safest and fastest way to California.

He pushed back from the table and crossed his legs, aware of the unusual weight in the outside seams of his canvas pants. He had taken the precaution of having mostly twenty dollar gold pieces sewn into tube-like pockets the full length of each pant leg. Gold was good anywhere. The obvious danger of carrying several thousand in gold on one's person was offset by the fact that it was well-hidden and that it was never out of his possession so he didn't have to wonder if some thief had stolen it from his luggage or his cabin. And he went to great pains to be sure it did not show, and that he was in a safe place before he dropped his pants to retrieve one or two of the coins for pocket money.

As he stood up from the table and started for his cabin, he realized that carrying extra weight in this way had had another advantage. It had strengthened his legs for what he knew would be an arduous march across part of the Isthmus.

As far as he was concerned, this was the point of no return. He could still change his mind and pay his return passage without ever leaving the *Lexington*. Before he debarked, he wished there were some way to find out how Emily was handling his absence. When he'd sat by her bedside and told her what he planned to do, he had elicited only a blank stare, and had found himself repeating, in stronger terms, the challenge he was putting to her. With the help of her maid, he had forced her to get out of bed and dress. He could not bring himself to slap her face or shake her in hopes of jarring her back to some sense of awareness. But he spoke sharply to her, believing that his tone and words, which had always brought an angry response from her in the past, would somehow seep into the depths of her mind and later prod her out of this hypnotic state. Even though he felt his overseer, Jason Biggers, was capable of running the place by himself, he desperately wanted his wife to take control. But he had no way of finding out, at this point, what was happening. What he couldn't control, he wouldn't worry about, he thought, throwing his dark jacket over his arm and picking up his scuffed leather grip and shutting the cabin door behind him.

An hour later, stepping ashore to the babble of river boatmen haggling with passengers over the price of their services, he had only one regret—that he hadn't thought to bring a broad-brimmed straw hat. The dark felt hat he wore seemed to soak up the heat, and streams of sweat were running down his face and neck, stinging his eyes.

According to the rough map he'd bought on board ship, the Chagres River ran nearly due south from this point for a distance of about thirty miles, winding through primitive jungle growth. The captain of the *Lexington* had told all the debarking passengers that the usual price a native boatman charged for taking a passenger to the headwaters of the river was $10 per person. However, the sudden and extraordinary demand had no doubt quadrupled the price since his last trip here. Other ships were off-loading a constant stream of human cargo, each of them in one hell of a hurry to get to the other side of the Isthmus and catch a coastal steamer to the land of gold. The captain warned them to be on guard against sneak thieves and robbers who would not hesitate to kill them for any valuables they might be carrying.

This was not what he wanted to hear, but Sloan felt that forewarned was forearmed and had carefully loaded and primed his Colt five-shot pocket pistol.

Carrying his small leather grip, Sloan stepped out of the longboat. Unlike the other men and women who disembarked on the sloping beach with him, he didn't scramble to be the first to reach one of the dozen or more native boatmen who awaited them. Instinctively, he considered the yelling and shoving to be somehow beneath his dignity. Besides, he rationalized to himself, it was just too damned hot and sticky for such frenetic activity. The way they were acting, you'd think California was just upriver.

As he looked around, two rowing boats from an anchored brig grated ashore on the gravel beach. The occupants came spilling out with their packs and bags and joined the rush. Sloan smiled to himself as he sauntered up the slope. The whole scene looked to him like someone had poured coal oil on a termite mound.

He perched on a convenient tree stump, after first checking it for bugs. All that weight of gold in his pants legs made sitting a lot more pleasant than walking. From where he sat, he could distinguish some of the conversations, and heard the dark-skinned, half-naked boatmen, in broken English, demanding, and getting, forty dollars a head to transport passengers the thirty miles upstream on the Chagres River. There was very little haggling. It was strictly a sellers' market—first come with cash in hand, first taken. The available transportation was quickly secured, and the lucky ones piled into the flat-bottomed poling boats with their luggage immediately to continue their journey while the rest milled about, grousing at the heat and the inefficient steamship line that had promised better accommodations. There were about two dozen wooden buildings that comprised the tiny town, but he preferred the outside air to any stores or saloons. On the only slight elevation stood the ruined fortress of San Lorenzo. According to the captain of the *Lexington*, pirate Henry Morgan had attacked this fort in 1670 and killed three-hundred people.

Sloan left the tree stump and found himself a shady spot on the grass under some tall trees. The untended grass had been tramped down by many feet, and he sat down, cross-legged, on the ground, fanning himself with his hat. He watched the sluggish current of the Chagres River debouching into the sea, staining the blue-green water of the Caribbean. His eyes traveled upstream, following the first of the rough-sawn wooden boats as the muscular natives, standing on either side in bow and stern, poled it around the first bend and out of sight. He leaned his back against a tree and closed his eyes.

"*Señor,* may I be of service to you?"

Sloan opened his eyes from a heat-induced doze.

"You are perhaps waiting for a boat upriver, *señor?*"

The pleasant voice addressing him came incongruously from one of the fiercest-looking men he'd ever seen. The lean, dark-skinned individual was of indeterminate age and was dressed in ragged cotton shirt and pants, apparently to cover his nakedness from the gaze of the foreign travelers. A loincloth sufficed for all the other natives he'd seen.

"All in good time," Sloan replied cautiously, noting the man's gaze dropping to the expensive leather bag on the ground beside him. "You got a boat for hire?"

"*Sí, señor.* A very good boat. It does not leak and has canvas top to keep off the sun and the snakes that sometimes fall from the trees."

Lovely, Sloan thought. Aloud, he said: "There's a group of people over there who are looking for a boatman. I'm in no hurry."

"But you go to California, the same as the others?"

"That's right," Sloan replied.

A look of confusion passed across the man's face. Then he grinned. "A man who does not hurry does not have fever for the gold, heh?"

Sloan squinted in the glare of the sun off the water, trying to figure out what the man was driving at. *Obviously thinks I've got money, or he wouldn't be soliciting my business,* Sloan thought. The man's brown face was still split in a wide grin, revealing a missing front tooth. Straight black hair hung down over both ears. He held a straw hat in his hands.

Sloan noted another boatload of passengers landing on the beach from the *Lexington,* and yet another pulling away from the bark anchored nearby. Why wasn't this man's boat filled immediately? There had to be some catch.

"How much?" Sloan asked.

"Sixty American dollars."

"Too much."

"I'm a poor man, *señor,* and must pole this boat many miles to feed my family."

"You'll be a rich man soon at those prices."

"It is too hot in this sun to bargain, *señor.* I will take you for fifty."

"Too much."

The fierce-looking boatman wiped his brow on his shirt sleeve and put on the disreputable straw hat. "For you only, today, I will make my new boat available for a mere forty dollars. Ah, what I must do to put bread on the table." He rolled his eyes to heaven.

"That's what the others were charging to begin with."

"But they are going only as far as Gorgona. I will take you another five miles . . . all the way to Cruces before we must go overland."

"You rent mules for the overland journey, too?" Sloan became interested. Perhaps he could strike a deal for the entire trip with this man. Cost was really no object, but he mustn't let this man know that.

"Oh, *sí.* My mules are very strong. To ride or carry pack," he added, looking around for any additional luggage.

"How far is it?"

"About forty-five miles by river and eighteen more by trail."

"I'll give you seventy for the whole trip," Sloan said, climbing heavily to his feet, feeling the weight of the coins in his pants. He picked up his grip.

"Ah, *señor,*" the man groaned. "You make a poor *hombre* work very hard for his money. I usually get eighty for the whole trip."

Sloan gave him an impassive look, not taken in by the whining act.

"But I must leave soon to make our stopping point by dark, so I will take seventy."

"Half now and half when we arrive in the city of Panama," Sloan said, digging into his pocket and handing over thirty-five in gold coin. "Where are the other passengers?"

"Only two others . . . boatmen who must return to Cruces where new boats are being made for them." He gave Sloan a gap-toothed grin over his shoulder as he started away through the trees toward the riverbank. His attempt at a friendly grin made him look even uglier.

The boat turned out to be a double-ended dugout canoe about fifteen feet in length. Two men wearing only cut-off canvas pants were waiting. They appeared to be of mixed Indian and Negro blood. Their expressions didn't change as they regarded him. Their lean torsos were corded with muscle.

"You will not be sorry you have hired the services of Septien Martínez," the boatman rattled on. He made no attempt to introduce the two others, who silently took their places in the bow and stern. Balancing himself with a hand on Martínez's arm, Sloan stepped into the middle of the unstable craft while the others steadied it. Sloan knew he was completely out of his element, feeling like a top-heavy walrus as he sat down clumsily in the bottom, the bag on his lap.

Martínez passed a pole to the native in the stern, took one himself, and stepped into the bow. With no further ceremony, they shoved away and started upriver. Sloan noticed that the promised canvas canopy was nowhere to be seen. But as far as the tropical sun was concerned, it didn't matter since they poled near the bank most of the time where tall trees shaded them.

Once the journey started, Martínez was all business, not talking. Now and then he gestured with an arm signal for the man in the stern who was standing up, poling. One thing Martínez had not lied about was the boat itself. It was dry and seemed reasonably new. Sloan watched the bubbles slide past on the murky surface as the dugout sliced upstream. As near as he could judge the normal water level, the Chagres River seemed high. Flashes of colorful plumage caught his eyes and raucous, unfamiliar cries pierced the heavy, dank air. A wide array of birds and monkeys, he guessed, as well as all manner of creeping, crawling, climbing things. When they rode close to the bank, he caught the odor of rotting vegetation. The water was stained the color of tea, and its smooth, swift-flowing surface was broken now and then by a splash. He'd heard about schools of flesh-eating fish in these jungle rivers that could devour a large animal, or a man, in a matter of seconds. He had no doubt that such things existed here just out of his sight beneath the surface a few inches away. He shivered inwardly and gripped the bag even tighter. He'd always considered himself a brave man, but he much preferred danger or an enemy he could confront directly, like the alligator he saw sunning on the muddy bank.

But, as the steady rhythm of the poling went on, hour after hour, his tense muscles relaxed, and his head gradually fell forward, and he dozed. During periods of wakefulness, he was aware of the river twisting back and forth in tight loops, the slanting sunlight throwing the shadows of the trees first one way and then another. If it hadn't been for the sun, he would have lost all sense of direction. Not that it mattered. The river was their only road with but a few feeder streams coming into it now and then. The natives did not speak to him, nor he to them. They were the hired servants, and he knew himself to be above them. But he also knew that he was at their mercy in this environment, and would have been much more comfortable if at least one other white man had been along. But he had his .32 Colt pistol in his right trouser pocket for emergencies.

He was perspiring freely, so had no need to urinate the entire afternoon. Which was just as well, since the boatmen made no stops. But by the time the natives poled the dugout into the bank near a small settlement just before dark, he was very thirsty.

To his great relief, there were about thirty other travelers there from the earlier boats who were also stopping for the night. It felt so good to be among his own kind again that he immediately struck up a conversation and sat down to eat with four other men he would never have looked at twice in Charleston. Their conversation, in which he took little part, was coarse and profane, but he shared a canteen of water with them, and then had a nip of homemade raw whisky one of them carried in a flask. That, and a supper of greasy pig meat tasted like ambrosia.

The owners of four rude huts that comprised this small village had long since rented out the few cots, hammocks, and sleeping space on the dirt floors to the early arrivals. Sloan and another dozen travelers, all of them men, made do outside on the dank ground. Sloan spread his jacket down to lie on and reclined against the lumpy grip like a fat pillow. He stretched his feet toward the log fire that, from its size and appearance, was kept burning day and night for cooking, light, and, most of all, Sloan guessed, to ward off night-prowling animals. Charleston was low and swampy, but, even to the first settlers, could not have appeared as wild and primitive as this.

He slept poorly, jumping awake at every squawk and screech and strange cry that came from the depths of the blackness that encircled them. Others around him were doing the same.

Toward morning he slept from sheer exhaustion, and awoke to a humid, smoky dawn, feeling like he'd been kicked and stepped on by a bull. He tried not to show his stiffness as he stumped to a cooking fire nearby where a large blackened coffee pot hung on an iron tripod. Two native women were frying some kind of pan bread in iron skillets while a third was collecting money for the fare from the travelers lining up to eat it like it was cuisine of the finest hotel.

An old woman thrust out her hand. "Three dollars, *señor,*" she enunciated in English with difficulty. "Bread and coffee," she said, pointing at each.

"How about some eggs and bacon?" Sloan muttered half to himself. A young American couple standing in a nearby line heard him and chuckled. Sloan thrust a hand into his pocket. His gun was there, but no coin. He tried the other pocket and then this jacket. He'd used all his ready cash on board the *Lexington* to buy his last meal before debarking. Embarrassed, he hurried off toward the shelter of the nearest trees, as if looking for a place to relieve himself.

After answering the call of nature, he thrust a hand down into his loosened pants and secured a small handful of gold double eagles from one of the tube-like pockets. Just as he was buckling his belt, he saw movement out of the corner of his eye, and Septien Martínez glided noiselessly out of the jungle behind him toward the village. Martínez flashed his gap-toothed grin. *"Buenos días, señor,"* he said, tipping his straw hat.

Sloan nodded, not changing expression. How much had the man seen. The native made no more noise than a hunting cat, Sloan reflected. The safety of his gold, and maybe his life, was dependent on his keeping the hiding place of his money a secret.

With this disturbing thought nagging at the back of his mind, he returned to the cooking fire and paid the old woman with a twenty-dollar gold piece. She returned only three five dollar gold coins and went on to her next customer. While more coffee was boiling, he chewed the tasteless fried bread.

"Hell, Sam, they ran out of sugar," a man commented, turning from a conversation with one of the women. "I can't drink this stuff black." He stared into his cup.

Even Sloan's mouth puckered at the sight of the bitter black brew, thinking how he had been spoiled by the finest honey.

In a matter of only a minute or so, Sloan saw a native girl of about sixteen come toward the fire, gnawing on a stalk of sugar cane. As he watched, she spat the juice into the boiling coffee, then bit off another mouthful of the cane. She repeated this process several times, until Sloan and a few of the more fastidious customers lost their thirst for the morning brew.

Martínez and the other two native boatmen indicated they were ready to leave. "We start now, we be in Cruces in two days," Martínez said. "They have beds there," he assured Sloan.

I must look like a soft, white slug to these people, Sloan reflected. By comparison to them, he had to admit that's exactly what he was. And he didn't at all like the pampered product of civilization he was presenting to these natives who were hardened to a primitive way of life. He hoped his

159

stolid expression gave no hint of the agony he was feeling when he thought of two more days in the dugout with these men. Mosquitoes had feasted on his pale flesh the day before and last night, and red welts dotted his hands, face, and neck. The itching was maddening. One ear was so swollen by their bites that it stuck out from his head like some ludicrous jug handle and was as thick as a piece of raw meat that he could flap back and forth. He knew he made a ridiculous appearance as he retrieved his grip and followed the three men toward the riverbank. *How narrow and quickly traversed the isthmus looked on a large map,* he thought, settling himself in the middle of the canoe. But experience should have taught him that nothing was ever as easy as it appeared.

During the next two days, Sloan saw more of the jungle than he'd ever wanted to see. He had to admit that Martínez and his two boatmen, who took turns poling, were skilled enough to keep them out of the whirlpools and eddies as they steadily thrust the log dugout upstream through the shallower, slacker water near the banks. Several times Sloan was treated to the sight of large, colorful snakes lying along the branches of overhanging trees, only a few feet from their heads. He spent most of one afternoon, gripping his pistol in his lap, waiting to be attacked by swimming anacondas, alligators, wild boars, and whatever else lurked just beyond that wall of growth where the fierce sun penetrated only as subdued, greenish light.

But gradually he toughened to the trail. He became inured to what he ate and drank at the stops, and to sleeping in the canoe or on the ground. Only the mosquitoes continued to torment him until he finally resorted to smearing a foul-smelling river mud over his face and neck and hands.

Bad as it was, this solution at least prevented most of their bites, except when he sweated the coating off, or when they were caught in a tropical downpour and the mud was washed off.

Since the river was high, the head of navigation closest to Panama was four and a half miles above Gorgona at Cruces, a slightly larger primitive village where the promise of a bed was kept, if a hammock could be termed a bed.

The next day, when they transferred to mules, Sloan was thankful for the change where he could be walking or riding astride most of the time. It was beginning to feel like the longest sixty-mile trip he'd ever made. But, at least, it was two-thirds over, and Martínez assured him they could make it to the city of Panama in one day.

The two native boatmen left them at Cruces, and Martínez engaged one muleteer to replace them. They started early, and the day was overcast, with intermittent cloudbursts. The trail, beaten down and churned fetlock-deep in mud, made for slow traveling. Yet, for several long stretches, Sloan was surprised to see the trail was actually paved with flat stones.

"This trail is part of the road between Panama and Porto Bello. Built in the time of the Spaniards many years ago," Martínez grinned, when Sloan remarked about it.

The weather, although wet, seemed cooler than before. Sloan guessed it was because part of the trail followed higher ground. It was not hilly, except where the travelers were forced to descend or climb up a streambank. The usually sure-footed mules even slid on these inclines in the black mud. All three men were forced to dismount and lead the animals, wading sometimes waist-deep. On these occasions, Sloan gritted his teeth, feeling the murky water sucking around his legs, imagining what might be down there, preparing to have him for a meal.

It happened that afternoon during a downpour when Sloan was trudging along, leading his mule. He had his eyes down, watching his step, water pouring off his hat brim. Something struck him in the back. His head snapped back, and he flew forward, landing face down in the mud. For an instant he thought the mule had kicked him, but then the mule packer was clawing at him. Sloan kicked a boot heel into the man's face and rolled over to see Martínez coming for him, knife raised. He saw the gap-toothed grimace, strings of black hair plastered to the face by the rain. Just as Martínez lunged, his foot slipped in the mud, taking some of the force from the blow. The knife arced down, ripping through Sloan's shirt, raking across his lower chest and abdomen. Sloan jerked away from the stinging slash, and tumbled backward off the slightly elevated trail. For a sickening second he felt himself falling. Then his head seemed to explode into a thousand painful lights, and everything went black.

Chapter Sixteen

Hastings Cut-Off,

South Fork of the Humboldt River

California Emigrant Trail

The bottom had fallen out of Lisa Sizemore's life. She was nearly paralyzed with shame and regret. Her pain was so over-powering that she could not even cry. As she watched the wagon train slowly disappear around a bend in the cañon, she fervently wished the earth would open up and swallow her.

She had killed Zeke Masters. As punishment, she and her parents were being banished from the party. It had been the worst day of her life. Oh, how she prayed that God would back up the clock by one day—no, only part of a day. She would make sure things were different; she would do something to avoid the terrible deed. But time ground remorselessly onward, leaving the pieces of human life in its wake.

The explosion had been simmering for weeks, but Lisa had still been caught off guard. She should have seen it coming, she told herself. But for many days following her decision to cut her hair and begin wearing men's clothing, Zeke Masters had not pursued her with the same rude ardor. She'd somehow made herself less attractive, she decided, or else he was just being patient and waiting for a better opportunity. She had smiled to herself when she thought perhaps he considered her one of those women who was attracted to her own sex, rather than to men. She did everything she could to foster such a notion by her actions, the way she walked, handled an axe, and talked. She even tried chewing some of her father's tobacco where Zeke could see her, and managed to get away with it until her tormentor was out of sight, at which time she promptly got sick.

But her efforts had the desired effect. As the Platte River Valley slowly unwound behind them, Zeke seldom spoke to her, and then only in passing. Several times she caught him staring curiously at her as if trying to decide what manner of person she was.

"Lisa, would you get me that saleratus?" her mother asked one evening as she was mixing biscuit dough. "It's in that box with the spices."

"Mother, I. . . ." She hesitated, on the verge of confiding the problem of Zeke Masters to her mother. But then she changed her mind and got up to go to the wagon. *I'm a grown woman and can fight my own battles,* she thought. Mother's got enough on her mind without my problems.

As she walked around the back side of their big wagon, she paused, catching the sound of her own name spoken on the far side of the next wagon.

"Thet Lisa Sizemore gal's not only a lotta woman, she's a lotta man!"

Several male voices guffawed.

"Rough as a cob, that one," said another.

"Aw, hell, leave Zeke alone," a third said in an aggrieved tone. "They've got a lot in common . . . they chew the same brand o' twist."

"Damn all o' you," Zeke's nasal twang interrupted the general hilarity. "I mean to mount that woman one day. After she's been rode a few times, she'll gentle down just like my saddle mare."

"Yeah, and I mean to be elected President along about the time that happens."

The voices gradually faded as if the men were walking away. Lisa's heart was pounding, but she hastened to climb into the wagon without being seen. Until that moment, she'd flattered herself that she'd succeeded in discouraging him. But now the old fear returned, and she secreted a broken-handled paring knife inside the belt of her canvas pants.

But the days passed and nothing happened, lulling her into thinking that maybe what she'd overheard was only a lot of male bravado. She even returned the paring knife she'd been carrying, pretending to find it in the wagon after Madeline Sizemore had given it up for lost.

Day followed day with nothing to break the monotony but views of distant antelope herds, or high-soaring hawks. If there were any Indians abroad on the high plains, they were staying well-hidden. Three different times the outriders came upon a few dozen grazing buffalo, but only once managed to kill three before the rest scattered out of range. The fresh meat was a welcome treat for everyone in the train. Some of the more enterprising travelers cut some of the leftover meat into thin strips and managed to dry it in the hot wind and sun during the next few days. One other thing the buffalo provided was dry dung for cooking fires. They gathered canvas bundles of these "buffalo chips" and carried them slung under the wagons to replace the available dry wood that had been scoured up by trains ahead of them along the high plains.

Several times the little caravan was pounded by violent

rain and hailstorms that could be seen coming across the wide sky from more than eighty miles away. Lisa had become accustomed to feeling exposed on the treeless plains as had the other emigrants, and they were all able to stop, unhitch, and corral the teams before the lightning and thunder got close enough to spook them. Even so, one particularly vicious hail storm in mid-June left many of the wagon tops looking as if they had been used for breastworks. But it wasn't all bad. Many of the men and women made up for the bruises received from the large hunks of hail by scooping up pails full of ice and enjoyed drinking ice water the rest of the day.

In spite of many diversions, the trail had been long and arduous from Fort Laramie on the North Platte, to Independence Rock, to the Sweetwater, to the broad South Pass. Lisa felt she could walk faster than the train was moving, and, exasperated by the plodding pace, she often did get out of the wagon to stride alongside. Beyond Fort Laramie, Lisa had written no more letters to her cousins since there was no way of sending them East after that.

According to Vincent Sizemore, Josiah Martin was elected wagon master because he was a former captain in the Mexican War, rather than for his trail experience. Thus, Lisa's father was not inclined to accept all the wagon master's decisions without question. However, Vincent did go along when Josiah Martin proposed following the Hastings Cut-Off. Martin had convinced the men in the train to try this alternate branch of the California Trail that crossed the desert south of the Great Salt Lake. Then, according to a guidebook that Martin kept handy, the trail doubled itself in a long loop around the Ruby Mountains before finally intersecting with the south fork of the Humboldt River.

"I don't know what this route is cutting off, besides

maybe our water," Lisa's father had growled after the first few days, raking a hand through his thick beard. "We should have stuck to the northern route. This sure doesn't seem to be saving many miles."

But they had not yet come to the worst of it. Traversing the Great Salt Lake desert in July was an experience that literally seared itself into Lisa's body and mind. And she knew it also left an indelible imprint on the other emigrants who hailed from places with trees and water. In preparation, they filled all water containers and cut grass to carry for the animals.

They set out to cross the Great Salt Lake desert just as the sun rose behind them, slowly changing the salt from a soft pink to a blinding white. Lisa rode the first hour, then got out of the wagon to walk alongside, hoping to relieve the mules of a little extra weight. It was probably a bad decision, she reflected later, since she seriously underestimated the power of the sun. By mid-morning, even though she only sipped at the tepid water, her canteen was empty. She was reluctant to refill it from the water barrel since the mules needed more than she, and the precious fluid had to last.

At noon the train was halted, and her father watered the mules with several hatfuls of water, being careful not to spill any. Nobody unhitched; nobody ate. The salt supported no brush for cooking fires.

"There's not enough wood within three-hundred miles to make a snuff box," Vincent Sizemore observed, squinting at the desolate landscape that stretched away in all directions, "and not enough vegetation to shade a rabbit."

A half hour later the caravan was moving again, the noon sun pouring its full force down on them. The mules' legs were caked with salt, and Lisa's boots were powdered white as well. The soles of her feet were burning, and, with every step, her boots broke a couple of inches through the surface crust. She was vaguely aware that she was being sucked dry by the heat pounding down from above and being reflected up from below. She thought she was perspiring, but her clothes remained dry. She slitted her eyes against the blinding glare and plodded on, her mind a blank. She wouldn't have needed Josiah Martin, or even the tracks of the previous wagon trains, to lead her across this waste, she thought. She could have found her way with her eyes closed or in the darkest night since dozens of horses and oxen carcasses littered the trail and filled the heated air with a noxious odor. Only when the wagons came close did the swarms of black buzzards flap heavily away from their gruesome feast. Lisa's eyes and mind recorded the sight, but it never penetrated her dulled sensitivity. She merely saw, then looked away to fix her gaze on the irregular line of blue mountains in the far distance with the longing of a soul in purgatory looking toward heaven.

Besides the dead animals, the trail was strewn with tents, blankets, iron skillets, stoves, and any item that could possibly be spared to lighten the wagons of those who had gone before.

As the afternoon wore on and the sun slanted directly into their faces, Lisa thought she had never been so hot in her life. Her head began to pound, and her mouth was parchment dry.

She was later to thank her parents for saving her from sunstroke. Apparently her father, who was driving, noticed her wobbling gait and halted the mules. He dragged her, red-faced and feverish, into the wagon where Madeline bathed her daughter's head and neck and dribbled water into her mouth from a dipper until she cooled and was able to drink small amounts. Then she dozed.

An hour before sunset, Josiah Martin halted the wagons. Everyone unhitched and watered the animals. Those who were able to work up sufficient saliva took some nourishment in the form of bread or jerky. But, mostly, they just rested as the sun sank beyond the mountains in a fiery ball.

Three hours later, they hitched up once more, and Martin led them on again, trying to cover as much distance as possible during the cool of the night.

White canvas tops wavered across the landscape in a slow motion to the creaking of wheels. Lisa watched the sharp black shadows of the wagons, thinking that the moonlight made the vast salt desert look like a snow field. The night was long, and she dozed on the wagon seat. Later she and her mother took turns relieving Vincent at the reins before the desert finally began to lighten again with the return of the sun.

They paused just before daylight for another three-hour rest. But now all of them, including the animals, were suffering from thirst, and the remaining water was doled out sparingly, not nearly enough for their needs.

Another day of hellish heat followed. Several of the horses and oxen dropped and refused to get up. They were shot and left by the trail. Meat was cut from a couple of the carcasses, and shared among those in the train. It was Lisa's first taste of horse meat, and the raw, juicy nourishment actually tasted good to her after a day's complete fasting.

During the thirsty traverse, those who'd imprudently loaded their wagons with chests of drawers, writing desks, and even the patent gold washers purchased at St. Joe, began dumping these heavy items by the wayside.

The hours and the miles began to blur in Lisa's mind. But, by the time they halted just before sunset, she did notice that the blue mountains were appreciably closer. Then, through the following endless night as they crept over the crusty surface under the millions of stars and some moonlight, she experienced weird hallucinations, or were they dreams? She couldn't tell. It was almost as if she were floating out of her body part of the time.

By daylight the mountains appeared brown and wrinkled, and sparse desert plants had begun to dot the desert as they left the salt behind. Lisa was completely numb and couldn't even feel elated when three men, who had ridden ahead, returned with full canteens and news of a spring several miles ahead at the base of the mountains. She was so exhausted all she wanted to do was drop down in her tracks and never get up again, as had several of their draft animals. Ribs and hip bones were beginning to push out the dusty hides of even the hardiest oxen who had all they could do to draw the lightened wagons. Lisa was proud of her father for selecting good mules who didn't seem to fare quite as badly.

The vegetation reappeared as they skirted the Ruby Mountains, even though it was mostly sage and low-growing desert shrubs. There was even enough grass to sustain the animals, if not to replace any of their lost weight. Periodic springs contained just enough water to keep the animals going, and partially to fill the water barrels, but not enough for such luxuries as bathing.

Thus it seemed to Lisa they had reached paradise when they pulled into camp along the South Fork of the Humboldt River. She never realized how good grass and water could look. She gathered fuel and built the fire as usual. She was very hot and tired, and cast longing glances at the small stream that went by the name of a river. Back home it would not have made a decent creek, she thought. She had to admit that wearing men's clothing on the trail was infinitely preferable to the customary garb that women wrapped themselves in. But she still knew she could never become accustomed to going weeks without bathing or changing clothes.

The heat had stolen her appetite, and she declined when her mother called her to eat the boiled beans and pan-fried bread. Even if she hadn't felt queasy, the everlasting sameness of diet put her off. Back in Tennessee, in July, she would have been eating and serving all manner of fresh vegetables. She tried to recall them individually—their color, their feel, their taste—ripe tomatoes, okra, onions, carrots, radishes, lettuce, squash, cucumbers, beets. This pleasant escape allowed her to blot out the fact that her family and most of the others had for weeks been subsisting on what she considered survival rations.

Consequently, she'd gladly left the smell of cooking food and stolen away to the river for a refreshing bath. There were no trees of any size to shield her, but she walked a half mile into the cañon, around the first bend, following the shallow water as it gurgled around boulders and over rocks and gravel to collect now and then in quiet pools.

Sitting down, she tugged off her short boots and set them aside. Her cotton shirt and trousers smelled of woodsmoke, bacon grease, and sweat. With no hesitation, she waded into the water, fully clothed. The water felt cool to her skin, and she sat down in the knee-deep pool. Then she lay back with a sigh of contentment and half floated, her arms wide. It was quiet, beyond all sights and sounds of the camp. She stared at the wide strip of blue sky above the cañon, watching a few birds, unfamiliar to her, fly up to perch in the branches of bushes that clung to the seams in the broken rock wall. The afternoon sun had warmed the rocks, but the water was deliciously refreshing. With little stretch of the imagination, she could envision herself as the last person left on earth. What a terrible prospect, if true. She wondered if Adam had felt a terrifying loneliness before God created Eve. Idle speculation.

She soaked and splashed for several minutes, letting her relaxed mind wander as her dry skin absorbed the wonderful moisture. As long as she was wet, she thought she might as well strip off her clothes and see if she could get them a little cleaner. She had not thought to bring any of their precious soap from the wagon. She'd heard that some Indians used pounded soapweed for washing. But she had no idea what the plant even looked like, much less if it grew here. They had plenty of bacon grease and wood ashes for lye, but her mother had not taken the time on this journey to make any lye soap. As she stood up and unbuttoned her shirt, she reflected that she had much to learn about the wilderness, probably more than an earlier generation of settlers had to learn about the Appalachians.

She was standing naked in the water, wringing out her shirt when the click of a stone made her jump and turn, fearing some animal had crept close.

"Whoa, now, but ain't she a ripe peach!" The man gave a low whistle, and his mustache stretched in a wide grin.

Two men were ogling her. One of them was Zeke Masters. The small, wiry man who had spoken was his first cousin who went by the single name of Bender.

Zeke Masters licked his lips and stared at her body like a starving man looking at a steak. He waded into the water toward her. She backed away slowly, still holding the wet shirt twisted in her hands and making no attempt to cover herself.

"Now's our chance, Lisa. There's nobody around," he said smoothly.

She glanced at his cousin, who was still grinning.

"Get on outta here, Bender. I can handle this," Zeke said over his shoulder.

The cousin, apparently fascinated by this tableaux, remained rooted to the spot.

Lisa knew there would be no bandying of words this time. They both knew what he had come for. She had no weapon, but that didn't mean she was completely defenseless. She feinted one way, then lunged the other, eluding his reaching hands as she splashed toward the bank. He caught her around the waist, dragging her back. She was amazed at his strength. Then he got a hand on her breast. She slapped the wet shirt into his face and started to scream. But he clapped a hand over her mouth, choking off the sound. The weight of his body on the backs of her legs brought her thudding down, half out of the water on a sandbar, knocking the breath from her. She barely felt the pain of her bare body against the rocks and gravel.

"You need some help, Zeke?" she heard Bender ask.

"Hell, no!" he panted, pulling himself up higher on her. "I said *git!*" he rasped.

He removed his hand from her mouth and gripped her windpipe from behind. "If you scream, I'll squeeze so hard you'll never breathe again," he whispered.

She believed him and kept silent, beginning to panic at the pressure on her throat. She saw Bender jogging away toward camp.

Zeke was struggling with something, and she twisted over on her back, scraping her skin. He apparently approved of the new position and allowed her this much movement. "Now you're gonna feel what a real man is like, you damned wildcat!" His foul breath was nearly in her face.

She saw he was struggling to slip out of his suspenders

and unbutton his pants. In order to do so, he had to remove both hands from her, even though he kept her held down with his weight. She acted submissive and terrified as she slid one hand slowly along the gravel bottom underwater.

Zeke was cursing the suspenders and fumbling with his wet trousers as her hand closed over a sharp, fist-sized rock. Wiggling her body just enough to keep his attention, she whimpered piteously as she slowly pulled the rock to her and brought it to the surface.

He glanced away from her to push his pants down, and she brought the rock around with all the power of an arm and shoulder strengthened from weeks of chopping firewood. It struck his head with the sound of a hammer on a rotten log. He fell without a sound.

She shoved him off onto his back and scrambled up, her legs bruised and scraped. He lay with his mouth open, his head in about three inches of water. Blood poured from the scalp wound, staining the clear water.

Almost in a panic, she struggled into her wet shirt, pants, and boots without bothering with underwear or socks. Her heart was pounding so hard she could barely get her breath. She started on a stumbling run for camp.

Reaching her wagon, she collapsed and gasped out her story to her father. Several nearby men came running to see what was wrong.

"Come with me. Trouble!" Vincent Sizemore said tersely, leading a half-dozen men on a run toward the river. Bender was one of them.

Madeline Sizemore held a cup of strong coffee to Lisa's lips, ignoring the curious stares from several men and women.

A short time later, six men came toward camp, carrying a limp Zeke Masters between them.

"Dead, by God!" Bender exploded, his eyes wide, as the men laid the body on the ground on its back.

Word spread quickly, and the whole party assembled. Suppers were left to burn on fires as men and women crowded in to see who had died.

Josiah Martin, carbine in the crook of his arm, jumped onto a nearby tailgate and yelled for everyone to quiet down. By the time the talking had died to a murmur, Lisa had recovered her breath and most of her composure, so she could tell her story. She stated it as simply and clearly as she could, leaving out nothing.

"That's a damn' lie!" Bender shouted as she finished.

All eyes swiveled toward him. "She's been wiggling her butt at my cousin ever since we left Saint Joe. Why do you think she's been wearin' those men's pants? And why do you think she was naked just now?"

"I was wearing those pants precisely to discourage him," Lisa replied. "I went for a bath in the river. If I were going to entice him, why would I have hit him?"

"You can say anything you want 'cause Zeke ain't here to defend hisself. You bitch! You didn't have to kill him!" Bender shouted. Restraining hands kept him from moving toward her.

Lisa saw the hard eyes of Zeke's three other traveling companions, and felt a sinking feeling in her stomach.

"That's enough of that!" Josiah Martin snapped, jumping down off the tailgate. Men and women fell back to clear a space around him. "All right, what did *you* see?" Martin asked, jabbing his rifle toward Bender.

"Just like I said. We was just walking down the river afore supper and come upon this woman, naked as a jaybird in the water. She give the come-on to Zeke. When he saw she was willin', he told me to get on back to camp, and I took off. Looked like she let him git his pants half down and then hit him with a rock when he couldn't move."

"I didn't ask you what you *thought* happened," Martin snapped. "I asked what you *saw*."

"That's all," Bender muttered.

"It doesn't make sense that she'd lead him on and then kill him," a woman said in a low voice. "What did she have to gain? The man looked to be as poor as a vagabond." She avoided Lisa's eyes as she spoke.

"Lovers' quarrel," a man said. "Maybe he got a little too rough with her."

"Fact remains, Martin, she hit him and kilt him," one of Zeke Masters's wagon mates said, stepping forward with a belligerent look. He was a raw-boned man, over six feet tall, dressed in homespun.

Before Martin could reply, Vincent Sizemore said: "A pure case of defending herself!" Lisa looked to her grim-faced parents who stood behind her. She found herself wishing she'd earlier confided in them. "That should be obvious," Vincent said.

"I tell you what's obvious, mister." The big man turned away from the wagon master. "Zeke Masters is dead, and your daughter did it. Look at her . . . there's not a mark on her. She must've hit him, sneaky-like."

There was a growl of assent from several others.

"Them are the facts. Now what the hell you gonna do about it?" the raw-boned man demanded of Josiah Martin. The growling grew louder.

"Damn you for a trouble-maker, Ray Hanner!"

"Hanging that woman would be about the only way to square things," Bender said, seeing an opening.

"The missus and I saw Zeke Masters hanging around her a few weeks back, but not lately," somebody volunteered.

"They didn't seem to have any problems, then."

Lisa realized she was gripping her mother's hand so tightly, her fingers were beginning to lose circulation.

"Well, what's it going to be, Mister Wagon Master?"

"Wait a minute! Hold on!" Josiah Martin leapt nimbly back up onto the tailgate to get the crowd's attention. "I don't know who's to blame here, but we're not having a hanging. There's no court of law here to sort this out. A young man has been killed, and what actually prompted this young woman to do it we may never know. But we can't tolerate conflicts like this on this train. And we must move on tomorrow." He took a deep breath, gripping his rifle in both hands. "Therefore, the Sizemore wagon will be cut out and left behind when we move out in the morning."

Lisa caught her breath, looking at the wagon master. She thought he'd been on the verge of ruling in her favor until pressured by Zeke Masters's friends. But now he'd rendered a Pilate-like decision. Abandonment in this wilderness could well mean death for her and her parents.

The crowd of some seventy people had erupted, talking and yelling, everyone trying to be heard at once.

Lisa shrank back against her father, who encircled her with protective arms.

"Hang the murderin' bitch!" came Bender's strident voice.

"You gonna let her off, scot-free?" a man rumbled.

"Martin made the right decision!" another voice shouted above the tumult. "That man was tryin' to rape her, sure as you were born ugly."

"Who you callin' ugly?"

Those in favor of the judgment and those against began to berate one another. Shoving matches broke out. Several women frantically tried to slide out of the crowd to safety as tempers flared and a punch was thrown. The crowd surged one way, and two men stumbled over the uncovered body on the ground.

Vincent Sizemore pulled his wife and daughter back against the side of their wagon and edged out in front of them, rifle in hand.

When Josiah Martin couldn't shout down the commotion, he raised his rifle over his head and fired. Lisa flinched at the explosion, and suddenly the crowd fell silent.

The wagon master's face was flushed, and he'd lost his hat. Long, graying hair fell across his forehead.

"Let's take a vote! The only way to settle this!" a man shouted. "She hangs, or she's banished."

"There'll be no vote!" Josiah Martin roared, gripping his rifle. "You elected me captain of this party when we started, and, by God, I'll make the decisions. Any man who doesn't like it can pull out and go his own way." He paused and glared at the men below him. "What about it, James? Walter? Martha Bigelow, can't you talk sense into that man of yours?" He singled out the leaders of both factions, one by one. They dropped their eyes and grumbled, but did not challenge him, and Lisa could see their will was broken.

"Now, get on back to your suppers. You'll see that I'm right, once you've had a chance to cool off and think about it. Hanner and Bender, I'm sorry for your loss, but you know damn' well what Zeke Masters was like." Then he continued in a softer tone. "Take care of the body. If you want to bury him here, I'll say a prayer over him in the morning before we start."

And so it was done. Now, as the last wagon disappeared around a bend in the cañon and the echoes of the rumbling wheels gradually died, Lisa's eyes, sore from crying and lack of sleep, fixed themselves on the mounded rocks and dirt marked by a board cross, torn from a packing box.

She'd gone over it time and again in her mind during a sleepless night, trying to discover if there were some way things could have been different. Even though she'd concluded her actions were justified, she felt a deep regret that she'd unintentionally killed him, rather than just injuring him enough to drive him off. But a human life had been snuffed out by her hand, and she would have to live with that fact for the rest of her life.

"We'll stay here today and rest up," her father's voice called from near the wagon. "Let them get a good distance ahead." He paused. "You know, things could have been a lot worse. Martin drew me a map from his guidebook. We'll be all right. We've got plenty of water and grass. The mules are in decent condition, considering what they've been through, and we haven't seen a single Indian. We have enough food to see us through for a good while yet. We'll join up with the main Humboldt River just the other side of this long cañon, Martin says. There should be good grass and wood and water there, too."

"I'm sorry I caused you all this grief, Daddy," Lisa sobbed, suddenly losing control.

"Never mind. It's not like you did anything wrong. I'd have been ashamed of you, if you hadn't resisted. We'll see this through to California. Everything will be fine from here on. You'll see. We're past the worst of it. God won't lay any burden on us that we can't bear."

Lisa nodded, wiping the tears from her cheeks with the back of her hand. She hoped with all her heart that he was right. But she couldn't shake the feeling he was only whistling past the graveyard.

Chapter Seventeen

Aboard the Inverness

South Atlantic

The Northeast Trade Winds lasted more than two weeks, giving Clayburn Collins time to recover from his strained and aching muscles and the bruises he'd received from the big hands of Abel Stark. His body toughened, and the rope cuts and blisters on his hands healed with the aid of salt water. In the balmy air of the night watches, he took his cue from the other men and went barefoot. Calluses formed on his hands and the soles of his feet. In fact, with the semi-permanent coating of pitch and tar that soon layered the soles of his feet, he could climb the ratlines and stand on the footropes with as little discomfort as if he were wearing shoes. He even had the advantage of being able to grip with his toes and felt more secure aloft.

Collins found himself requiring little sleep in the warm weather as less work was required. Several of the men brought their bedding from the forecastle to sleep in out of the way places on deck.

At the beginning of the Trades, both watches had worked to strip all sail and send aloft their oldest, thinnest sails that were kept for just such weather. Since no sail-maker was aboard, Stark trained two volunteers in the art of cutting and sewing new sails and repairing old ones from spare canvas. The two men, one Cuban and one Vermonter, sat on the forehatch during the daylight hours, stitching with leather palm and needle, while Stark looked over their shoulders, now and then giving pointers. For the time being, they were relieved of watches and slept in all night. Their work was not missed. Collins found himself fighting drowsiness as he stood about the main deck on night watches, waiting for some order to be given. He even welcomed a two-hour trick at the wheel when his turn came. While at the wheel, he loved to watch the glowing phosphorescence sweeping out on either side of the bow as the ship plowed through the warms seas. He breathed the night air as if it were some heady tonic, and couldn't seem to get enough of it into his lungs. The bellied square sails above him were wind-steadied arches leaning on the night. The wind seemed to caress the ship, but its power was deceptive. The noon sightings showed twenty-four hour runs of two hundred thirty, two hundred forty-seven, and two hundred sixty-four miles on three recent days. Abel Stark, as the only one with skill in celestial navigation, shot the sun with the sextant and worked up the calculations; Gilbert Malloy, as captain, kept the log and posted on the mainmast the number of nautical miles sailed in order to foster morale among the crew. What it fostered was betting pools on what the next day's run would be.

On the day watches, the men were kept busy tarring and tightening the slack in the stretched standing rigging, holystoning the decks on hands and knees—a job that Collins and all the other crewmen hated. Very few sail adjustments were necessary.

When off watch, Collins even resurrected his neglected sketchbook and took up drawing again. He gained a satisfaction from art that nothing else gave him. During these periods of leisure, he often thought of Lisa Sizemore, the beautiful Melungeon girl he had sketched that snowy day in the mountains. Would he ever see her again? It was unlikely. If he ever got back to the Tennessee mountains, she would probably be married and gone. But he could carry that image of her as she was that morning—bright and vivacious. He felt a deep regret that he could not have stayed there and gotten to know her better.

With ample food, no alcohol, and light work, the men in the forecastle fattened up, if filling out and hardening up could be called "fattening."

The immutable Abel Stark went on as before, standing watches, showing no favorites when it came to work, keeping to himself even more than before. However, he did unbend now and then in the relaxed atmosphere of the warm Trades, to reminisce about his days at sea. It helped pass the time in the long night watches when there was nothing else to do. Collins assumed the mate talked almost exclusively to him because of his being a former passenger and not a man who followed the sea, and because he didn't cower before the mate. Besides the look-out and the helmsman who had something to do, the other three men of the watch stayed away from Stark.

One night Collins was leaning on the starboard rail, watching the glow of the phosphorescent bow wave curling away from the ship. Lost in thought, he suddenly started when he realized the mate was standing beside him.

"A great thing, the sea," Stark remarked, holding to a shroud with one hand. "She can be beautiful and caressing, like now, or she can be hard and unforgiving. Like a woman. I guess that's why they refer to her as female."

Collins merely nodded, feeling the comment needed no response.

"I know how Captain Blackwell must have felt, having to leave all this . . . especially against his will. He may never get another command, even though it wasn't his fault. Sometimes even a captain can't dodge bad luck." He was silent for a moment. "Just like the captain who first promoted me to mate forty-five years ago. Adolphus Zucker was his name. A German from the old country, and hard as nails, he was. But fair, and the best seaman I ever knew, bar none. I served five years under him, and then went on to other ships. He retired from the sea fourteen years ago. But he didn't have a chance to enjoy life before some slimy coward murdered him for all his life savings, within a month after his retirement."

"Damn," Collins breathed softly, feeling he needed to let Stark know he was listening. "Did they hang his killer?"

"Never caught him. Before he died, the old man managed to draw a figure in blood on the floor. When his wife found him, he only had breath enough for one word before he died."

Collins waited.

"He said the word, 'tattoo.' What he drew in his own blood was a horned devil's head with an anchor under it and the letters G-A-M."

"That was it?"

"The police had no other clues. They figured the killer was somebody who probably knew him, and was a man of the sea because of the anchor. But Zucker had had such a long career and had commanded hundreds of sailors, so it could have been anyone. They checked all the tattoo artists they could find, but came up empty. Most likely done in some other country. Well, the law finally gave up, but I've been looking for a man with a tattoo like that for the last fourteen years. Any damned weasel who would hurt a fine

183

old man like Adolphus Zucker deserves. . . ." He paused with a choking sound in his voice. "This!" he finished, slamming a belaying pin down on the rail with a force that made Collins jump back and catch his breath. Stark turned on his heel and walked away, smacking the pin into his open palm and muttering to himself.

Collins's heart was pounding as he ran a hand over the rail and felt the deep dent in the wood. He gave thanks he was not the object of Stark's long search. And he was equally glad when four bells sounded so he could go on the poop to take his trick at the wheel.

Over their evening meal that day Collins related the incident, and Merriman was of the opinion that Stark, with more than a half-century at sea, had pretty much seen it all.

"What's another mutiny, more or less, to him? As for this murderer he's looking for, if he hasn't found him in fourteen years, it's not likely he ever will. The man probably left the sea with the money he stole, or he could even be dead by now. Who knows?" He shrugged. "I guess it's just something to keep him on edge and angry when he thinks about it. Can't afford to let himself get soft in his old age."

"The man's a marvel," Collins said. "He came topside to stand the midwatch the other night wearing just a pair of cut-off pants. I've never seen a man so fearfully muscled. You could strike a match on him anywhere. Amazing for a man pushing seventy. Just an easy swipe from the back of his hand lifted me off my feet one day. Knocked the wind clean out of me. It was like getting hit by a bear."

"His condition isn't because he takes good care of himself," Merriman continued. "My guess is he inherited a lot of that, and hard toil has done the rest. The only thing I see physically wrong with him is a slight limp, probably from some old injury."

"I've smelled liquor on him since Captain Blackwell was put over the side," Collins said.

"He must have his own private stock. If there's any in the ship's stores, I don't know about it."

"The cook might have some for medicinal purposes."

"Stark's not hard up enough for a drink to rob the cook."

"Well, he's no drunkard. If the drink does anything to him, it makes him more short-tempered," Collins said.

"But he knows his business. Not a detail of the sailing of this ship escapes his attention," Merriman declared.

"I'm surprised he hasn't gotten his own command before now."

Collins shrugged. "Maybe he has, then fouled up somehow and lost it."

"Well, the men respect him," Merriman said.

"Fear him is more like it."

"No. If you'll notice, the older men in the crew . . . at least the ones who don't seem to be the criminals . . . give him a lot of respect as a professional. I believe they sense he can somehow get them to California, come what may. The younger ones, by and large, plus an old wharf rat like Jacobus take to the easy-going ways of Mister Malloy, and ridicule Stark behind his back."

"Not a healthy situation. That might explain why I'm hearing rumors of fights in the fo'castle," Collins said thoughtfully.

Four days later, Collins had reason to believe his guess was correct. They'd just crossed the equator, under full sail, in the early afternoon. The event was marked, not by any ceremony involving King Neptune, but rather by a murder. Will Fjelde ripped open the throat of Rafer McCook, a New Yorker, during an argument in the forecastle.

Fjelde had calmly turned over his broken knife to Stark who had rushed to investigate the commotion. The off watch laid the body out on the main hatch cover, sluiced a bucket of sea water over it, then set to work, grumbling, to clean up the mess of blood that had spewed all over their quarters.

"Damn you, Fjelde," Stark fumed. "I should have left you in the water. What the hell did you do that for?" The mate was opening and closing his huge fists as if having a hard time controlling himself. "I don't care what started it. In the old days I'd have swung you to the yardarm. And I ought to now, but that would just put us another man short. But, by God, I'll see to it that you do two men's work from here on."

Collins could see his jaw muscles working as he ground his teeth.

Eight bells was struck, and the watches began to change. Malloy came on deck and saw the crowd around the main hatch. "What's the trouble, Mister Stark?"

"One of your men just committed murder!" he snapped, pointing at the body.

Malloy calmly surveyed the bloodless face. "Well, if we had to lose someone, I'd rather it be him," he said dispassionately. He looked at Fjelde. "Want to tell me about it?"

"He was bad-mouthing you, sir, and Mister Stark. Bragging about what he was gonna do to the both of you when we got ashore."

"That's hardly reason enough to kill a man," Malloy remarked.

"Well, sir, then it got personal. One thing led to another. . . ."

"I'm sure you know a Finn's reputation for bringing bad luck, Fjelde. You're just adding to that reputation."

If that was meant to be a reprimand, it didn't come across as one, Collins thought.

After a short silence, Malloy said: "You're confined to the midship house for a week on bread and water."

"Hell, that's no punishment!" Stark burst out.

"You'll address me as 'sir'," Malloy corrected him mildly.

Stark grew red in the face as the crew looked on expectantly.

"It seems he should at least be lashed, *sir,*" Stark said, controlling himself with an obvious effort.

"As you know, Mister Stark, we need him. He's just now mending from his broken ribs. Flogging would only weaken him further. You can bring charges of murder against him in court when we get ashore, if you are still inclined to do so. In any case, you and I will discuss this privately, later. For now, Fjelde, you will be confined as ordered. Jacobus, as bo'sun, you will have the key to the midship house." Malloy turned to Collins and Merriman. "You two will take your meals in your cabins while his sentence is carried out."

The next morning, the ship was moving through the water too fast for a proper burial. Growling and sour-faced, Stark ordered the mainsail backed to slow their headway while the crew assembled at the starboard rail. McCook's body had been sewn into a rotten piece of canvas as a shroud with a lump of lead at his feet. The body rested on a hatch cover and four sailors balanced it on the rail, while Gilbert Malloy read from a book he'd apparently found in the captain's cabin, as the men stood, bare-headed and silent.

" 'Lord we beseech thee to be merciful to the soul of our shipmate, Rafer McCook. We commit his body to the deep in the sure and certain hope of the resurrection to come when the sea shall give up her dead. All things will be made whole once again, and there will be no more death or pain or weeping.' " He closed the book. "Until that day, grant us fair winds and a fast passage. Amen."

He nodded, and the men tilted the hatch cover, and the canvas-wrapped body slid into the sea. A slight splash, a swirl of bubbles, and Rafer McCook was gone. Once his sea boots, clothes, and a few personal possessions were divided among the crew, as was customary, there would remain no trace that the man had ever existed on earth. How vain man was to think that all his struggles and accomplishments amounted to more than a few square feet of canvas and a lump of lead at the feet, Collins thought as he moved away. Without a belief in an afterlife, everything was certainly a waste of effort.

"Get 'er before the wind again!" Stark snarled. "We're losing time!"

As the men dispersed, Collins found it difficult to work up any sympathy for the departed McCook. He'd only known him by way of a few insulting remarks the New Yorker had thrown in his direction. Yet he felt somehow diminished by his loss. "If it can happen to him, it can happen to me just as quick," he muttered to himself.

"Well, that's one more the New York City police can mark off their list," one of the sailors remarked as the men moved to the main brace.

That evening the Chinese cook surprised them by preparing lobscouse—a sort of hash made with boiled potatoes, onions, salted meat, hardtack, rice, and beans. Collins found it delicious and had two helpings. "Mighty good dish to have such a strange name," he remarked to Merriman as they sat on the bunk in the latter's cabin to eat.

"You're right. Don't know where the name came from,

but this stuff has been made for more than a hundred years. I think it's the seasoning that makes it so tasty."

"Or my appetite."

"You know, I never figured Fjelde for a violent man," Merriman said, changing the subject.

"Me neither. Must've been a matter of self-preservation. I'm sure we don't know the full story," Collins said.

"A week's confinement on bread and water hardly seems appropriate, though."

"That's what Stark thought. Any slight differences are liable to turn violent, if that's all the punishment the winner can expect."

"You know, Malloy had a loaded pistol he was holding on the captain during the mutiny. He must have some powder and balls and caps somewhere. Wish I could get my hands on some of that for my Colt," Merriman said. "I'd feel a lot more secure with a loaded firearm handy."

"I'm in Stark's watch," Collins said. "If I get a chance to get into Malloy's cabin while he's on watch, I'll see if I can find it."

"Is there any powder in the ship's stores?"

"I doubt it. I can't think of any reason they'd have it, unless it would be to scare the natives when they were slaving. Black powder is dangerous to haul."

The Northeast Trades drove the *Inverness* almost into the Southeast Trades. But for several days the bark rolled in the doldrums between the two predictable weather patterns. The change was expected, Merriman told Collins, but still Stark seemed to take it as a personal affront. He stumped about the decks, sour-faced and mumbling to himself. The sailors knew to stay out of his way when he was in this mood, and Collins made sure to do nothing to irritate the mate.

"Give him a good wind and he's happy," Merriman muttered one afternoon, as he stared out at several patches of sargasso weed floating on the glassy surface of the sea. "But take the driving force from the ship, and he can't stand it."

Day after sweltering day with no breeze, the tropical sun bore down in force, heating the ship until pitch bubbled up from the seams between the deck planking.

Fjelde's week of confinement was up, and he rejoined his mates in the forecastle, happy to be out of the hot midship house and back on regular food and work.

Malloy and Stark took advantage of the calms to prepare the ship for what was to come. The crew was kept busy hauling down the fair weather sails from the yards and replacing them with the newer storm sails of heavy canvas. A thorough scrub-down of the decks, fore and aft, was ordered. All worn rope was replaced; the longboats were painted and seams caulked. As a precaution against Cape Horn seas, the door leading from the main deck into the after cabins under the poop was sealed and caulked, and double strength timbers were prepared to cover both fore and main hatches.

One sweltering evening, as Collins was preparing to go on watch, Louis, the Chinese steward, appeared at the open door of his cabin with an empty tray in his hands. He paused, looking carefully around him. "Mister Clayburn Collins," he began with polite formality.

"Yes?"

"I bring you something to eat or drink?"

"No, thank you, Louis. I'm just going on watch." Collins winced from a fresh rope burn on his hand as he pulled on his shirt.

"I bring you salve for sore hands. Make up special. Work every time. Heal fast." He grinned, and his slanted eyes nearly disappeared in the pouches of fat. His round, bald head was shining with perspiration in the lamplight from the hallway.

Suddenly Collins had a thought. "Come in a minute."

The old steward stepped into the cabin, and Collins moved to shut the door behind him.

"Do you serve Mister Malloy in his cabin?"

"Oh, yes. All time. Him take more meals there now."

"Is he drinking rum with his meals?"

"Him drink rum all time alone. Not just with food."

Collins nodded. The steward had confirmed what he suspected. Malloy apparently had a weakness for the drink. He couldn't imagine why, but the acting captain was taking advantage of his new rank to stay partially inebriated most of the time.

"I want to ask a favor of you. You'll be paid. If you don't want to do it, just say so, and we'll forget all about it."

Louis gave him an inscrutable look.

"See if you can find out where he keeps the gunpowder, lead balls, and percussion caps. I know they have to be somewhere in his cabin. If you can find them, I'll pay you to steal them for me. A man who drinks all the time can't be trusted with a pistol," he added as if by way of justification.

The old steward grinned conspiratorially. "Maybe all same take pistol bye-m-bye."

"No. He carries that pistol constantly. He'd miss it right away and raise hell. If you could somehow get away with his ammunition, he might not be aware of it for a while."

"Him sleep with gun under pillow," Louis informed him.

"I know it will be dangerous for you. Can you get into his cabin when he's on deck?"

"Captain lock all tight. Me no get in but for meals. But Louis find powder and shot, you bet."

191

"Thanks. But be careful and don't take any big chances. If you can get them, I'll make it worth your while."

The steward smiled, nodded and retreated out the door.

Finally, just before dawn a few days later, some puffs of wind began to move the ship, and by noon they were making a steady five knots through the water. Porpoises began following the ship, their sleek bodies slicing in and out of the blue sea as they leapt alongside the cutwater.

Several of the men off watch baited large hooks with salt pork and trolled alongside. After an hour they managed to hook one of the creatures and hauled him aboard, clubbing him with a belaying pin. The cook was able to serve fresh porpoise fillets for supper, a welcome change for all hands.

Two days later, shortly after sunrise, the look-out's shout of—"Land ho!"—brought Collins and Riaz away from the pumps where they'd been sucking the few inches of seepage out of the bilge.

The high mountains of a distant coast were in view as the morning haze burned off.

Stark took a small brass telescope from his pocket and strode to the rail. After several seconds of study, he snapped the glass shut. "The port of Río," he said. "Right where it should be." He almost grinned. "Told Malloy to allow for drift," Collins heard him mutter in a low voice. "I reckon my navigation's dead on."

All sail was set to the quartering breeze, so the mate went aft where he climbed the ladder to the poop. Collins saw him giving instructions to the helmsman.

"Why are we putting into port?" Collins wanted to know as he and Merriman passed at the eight o'clock change of the watch.

"I heard Mister Malloy . . . 'scuse me . . . *Captain* Malloy say we're going to sell our cargo of molasses to buy stores for the rest of the voyage."

"We won't be arrested as mutineers?" Collins was incredulous.

"We're a couple thousand miles from where that happened. No way word could have gotten here ahead of us. Besides," he winked, "it's a safe bet that these officials don't take sides as long as the money's right."

Collins got an exhibition of Stark's sailing skill when the mate, conning the helm, sailed into the Río de Janeiro harbor without a pilot, in spite of fluky winds deflected by the steep mountains. Most of the men of the off watch stayed on deck to watch the Brazilian port approach and to reef sails willingly as Stark worked the *Inverness* into within a cable's length of the wharves before dropping anchor.

Malloy, in spite of the language barrier, apparently dealt in a smooth manner with the port authorities who came out in a steam launch. Whether he passed himself off as Captain Blackwell, Collins never knew. But, whatever papers he showed them seemed to satisfy their requirements, and the uniformed Brazilian officials left.

Shortly after their departure, Malloy had both remaining longboats swung over the side, and most of the crewmen were allowed to row the short distance to shore. Juan Verdugo was taken by Malloy as interpreter, since he could come closer to speaking and understanding Portuguese. Apparently Malloy had no trouble finding a buyer for their cargo, because he returned in early afternoon all smiles and conferred with Stark privately.

The next morning, lighters came out to the ship. Stark had the main hatch cover taken off. A block and tackle was rigged to swing the small kegs of molasses up out of the hold and over the side. The operation, with all hands working, took most of the day. When it was done, the ship rode considerably higher in the water.

As soon as the last of the molasses kegs were off-loaded, Malloy ordered the ship's hold thoroughly washed down with sea water and all rats they could find killed and pitched overboard. Then the hold was pumped dry. The whole thing was a disagreeable job, Collins discovered, sweating in the airless space below deck with squeaking rodents trying to scramble out of the water that was flooding the bilge. He wondered how the African slaves had stood weeks of confinement, lying on these wooden shelf-like platforms built out from the sloping sides of the hull. Apparently a number of them died on every voyage, leaving only the strongest, which fetched a higher price at market.

After things had dried out, Stark took a lamp and made a complete inside inspection of the hull for leaks or damage or wood rot. Then Fjelde took a longboat and went around the outside of the hull, paying special attention to the rudder fittings. Four sailors were put to work from the longboat scraping all the weedy sea growth and barnacles from the waterline down under the ship as far as their arms and four-foot flat shovels could reach. The hull was copper sheathed against borer worms, Merriman told Collins as they watched the operation from the deck.

The next day the cook and Verdugo went ashore to buy stores. Collins and Merriman anticipated they would be going ashore with the rest of the crew for some sightseeing. But it was not to be. Gilbert Malloy made up a list of ten men who would be allowed to take the other longboat ashore for the day. But Collins, Merriman, and Stark were not on the list.

"Afraid we'll jump ship," Merriman said, examining the list tacked to the foremast. "Notice all those names are the sailors who backed him the strongest in the mutiny. Malloy's no fool. He won't risk losing part of his crew. Did you notice he's been wearing his pistol on a belt holster ever since we got to port?"

"Damn," Collins said softly. "I'm sure getting tired of seeing nothing but this ship."

"Well, take a good look. There's Río," Merriman said, waving a hand at the distant buildings.

Collins shook his head disgustedly.

Later that day a flat-bottomed lighter came alongside, rowed by several boatmen with long sweeps. Stark directed the crew in bringing aboard coils of new rope, spare canvas, several long timbers to be used to repair any broken spars or sawed up for braces in case of damage, a length of chain, and boxes and barrels of foodstuffs.

Collins and Merriman formed part of a line of men handing up the stores and stacking them on the deck.

"Looks like Malloy operates on the premise that a contented crew is a trouble-free crew," Collins muttered as he swung a box from his hands to Merriman's.

"Why's that?"

"Food takes on exaggerated importance at sea," he said. "From the looks of this stuff, he's given the cook a free hand to buy the best. Not just preserved food, but look at these fresh vegetables and melons. Lots of dried fruits and meats and sugar, too. There's even a few live chickens in pens coming aboard. It'll be plum duff for dessert twice a week for a while." He grinned.

Malloy came striding up at that moment, all smiles, to watch the operation. "You can thank the Boston owners of the *Inverness* for all this," he said. "Their molasses paid for it. But you can be assured that their sacrifice won't cause them to lose an inch off their ample waistlines. None o' your tainted salt horse for us the rest of this trip."

"Oh, stow that in my cabin," Malloy called, stepping away to direct the sailors who were lugging two small kegs of rum. Collins and Merriman exchanged knowing glances.

Some inside ballast, in the form of stones, was swung aboard and placed in the bilge on either side of the keel. Stark personally supervised the trimming of all weight, fore and aft.

Late that night, Collins was awakened by the tramp of feet on deck and some loud, raucous voices. " 'Oh, whisky killed my sister Sue'," someone wailed. " 'And whisky killed the old man, too!' " sang another drunken voice. " 'Whisky for my Johnny!' " roared several in unison with the chorus.

Collins, suddenly glad he hadn't gone ashore, rolled over and went back to sleep.

A few short hours later, Stark showed no mercy to the hungover men. In fact, Collins thought the old man took a grim satisfaction in snarling out orders to three men to go aloft who had just been heaving over the side.

The anchor was winched up with the windlass, and the *Inverness* swung toward the mouth of the harbor on an ebb tide, keeping well clear of two other ships getting under way at the same time.

It was a sunny day, and, with yards braced, they cleared away on the port tack with a good southeast breeze. The watches were set, and the regular routine of shipboard life started once more.

Besides the stores, the only other thing of note they brought away from the Brazilian coast was two cases of fever, picked up by Will Fjelde and a young sailor named Jack Morrison.

Collins was sketching on the poop two days after their

departure, when he noticed Will Fjelde, who was steering, continually resting his forehead on the rim of the tall wheel. Collins assumed the Finn was just tired until he looked closer at the older man and noticed his fair face was flushed and sweating, even though the weather was moderate.

"Are you all right?"

"Yeah. Yeah. Just a little hot is all." Fjelde straightened up and glanced at the drawing sails and then into the binnacle.

But the man was obviously in distress. By the time he was relieved from his two-hour trick, some thirty minutes later, he reeled away and down the ladder like a drunken man.

That afternoon, Collins and Riaz were reefing a topsail, side by side on the yard in a freshening wind.

"Will is in his bunk with fever," Riaz yelled without turning his head.

"Who?" The wind was whipping their words away.

"Will Fee . . . Fee. . . ."

"Fjelde," Collins prompted.

"*Sí.* He is the one. Very sick."

Collins threw a knot in the reef points, and the two of them slid their feet carefully along the footrope back in toward the mast.

Fever was not uncommon, and Collins thought nothing of it until Fjelde didn't report for duty at the change of the watch. *Either Malloy is being easy on him, or he's really sick,* Collins concluded.

The next day Fjelde was up and tottering around, making a try at working, but Collins noticed him wrapped in a heavy coat and his teeth chattering even though it was a sunny, mild day.

After that the Finn seemed to improve as they sailed

southward the next few days, and Collins forgot about him as the ship entered a region along the Argentine coast that the older sailors said was noted for its spectacular sunsets. The heavens were suffused with golds and reds and purples and gray-blue, shot through or backlighted with brilliant rays of sunlight. Night after night the panorama of mushrooming cloud banks stretched across the western sky, sliding and changing into breathtaking tints.

"Stark says they're caused by dust blown high into the sky from the Argentine pampas," Merriman said, coming up to stand beside Collins at the rail one evening just after supper.

"Spectacular!" Collins breathed. "Gorgeous. A good thing I don't have a palette and brushes right now."

"Why?"

"I could never capture it . . . it would frustrate me. Maybe it's caused by dust rising high and the world turning so that the sun shines at the just the right angle, and the heat sucks up enough moisture to form clouds, but the hand of the Master Artist is at work here."

"Hard to believe it's the same Artist who's behind all the ugliness in the world," Merriman remarked.

"I can't explain the nature of God. I just believe coincidence is His way of remaining anonymous," Collins shrugged.

"Well, whatever's behind that sunset, I've never seen anything to equal it . . . except maybe this one girl I used to see in Nashville. . . ."

"Different kind of beauty."

"Whatever pleases the eye . . . ," Merriman said.

Chapter Eighteen

Collins rested his sketchbook on the taffrail. With quick, deft strokes of his pencil, he was making the towering masts take shape on the page before him.

It was the next afternoon, and Malloy had the watch. He strolled over and stood observing for several seconds.

"You have a rare talent there," he said politely.

"Thank you, sir. I'm afraid it's nothing I can take credit for. It's a pure gift. I've been able to draw and sculpt since I was a boy."

"Nevertheless, it's a pleasure to watch. You do this for a living ashore?"

"Yes and no," Collins replied evasively, having no intention of revealing his engraving of counterfeit coins.

Malloy merely nodded, then strolled away, hands clasped behind his back.

The *Inverness* was slipping through a quiet sea, all sail set. Jack Morrison, the lean young sailor who'd recovered from the touch of fever, was steering.

Collins put the finishing touches on his drawing. Then, as an afterthought, he added a huge albatross to the sky in the background. He took a last look. Satisfied, he closed the book and started to go below, when the stocky Malloy sprang across the poop in front of him.

"Hard a-lee!" he yelled, shoving the helmsman aside and spinning the big wheel himself, all the while fixing his gaze ahead with a wide-eyed look Collins had never seen before.

Collins jumped back, startled, as the bow of the ship began to pay off. He followed the direction of the captain's gaze and felt the bottom fall out of his stomach. Boiling toward them from the unseen coastline was the blackest cloud he'd ever seen. It was moving with breathtaking speed, apparently pushed by a tremendous wind. Lightning was flashing and flickering from this massive, roiling substance that was spreading out and rising higher with every passing second.

"Clew up! Haul down! Let go on the run!" Malloy was shouting, holding the wheel hard over and watching anxiously as the ship answered slowly, turning away from the black monster that was bearing down on them. "Jump to it, or we'll be caught aback!"

Jack Morrison ran to lend a hand.

Collins flung his sketchbook through the open doorway of the charthouse and sprang to cast off the sheet of the big spanker that was secured to a pinrail near him. Then it was down the ladder of the poop in two bounds to help the other half-dozen men get as much sail off her as they could before the squall hit them. Fairleads skirled as ropes were released and sang through the blocks. Feet thudded and voices yelled back and forth as too few sailors tried desperately to douse too much canvas.

Like a black panther pouncing on a white sheep, the blast of wind hit as the *Inverness* was just about broadside to it. The tall ship lay over on her side, and Collins was thrown off his feet and sent sliding into the wall of the midship house. He was aware of three things—a roar in the rigging, sudden blackness, and the ship's time bell clanging. And the wind! He was pinned against the side of the midship house by an unseen pressure that forced the breath back into his lungs. He had to turn his face aside into the lee of the draft to breathe. Squinting up through the slashing rain, he could see figures on the yards. The first blast had blown out the two jibs and the fore topsail, while several others had departed in shreds. The remnants of canvas were whipping straight out like pennants, adding to the thunderous noise. Lightning flashed and popped.

Collins could feel the ship, even in ballast, being pressed over and down, farther and farther. Either the *Inverness* would lose her masts, or she would rise and leap away before the wind, or she would never rise again. He was lying nearly horizontal against the wall now, and the longer, lower yardarms were almost touching the sea. Her lee rail was buried, and water was creaming along the deck almost to her hatch coamings. He clung to the iron handrail on the wall and awaited the outcome. He could feel the midship house vibrating under him and looked to see the huge mainsail had burst its gaskets. It was flogging with tremendous force. The whole ship was being buffeted as if shaken in the maw of some gigantic monster.

How long she lay like that, Collins never knew. Time meant nothing. Everything had ceased but the life and death issue of the present moment.

Yet, somehow, the *Inverness* gradually began to right herself. The big mainsail finally tore itself loose and disappeared into the murk. Slowly at first, then with a grand dignity, the ship rose, her mostly bare masts erect. The bow paid off, and the ship plunged away through the sea, with only her spanker on the mizzenmast and two of her staysails still intact to drive her before the gale.

Through the stinging rain, Collins could see a figure clinging to the wheel as the *Inverness* ran before the storm at a good fourteen knots. The stocky man who held the ship before it was Malloy.

★ ★ ★ ★ ★

"Well, you've had your first taste of a Pampero," Abel Stark said to Collins as the two descended from the charthouse to their cabins more than two hours later.

"Whatever it's called, I don't want to see another one of them."

Collins had to grab the newel post as a following sea flung the stern of the ship skyward, and the stairway became horizontal.

"Oh, you'll see more of them before we get farther south," Stark said. "This region just off the Plate River is notorious for these sudden storms. One of the worst in the world. I was dismasted right here, off the Plate, twenty-seven years ago, when I was second mate of the *Capricorn*." He paused to steady himself as the room dropped sickeningly. "Took the sticks right out of her the first whiff, or we'd have turned top for sure. As it was, we had to chop away the rest of the rigging and were adrift for a week before we were sighted by a Danish brigantine and taken aboard."

Collins never ceased to be amazed that this hard-bitten mate would pass the time of day with him. But as the subject was ships and the sea, the mate would talk to anyone.

"Did we suffer any damage?" Collins asked.

"I don't think we've sprung anything, but I counted ten sails blown out. Might be able to salvage about half of them for spares." He nodded and turned abruptly away toward his own cabin.

The *Inverness* ran before the gale with only a storm trysail set. But, for many hours, the ship rolled and plunged in the huge seas thrown up by the wind.

The storm blew itself out some time after midnight. When Collins came on deck to stand watch at four o'clock, he was surprised to see stars shining overhead and more sail set. The ship was back on her southwestern course.

"*La Plata* is very bad," Verdugo greeted him with a flash of white teeth in the moonlight.

"Very bad is right. I thought we were all goners."

"One must be alert, or the Pampero will pounce on him like a jungle cat," Verdugo said.

"I don't think my heart will stand another one of those."

But, the next day, another one threatened during Abel Stark's watch. The sun was sparkling on a cold sea, but the barometer had been falling for hours. Collins was in the rigging of the mainmast when Stark shouted at them to begin furling and clewing up as fast as possible. From his lofty perch, Collins could see the blackness building again in the west, with bolts of lightning flickering from it. It rose higher and higher until it blocked the sun, and the blackness turned a greenish color as it rushed toward them. All hands were called, and this time it was buntlines and clewlines and a lowering of yards as the topgallant sails were stripped off. The big, fore-and-aft spanker sail was lowered and furled on its boom. The dim twilight became very calm and still. Through some peculiar condition of the atmosphere, Collins could hear words spoken on deck, far below, as clearly as if they had been beside him. He finished his work and slid down a backstay to the deck where the crew gathered to await the onslaught.

But it never came. After threatening and grumbling and flashing lightning for a good half hour, the storm slowly moved around to the west and north of them and the sun reappeared. They were left rolling in a calm with bare poles.

"You can't ever tell about these Pamperos," Stark said, ordering them aloft to get sail back on the ship. "I'd rather have it promise and not deliver any day."

The crew of the *Inverness*, in spite of differences among themselves, operated with a maximum of teamwork as they drove the ship south out of the region of the Pamperos. The weather began to grow chilly at night, and then much colder. Collins and the rest of the crew donned shoes and jackets for the night watches. They had traveled through three of the four seasons in less than four months—from the chill of early spring along the coast of the Carolinas, through the heat of tropical summer, and were now well into fall weather.

"It'll be winter off the Horn," Stark had told them. "And we'll be rounding east to west, against the prevailing wind. Wind? Huh! I shouldn't even use that word for a regular Cape Horn snorter!"

That night Louis, the Chinese steward, appeared at Collins's open door just after dark, carrying a covered tray. "Supper, Mister Collins," he said, entering and closing the door with his heel.

"Supper?" Collins wasn't in the habit of being served his meals.

"Special hot beef you ask Louis for." He swept the white cloth off the tray and set it down on the bunk. Steaming slices of beef lay on a cloth napkin, but Louis pulled the napkin and meat aside to reveal a two-pound sack of black powder, a canvas sack of lead balls, and a circular tin of percussion caps.

Collins looked up in astonishment at the grinning Oriental face. "I don't know how you did it, but thank you. You'll have fifty dollars in gold within the hour."

"Louis very good. First find out where likely spot to keep powder inside cabin. Come back hour after meal to pick up dishes. Captain very drunk by then. Him pass out on bunk.

204

I look in drawer below bunk and find this." He grinned again. "Cabin very cold, and captain not have shirt on. I pull blanket over him before I leave. Cover evil spirit on shoulder."

"What evil spirit?"

"Him have mark of Satan here." He indicated a spot high on his upper arm.

"You mean a tattoo?"

Louis nodded.

"A tattoo of a devil's head . . . with horns?"

"Yes."

Collins felt a chill begin to creep up his back. "Was there anything else . . . any other mark besides the devil?"

"Anchor below, and letters . . . G-A-M."

Collins swallowed hard. Louis was describing the tattoo of the murderer of Captain Adolphus Zucker! "What is Gilbert Malloy's middle name?"

"Name of Gilbert Arthur Malloy on sea chest."

G-A-M . . . the initials matched, Collins thought. No wonder Malloy was drinking just when he seemed to have everything going his way. Malloy must have discovered, through some casual conversation with Stark, that the mate was looking for Zucker's killer. And the fear that Stark would see that tattoo was eating him alive, driving him to steady his nerves with rum.

"Louis, you've trusted me. I've got to warn you of the grave danger we're in." Collins told the steward of Stark's quest for the tattooed killer.

Louis listened impassively to the story, then said: "Bad men. Bad luck. All rotten, damn to hell." With that he picked up his tray and departed.

"Land ho!" shouted the look-out one morning just after

a squall of hail and heavy wind had passed them. They were driving south under fast-moving storm clouds, alternating with bursts of sun. Spray showered over the port bow as the ship shouldered aside a steady succession of rollers.

What land? Collins thought they were far offshore. But the look-out was pointing off the port side, and Collins saw two rounded hilltops of different heights in the blue distance, most of the land lying below the horizon.

"The Falkland Islands," Abel Stark said.

Several hours later they sailed beyond the islands in the northeast without coming any closer.

Later that day, the masthead look-out reported sighting land off the starboard bow in the far distance.

The next day broke to a fierce, cold wind and scudding black clouds. Snow squalls began to pass across the ship, one minute blowing a horizontal snow so heavy Collins couldn't see twenty feet, then the cloud would be gone and a wan sunshine brightened the day for a half hour.

"I slipped into the charthouse and took a look at the course Malloy's been plotting," Merriman said that evening during the dog watch as they sat eating in the relative warmth of their adjoining cabins. "That land the look-out sighted yesterday, off to starboard, was Staten Island. We're in the region of the Horn."

"Is Cape Horn really as bad as its reputation?" Collins asked, tearing off a hunk of fresh bread and dunking it in his steaming soup.

Merriman shrugged. "I've never been this far south, but I don't think the old hands are trying to josh us when they tell horror stories about it. Even Stark speaks of it with respect. And *nothing* scares him."

"I hope to God he doesn't find out about Gilbert Malloy," Collins said in a low voice.

"If he does, we'll have more bloodshed, that's for sure. I've got that powder and shot stowed in the cabin where it would be hard to find. And I've loaded my Colt. Lucky the balls were Thirty-Six caliber. But if the mates go at each other, the crew is liable to take sides in an all-out battle," Merriman said.

"And this ship is coming up on the most dangerous piece of ocean in the world," Collins said with a sinking feeling in the pit of his stomach. He set the rest of his food aside.

"Well, so far the only ones who know his identity are the two of us, Malloy, and Louis. And I think the secret's safe with all four of us."

"Louis is a good friend of the Chinese cook. Let's hope he doesn't even tell him."

Over the next twenty-hours the wind died. For more than a day and night they wallowed in huge glassy swells, leftover reminders of the perpetual storms that blew, unimpeded, around the bottom of the world. Cold air also filtered up from the polar seas across the warmer ocean, wrapping the ship in a dense, cottony fog.

And Fjelde had a relapse of the fever. He had taken to his bunk two days before, this time much worse, Verdugo told Collins. Stark ordered the sick man carried to one of the several empty bunks in the midship house. "Might be something catching," as he put it. "And not a damn' bit of quinine aboard," he grumbled as Collins, Merriman, Riaz, and Verdugo carried the Finn into the midship house and laid him down on his own thin cotton mattress, covering him with a blanket.

"Should have bought some quinine in Río," Stark continued, "but I figured there was some in the medicine chest." He looked down at the sick man who was only semiconscious. "Spread the word that any of you who wants to can sit with him on your off watches. Swab him down when he's burning up, and pile on the blankets when he's shivering. He'll have to come through this as best he can. Sure as hell hate to be another man short. You saw how it takes twice as long to make sail or shorten sail with the crew we've got. We lost a good mainsail in that Pampero because the few hands we had botched the job of putting on the gaskets."

Collins came on watch that night to a fog so thick that he knew it was of little use to have a look-out posted in the bow or at the masthead. He would never be able to see another ship before a collision, or any rocks in time to avoid them. Luckily, they had plenty of sea room; there was no charted land anywhere within many miles. As for other ships, it would be an extremely long chance that they would encounter another vessel in this vast expanse of southern ocean. A collision, in any case, would have to be minor, since both ships would be rolling in an oily swell with no headway. Yet, with the number of ships headed for California, several of them could be converging near the tip of South America.

As he strolled forward to find one of his Cuban friends to pass the time, he heard a sound like a slow wave washing up onto a still beach. He froze, and a chill went up his back. He held his breath and listened. It came again, this time accompanied by a sighing noise. He sprang to the rail of the ship and strained his eyes into the darkness. Had they somehow gotten off course and drifted onto a lee shore? Were there some uncharted rocks nearby?

Suddenly Verdugo appeared at his side. "Collins," he said, "you hear it, too." They stood for several seconds, gripping the rail. Then they heard a swishing of water and a low, groaning noise. Collins couldn't tell from whence it came because of the fog that seemed to be playing tricks with the sound.

"It is the spirits of Rafer McCook and other lost sailors," Verdugo whispered. "They are calling for us to join them."

Again a chill passed over Collins. He wanted to reply that the idea of sailors' ghosts was ridiculous, but fear glued his tongue to the roof of his mouth.

There was a *whooshing* sound and another small splash. "Get Stark," he managed to mutter, trying to keep the tremor out of his voice.

Verdugo disappeared. It seemed a long time that Collins stood listening to the whistling, sighing, groaning sounds and the splashes coming from different directions before Abel Stark came striding up. "What's the problem?"

"Listen!"

After a few seconds, the noises continued. Stark listened, then emitted a low chuckle. "Whales," he said. "Hear 'em blowing when they come up to breathe? Not uncommon to see them in these waters."

Collins's knees were weak, and he was sweating, more from relief now, than from fear. He couldn't believe he had been so frightened of something for which there was a natural explanation. The unknown, he reflected, always seemed more terrifying than the known, even if the danger might be real. Imagination could create some beautiful images when it was applied to art and engraving. But, when allowed to run wild, the same human imagination could create horrifying monsters.

Before the four-hour watch was over, the fog had become patchy, allowing some moonlight to penetrate the wispy gaps. Collins and the other four men, including the look-out and the helmsman, were able to make out the long, black backs of the nearby whales, sliding up and over, making glistening humps in the water. Now and then they could see one spouting through his blowhole. Magnificent creatures of the deep, Collins thought. He wondered if the giant sea monsters, depicted in many stories, were actually real. If the limitless oceans could shelter things the size of these whales, why couldn't there be other creatures who lived in the unplumbed depths, creatures that could crush ships with their tentacles or jaws as if they were toy boats? There was no logical reason why it could not be.

When eight bells sounded for the change of watch at four o'clock, he stepped into the midship house to see Fjelde. To his surprise, he found the sick man awake. Collins sat down on the edge of the bunk. "How are you feeling?" he asked, placing the back of his hand on the Finn's forehead.

"Fit for duty," he replied cheerily. But the unusually bright blue eyes and the heat of the forehead told Collins otherwise.

"Maybe not quite yet," he replied, dipping a cloth in a pail of water on the floor beside him, and placing it on the man's head.

"Ah, that feels good."

"Whales spouting around the ship," Collins said, when Fjelde seemed to doze.

"A sign of good luck," the Finn said without opening his eyes. "But killing that porpoise a while back was not good. They're of the same family, you know." He looked up at Collins, pushing back the wet rag on his forehead. "How many days to California?" he asked.

"Don't know. We haven't passed the Horn yet. You've gone 'round before, haven't you?"

"Ah, yes. And each trip I swear will be the last. But then time passes, and I forget how it was." He paused. "But I

210

have good reason for going this time."

Collins waited.

"The gold. All my life I've struggled to . . . to. . . ."

"Get rich?"

"Oh, no. Only to have enough so I could relax, pay my debts, not worry if I would be crippled from an accident at sea and have to beg in the streets while my family starved, or were thrown on the parish for charity."

"You have a family?"

"Three children, all grown now and doing well. My wife . . . well, patient woman that she was, couldn't stand my being at sea for months at a time. She finally got tired and went back to live with her mother's people in New Brunswick. We still see each other now and then, but . . . well, I'm alone in the world."

Collins didn't reply at first, not knowing what to say that might cheer him.

"Water."

Collins scooped up a dipperful of water and held it while he drank.

"More."

Collins repeated the process. "Hungry?"

Fjelde shook his head.

The two sat silently for several seconds as the sick man lay back and closed his eyes. Collins thought he had dozed off and was on the verge of leaving. He needed to get at least three hours of sleep before his next watch. In the dim light of the gimbaled oil lamp on the bulkhead, Fjelde's face looked scarred and seamed with years and work. The lined cheeks and strong chin bristled with several days' growth of white stubble. Only a trace of blond remained in the curly white hair. Without the light from the blue eyes, the face was old and worn.

Then the eyes opened again. "McCook," he whispered.

Collins waited for him to continue. When he didn't, Collins said: "Verdugo thought the sounds of the whales was McCook's spirit calling us to join him."

"He's where he belongs."

"Did you really mean to kill him?"

"Not until I saw that it was him or me," the Finn answered. "To him, there was no argument that could be settled with fists. It was all or nothing, kill or be killed. Maybe that's the way he grew up fighting in the streets of New York. No wonder he was running from the law." He paused and tried to take a deep breath. "What really started it was that he was cussing you."

"Me?" Collins was surprised. "I thought you told the mates he was threatening *them*."

"That was only half true. He was cussing Stark."

"Everybody on this ship has probably done that a few times."

"Not like this. He was bragging about how he was going to put a knife between his ribs one dark night. And McCook was the kind who would really do it. Now, Malloy's my man, too. I have no use for Stark. But Abel Stark's the best sailor on board, and I figured we needed him to get this ship around to California. Slave-driving bastard that he is, he's the only one who can hold this crew together and get the job done."

He motioned for another drink, and Collins helped him with the dipper.

"Ah," he said, his breath coming rapid and shallow. "But then McCook started on you again, calling you a half-breed nigger who wasn't worth the sweat off his balls, and why would a nigger who didn't know a reef point from a knife point have his own private cabin in the after part of the ship, and so on. Well, I told him to shut his mouth and go to sleep. It was like a red rag to a bull. When he started in on me, I was having none of it. If you let a man like that think he's got the upper hand, you'll never be free of his bullying." He paused, sweating and breathless. "I've had fever before, but I don't think I ever felt this bad."

"You need to get some sleep."

"Yeah. Otherwise, Stark will think I'm a no good, malingering Finn. I'll show him. I'll be standing my watches tomorrow. Then, by God, it's on to the gold fields. Riches to pick up off the ground, they say. But I don't mind doing a *little* digging or panning. A man can't have things too easy. . . ." His voice trailed off as he lay back and closed his eyes, visions of golden nuggets no doubt filling his mind.

Collins waited for several minutes. When the old man did not rouse up, he stood and quietly went out the door.

Fjelde died of fever and congestion of the lungs about three hours later.

When Collins came on deck again at eight o'clock, the fog had lifted. Merriman and Stark were just coming out of the midship house.

"Was anyone with him when it happened?" Merriman asked.

"Naw," Stark answered. "Died sometime early this morning, I figured. Nothing we could have done to save him. Probably lucky it happened now," he mused, almost to himself. "The Horn would have done for him anyway, what with the bunks being washed out and cold all the time."

Collins listened to this dialogue, then caught Merriman's eye and shook his head, sadly.

A man can't have things too easy. . . . Collins recalled the Finn's last words. A battler to the end. Did he know he was dying? He had mentioned nothing about God or a belief in the afterlife, if he even thought about such things. His last thoughts and words were of gold and earthly riches. To Collins, this only proved the existence of the soul. Whatever it was that infused the body with life was always strong and never-changing. It did not get tired and never broke down. Even as Fjelde's body was wearing out, the soul was still planning the next great adventure in the gold fields, as if it didn't realize its means of functioning would soon be gone. At least, that was the way Collins envisioned such an abstruse concept as the human soul. Instead of the soul being snuffed out like the flame of an oil lamp when it ran out of fuel, he pictured the soul as a gull flying up and away from a sinking ship, to live on somewhere else.

But it seemed a fitting time to go. Fjelde had departed during the calm and the fog and the eerie sighing of the whales. Maybe it *was* the ghosts of McCook and the drowned sailors calling the old Finn, and not the blowing of whales at all. Had his spirit gone to join them?

"What's wrong with you?" Merriman asked, as Collins continued to stare at him.

"Nothing." Collins collected himself with an effort and saw that Stark was gone. Riaz and Verdugo were passing through the door into the midship house, presumably to haul out the body for burial.

Collins turned away to go aloft and relieve the look-out on the foretop—a small platform near the top of the fore-mast. The sky was overcast and a cold, favorable wind was blowing over their port quarter as Collins climbed into the rigging. *Every hour of this brings us a few miles closer to the Horn*, Collins thought, settling himself on the wooden platform, with the wind at his back and snugged into his oilskins and southwester. If there was anything he really loved about a sailing ship, he found, it was to be aloft when he had time to observe and reflect. And serving as masthead look-out provided just such an opportunity.

While he sat there, gazing out over the empty sea, he wished he had brought his sketchbook from his cabin, although he knew Stark would never stand for it. He was on watch.

The fresh wind began to lessen, and the *Inverness* slowed over the next hour until she was making only four or five knots through the water. The horizon had also become obscured with a mist that seemed to blur sea and sky together. Finally, the wind ceased entirely, and the ship rolled. A light snow began to fall, and Collins could see nothing beyond a gray wall of mist. He marveled at the thousands of tiny flakes that fluttered down noiselessly around him, furring every rope and spar. If only he had his sketchbook!

Then the snow shower passed, and the cloud-dimmed sun tried its best to appear. A few brief shafts of light stabbed through the pall, then were blocked again. Collins swept a look around as far as he could see. Malloy's hopes of sneaking around the tip of the continent with a fair breeze were not to be realized, he thought. Some sea birds were wheeling and mewing past the ship. Ahead of them, the dimness quickly dulled to black, and he heard Stark's voice barking commands. Collins saw the men springing into the rigging and others loosing halyards.

"Rouse up the other watch! By God, it's here!" Stark thundered. "What's wrong with you, look-out? You asleep? Why in hell didn't you sing out?" he snarled up at Collins.

But Collins could only stare ahead in fearful fascination. From the southwest came the end of the world.

Chapter Nineteen

Panama City,

Republic of New Granada

Trevor Sloan ran his fingertips gently across his lower rib cage where the cotton shirt was snagging the stitches of his wound.

"Damned lucky it didn't penetrate the abdominal wall," the American doctor had told him two days before as he swabbed the long gash with rum and prepared the needle and thread.

At the time, Sloan had been feeling more nauseous than grateful and had taken a swig from the rum bottle the doctor had handed him.

All of his fifty-five years weighed him down this morning as he seated himself on a stone bench in the partial shade of a crumbling wall. Sweat popped out on his forehead, although the sun had only just begun its daily grilling of the old Spanish city.

He had come close to death at the hands of his attackers—as close as that day twenty years before on the field of honor when his opponent's ball had deflected off a brass button on his coat and only broken a rib. Septien Martínez had taken him in too easily. Sloan had gotten careless and had let down his guard after three days of traveling with the boatman and guide. A man of his experience should have known better, he reflected ruefully. Since his arrival in Panama City, he'd heard numerous tales of brigands who robbed and murdered along the jungle trails between here and Chagres. It was more common than not where existing law looked the other way and let these foreigners fend for themselves.

But, if survival was the name of the game, he'd won. It didn't really matter that his gold was gone, along with his steamship ticket to San Francisco, his pocket revolver, and his leather grip with his clothes and personal items. All of that could be replaced—somehow. But he had no idea how, among thousands of strangers, many of them nearly as destitute as himself. Even the shirt, pants, and sandals he wore were gifts from a stranger—one Roscoe Caldwell, from Vermont, his rescuer and benefactor. When Caldwell and his guide, Ruben Sanchez, had come upon him, they had thought he was dead. But he had knocked himself senseless by hitting his head on a rock in his fall from the steep trail where he lay, bloody and muddy and partially stripped. These two Samaritans had stanched the flow of blood and slung him on a blanket litter between two mules, carrying him the rest of the way to the city of Panama, where Caldwell had found and paid a doctor to tend Sloan's wounds.

If he lived to get home, he resolved not to forget these two men—if he could ever find them again. Caldwell had even given him ten dollars to eat and find a place to sleep. Now, two days later, the money had dwindled down to one dollar, and his prospects were bleak. He leaned back against the stone wall, still feeling the sore bump on the back of his head, and surveyed the old town. He saw mostly two- and three-story buildings of brick and stone with red tile roofs, and a few enclosed courtyards adjacent to aging mansions. From where he sat, he could even see the pearl-gray sheen of the cathedral's twin towers that had somehow been coated with the insides of oyster shells. He had walked as far as he was able in an effort to regain his strength, and had found that the old, walled portion of the city was just over a mile in width. There were many shops on the ground floors of the old buildings, selling everything imaginable. Several of the dilapidated hotels were run by Americans, but everything in a town filled with transients was on a cash only basis. Cash—it was the one thing he lacked, the one thing that could purchase the necessities of life, the one thing that he'd had no real need of for years, the one thing he'd only played with in his game of buying and selling in order to accumulate more.

But now he was looking at the economic structure from the bottom up, and it was no longer a game. In the two days he'd been here, he'd discovered two things—first of all, no one had any use for a man with no money. And secondly, several thousand people—mostly men—were waiting here for the first available steamer up the coast to San Francisco. Rumor had it that the majority were holding through tickets they'd purchased before leaving home, only to discover that there was no ready transportation available on the Pacific side. Many of them had been here for several weeks, and the longer their wait grew, the shorter their tempers became. The complaints he overheard in the saloons and on the streets were vociferous. If Sloan didn't know better, he would have guessed the two steamers that arrived the day before were giving away spaces as he watched the arguing, shoving, and fist fights that broke out among the hundreds trying to get aboard the native boats to be ferried out to the ships. Men were scalping tickets, and there was no shortage of eager bidders.

The two sidewheel steamers had gone north with every

square foot of space crammed with human cargo—at least three or four times the number the vessels were designed to carry. Even steerage was going for upwards of $700. And these were people with tickets and money in their pockets. Under such conditions, he might be here for months, or even years, Sloan figured, provided he didn't starve to death or die of disease first.

It was a bleak prospect that presented itself as he sat on the stone bench that morning. He'd been a fool to come on this trip alone, but that couldn't be helped now. He couldn't ask Caldwell, his rescuer, for more money. Even if Caldwell hadn't departed on one of yesterday's steamers, Sloan already owed the man his life, and he couldn't ask for more. The thought of being reduced to the status of a common beggar appalled him. He still had money in the bank in Charleston, and large land holdings and slaves, but he had no way of getting at any of it. Even a letter would take weeks to reach home and weeks more for Biggers to send him enough to get him out of this.

He rubbed a hand across the stubble on his face and looked at the sky that was fading into a lighter blue as the sun climbed higher. *At least I'm not sitting here in a tropical downpour,* he thought. For some reason this struck him as funny, and he laughed aloud, impervious to the curious stares of several men walking past on the street. He laughed at the ridiculousness of the situation, pausing only when his sutured wound began to hurt.

It was early that afternoon before gnawing hunger pangs drove Trevor Sloan to beg. After an hour of sitting on the edge of the street with his hand out and collecting only twenty-five cents, he reluctantly began accosting passers-by. Mostly, he was ignored or pushed aside or cursed by those hurrying about their own business. But several men, on seeing the fresh wound that he allowed to show through his open shirt, handed him change from their pockets.

By the end of the day, he was eating some beef and beans in a fly-ridden saloon and feeling much better with more than six dollars remaining in his pocket. The experience of being a beggar was a revealing one. He had pretty much ignored the down-and-outers he'd encountered in Charleston, but now he saw the world from their perspective, and it was a humbling, humiliating experience. He had always thought of panhandlers as alcoholics, too lazy to work. But now he could see how a man, through no fault of his own, might wind up at the bottom of the social and economic heap and be forced to do what he had done just to survive.

That night he slept under a bush in an out of the way corner of a courtyard, carefully avoiding any other people. He was instinctively aware of the dangers of sleeping, unprotected, on the streets of any city, but especially this one with a large, transient population and little protection from the police.

For the next three days, in order to save the money he managed to cajole from people on the streets, he begged for his food at the back door of the cathedral rectory, where two kindly Spanish priests fed him.

At the end of a week, he realized that he could survive rather precariously for an indefinite period, but it was bringing him no closer to California. Living as he was, he became aware of other beggars and street drunks, as a stray dog becomes aware of others of his kind. He shied away from them when he could. If they happened to approach him, he was careful to conceal his wound and not show any signs of weakness. In this underworld society there was no rule of law; the strong dominated the weak. He was subsisting in a predatory world, and he had no weapons but his cunning to keep himself safe from others who thought he might have something worth stealing.

It was clear, being unable to do any physical work, that he would have to take some drastic measure to pull himself up from his present position. One hot morning he saw his chance. While a merchant in an open, store-front shop was haggling with two customers, Sloan, his heart pounding, managed to slip a soft leather pouch from a wooden peg and sidle away with it concealed in front of him. Before the hour was out, he had sold the beautifully tanned leather bag to a departing Argonaut for $10 "to hold your gold when you get to California." With this money and what he had managed to save from his begging, he now had $34 and looked to get into some kind of poker game. The town was full of gambling halls, but the odds were all weighted in favor of the house. Not having bathed or shaved in almost two weeks, he knew he could not get into any kind of respectable private card game, so he convinced the white-haired priest at the back door of the cathedral rectory to allow him to bathe in the horse trough. The priest also gave him some old, worn clothes and lent him a razor and a bar of soap. He even soaked and pulled out the stitches from the long red scar across his midsection. In this moist climate where everything seemed to rot and fester, he felt very fortunate that the wound was well on its way to healing without mortifying.

Thus rejuvenated, he went forth to find a poker game. If he lost what he had, so be it. He would be no worse off than he was now. He had nowhere to go, but up. Before he sought out a poker game, he bought some paper and pencil and wrote letters to his wife and to Jason Biggers. He told them of his situation. Having no confidence in the local mail, he told Biggers to send him money by way of the post office in San Francisco. He didn't want to have to wait here for a reply that might never come. Given the precariousness of the mail service and the distances involved, the letters might never get back and forth, but he had to try.

In his younger days he had been an astute poker player; he hoped that skill had not deserted him. At one of the saloons, he managed to insert himself into a private poker game with three other Americans who were idling away their time, waiting for a ship. He lost and won small hands, and, at one point, was down to his last two dollars. But, by six o'clock that evening, he left the game to the grumbling of the other players, with $123 in his pocket. He was elated and at the same time depressed that this amount was not nearly enough to purchase a steamer ticket. In the attempt to increase his stake the next day at the poker table, he lost $57 before he abandoned the game and went back to begging.

The following day, a California-bound steamer lay anchored in the harbor. With the rough outline of a plan in mind, he joined the crush of men trying to get aboard the native boats to be ferried to the ship. Men were pushing and shoving and shouting, as usual. Sloan slid into the crowd. Watching his chance, he bumped a man who was waving his ticket and yelling drunkenly. The man teetered on the edge of the stone pier, flailing his arms, before losing his balance and toppling off the stone wall into the two-foot deep water of low tide.

"Hang on, I'll help ya!"

As Sloan jumped in, he brought a forearm down on the man's wrist, knocking the ticket out of his hand.

"Gaw damn! Where is it?" he cried.

"Where's what?" Sloan asked, looking concerned as he pulled the man to his feet in the water.

"My steamer ticket!" the man bawled, twisting and turning, looking in the lapping waves around his knees.

Sloan splashed about, pretending to look, but the wet pasteboard ticket was already tucked safely inside his pants pocket. He left the cursing man standing in the water and lunged toward one of the boats that was rapidly filling.

There was no way he was going to miss that ship.

Chapter Twenty

Confluence of the Humboldt River and the South Fork of the Humboldt

"We'll camp here for the night," Vincent Sizemore announced, looping the reins around the brake handle and climbing down from the wagon seat.

The tired mules lowered their heads and began to graze on the plentiful grass.

Lisa sighed with relief as she picked the axe from the wagon and set out to find some firewood before dusk.

It had been an exhausting day, she reflected, to have covered only ten miles. But it was ten miles of a twisting cañon that enclosed the South Fork of the Humboldt River. As the wagon trail beside the river was pinched off by steep slopes or sheer walls, they had been forced to cross the shallow river six or eight times. She had lost track of the number.

Aware that they were now completely on their own, her father had taken extra care in easing the heavy wagon across the many fords, lest a wheel fall into a hole or an axle break in the rocky river bed. Lisa had spent most of the day on foot, constantly wet to the waist, wading the river, testing the bottom with a stick, guiding her father to the easiest crossings. But mainly they followed the marks of the wagons that had preceded them.

Even though she was with her family, Lisa felt very iso-

lated. She had taken for granted the presence of many other
people. They were part of the background, a protection, a
shared comfort in the wilderness—even those with whom she
had only a nodding acquaintance. But now they were gone,
taking with them the familiar sounds of voices, the noise of
their wagons and livestock, the harmonica and fiddle music
that drove away the fearful silence in the evening camps.
Here the pitifully thin sounds of their own passage echoed
off the stone walls that loomed above them. Banishment had
not seemed like a severe penalty at the time, especially considering what might have happened, but now she saw why
emigrants formed companies and traveled in trains. They
banded for mutual assistance and protection. One accident,
one slip of the axe and a leg could be gashed—one large rock
in the trail could break a wheel spoke—a rattlesnake could
strike human or animal—a single wagon could present an inviting target for any band of marauding Indians.

At least, they had reached the confluence of the
Humboldt and South Fork Humboldt rivers, and had rejoined the main California Trail, where they were bound to
encounter other people. After all, they had seen wagon
trains ahead of them and behind them on the plains as the
vast migration of the "Golden Army" proceeded mile after
endless mile. And at night, campfires of other trains were
often visible when the terrain were flat enough. But her father had made it very clear he had no intention of trying to
join up with any other train. She suspected that pride was
part of it, but, also, the embarrassment of having to explain
why they happened to be traveling alone. And she had never
known her father to lie.

Supper was a quiet affair that evening, each of the three
with their private thoughts. Lisa had changed out of the wet
denim pants and into a dress. It was a comfort to be in dry

clothing. As she ate in silence, she wondered if her parents were silently blaming her for what had happened. Or were they just dulled with fatigue? She was hardly able to keep her own eyes open as she chewed her food mechanically and stared into the hypnotic flames.

They spent an extra day at this campsite to rest themselves and the mules. They were still ahead of schedule, her father said, so weren't obliged to push too hard. Even though it was early August, the air grew chill as soon as the sun dipped behind the western mountains. And in the morning, there was a skim of ice on the bucket of water Lisa had left near the wagon.

"We're at a higher elevation where the air is very dry," her father said when they shivered themselves warm after sleeping in their clothes under blankets. "Before noon we'll be sweating like it's really summertime."

For the first time Lisa felt a real pang of homesickness for her humid woodlands in the Tennessee mountains. Thoughts of Clayburn Collins, the handsome, green-eyed artist, came flooding back to her. She fixed her thoughts on him, fantasizing about making love in the safe, familiar surroundings of the Sizemore Inn. She felt ashamed at entertaining such thoughts, but they seemed the only way completely to detach her mental self from the reality of her harsh surroundings. She tried to shake off the daydreams by staying busy, and spent most of the day washing their clothes and spreading them over nearby bushes to dry.

Using the jack, her father removed the wheels, two at a time, and soaked them for several hours in the shallows of the river. While waiting for the wood to swell and tighten the spokes, he rubbed some of the extra axle grease into the leather harness that had been stiffened with mule sweat and repeated wettings.

The two stout mules, although grown lean, ate their fill and then rolled in the grass, then grazed again, often wading into the river to drink and refresh themselves.

When her chores were done, Lisa sat in the shade and caught up on the diary entries she had neglected since the traumatic events of three days before. Dredging the details out of their shallow grave was a painful process. But for some reason that she couldn't explain, she felt obligated to write out these happenings to the best of her ability. Maybe it was for the historical record of the trip, maybe to put down her side of things if any legal action was ever brought against her. When she finished, she put the book away in her trunk with the feeling that transferring her thoughts to paper might free her from the anguished dreams disturbing her sleep.

They set out the next morning, somewhat refreshed, but not fully recovered from their three-month ordeal on the trail. The mules were lean, but Vincent had been careful to treat with salve and padding any galls that had begun to develop from the rubbing of the harness. As worn down as Lisa felt, she knew her parents who were twenty-five years her senior had to be feeling the grinding effects of the long summer march. The spring was gone from their step, along with their optimistic attitudes. Lisa noted that her mother, a stout, buxom woman for as long as she could remember, had to cinch her dress around her middle to keep it from hanging loosely on her. The dark skin of their exposed faces, hands, and arms had been burned even darker by the sun until their clothing and light eyes were the only outward signs distinguishing them from Indians.

For the next ten days Lisa and her family, the span of mules pulling the wagon, followed the Humboldt's sinuous course downstream, treading generally in a westerly direction. The weather remained broiling hot in the daytime and cold at night, but at least there was plenty of good water and grass. Now and then the wagon had to ford the river or follow the trail as it snaked up and away from the river for several miles to wind around a projecting ledge or escarpment. Lisa saw her father referring to the hand-drawn map Josiah Martin had given them, but mostly the way was clear, cut by hundreds of wagon wheels into the soft soil.

Then the river began to bend southwestward, and, on the eleventh day, they came to a fork in the trail in a large, grassy meadow. Here several sign posts were stuck into the ground. Tacked to these posts were notes to friends following, and directions and advice for any and all. One large, crudely-lettered sign indicated the right-hand fork of the trail that went straight west toward the mountains was something called Lassen's Cut-Off. Below this sign were the names of several parties that had taken this route, and the dates, all of them within the past month.

There was also a small wooden barrel, about the size of a whisky keg, painted red, and partially buried in the sand. On the side of this barrel the word **MAIL** was painted in white letters. The round top could be lifted by a loop of rope

"Who's going to be delivering this mail out here?" Lisa wondered aloud, lifting the lid and noting the small pile of letters and notes.

"Whoever happens to be going back East," Vincent said, unhitching the mules for their noon stop. "And from the looks of some of those messages on the post, there've been more than a few."

Lisa took a closer look where he pointed, and read the names and dates and remarks of those who'd given up the effort and were returning to more civilized places. As she read their cryptic notes of bad water and heat and desert to the south, animals dying, wagons abandoned, a knot began to form in her stomach. Were conditions really that bad farther on, or were these just the words of discouraged men who didn't have the fortitude to continue and were leaving these jottings to justify their own failures? One returnee, with grim humor, had written the following:

> **I crawled out and started on,**
> **And managed very well,**
> **Until I struck the Humboldt**
> **Which I thought was nearly Hell.**
> **I traveled till I struck the Sink**
> **Where outlet can't be found;**
> **The Lord got through late Saturday night—**
> **He'd finished all around,**
> **But would not work on Sunday,**
> **So he run it in the ground.**

Surely, most of the wagons had gone on, she thought. Apparently there was another terrible desert to the south. Could it be any worse than the Great Salt Lake desert they had crossed? She shuddered, feeling the weakness of discouragement in every part of her. So far, the Humboldt, or Mary's River, as some of her former companions had referred to it, was reasonably good with potable water and adequate grass for the mules. But now, the river was making a big bend from west to south, and things were apparently going to change.

"Lisa, are you going to help me or not?" Madeline Sizemore snapped, sounding tired and irritable.

"Yes, Momma." She went to gather some dead brush for a fire.

As they ate their bacon and fried hoe cakes, Lisa wanted to ask her father which route they would take, but she held her tongue as she noticed him walking away from the wagon to study the routes in both directions.

Finally he returned and sat down on the wagon tongue, chewing the last bit of his food. He was silent for several seconds, then said: "The route straight west on this cut-off looks inviting, but it appears to have been in use only a few weeks, and there aren't any notes to tell us what it's like. I'm sure Josiah Martin took our train down along the river. It's not like him to go into the mountains until he has to."

"How will we get the wagon across the mountains?" Madeline asked in a dull voice, raising her eyes toward the snow-capped peaks in the distance.

"There must be passes through there," her husband answered. "Others have done it, and we will, too. If worse comes to worse, we'll leave the wagon and pack our things on the mules and walk," he added in a grimly determined voice. "But I'm not inclined to take this cut-off. As long as we're on our own, we can't afford to take unnecessary chances. We'll follow the river as long as we can. We'll deal with the mountains later."

"That map Martin gave us doesn't show all the routes," Madeline said.

"No." He pulled the paper from his shirt pocket and unfolded it. Lisa looked over his shoulder at the squiggled lines that the wagon master had hastily drawn. She didn't know how her father could make heads or tails of it.

"Why don't we wait for the next train that comes along and ask for help?" Madeline suggested. "Surely others will pass here within a few days."

Vincent's lips compressed as he refolded the map. Because of the heat, he had recently shaved his beard, and his cheeks and chin were not yet as dark as the upper part of his face. "No," he replied, not offering an explanation. "We can't waste any time. We'll just keep on in this direction for now." He got up and went to retrieve the mules that were drinking at the edge of the river.

Lisa noted they had not discussed the option of turning back, maybe to reach Fort Hall and possibly join up with some of those going East. She knew there was nothing for them to return to. They had sold their inn, and used most of the money to outfit themselves for this journey. It was either continue until they somehow reached the benign climate of the Sacramento Valley, or die in the attempt.

As if the passing of Lassen's Cut-Off were a signal, everything began to change. Slow day followed slow day, and the grass began to give out, while the water, once clear, began to turn brackish. Lisa had delighted in calling the river by its earlier name—Mary's—since it connoted to her a lighter, more delicate and graceful watercourse. But now it became the Humboldt for certain, with all the appropriateness of the name's blunt, hard consonants.

Some boiling hot springs were encountered some way back from the riverbank as the grass disappeared to be replaced by scattered sage and greasewood. The whole floor of the broad valley sloped back to the low desert mountains. The earth was covered with a dried mud that had apparently been belched forth at some earlier time by subterranean geysers and springs. This mud had dried and cracked in the sun, and the daily wind picked up the fine powder, whirling it into dust devils that danced and spun across the distant flats like so many plumes of white smoke.

Lisa watched these distant whirlwinds form and dissipate in the hot wind. And she saw the circling buzzards that were only black specks against the pale blue sky as they were drawn to the carcasses of some carrion. What a silent, lonely vista, she thought, walking several rods to one side of the wagon and squinting her eyes against the chalky gray-white dust being churned up by the hoofs and wagon wheels. A human could have plenty to eat and drink and still die of starvation of the soul from absolute loneliness in a place like this.

The river spread out and became sluggish while the water, now full of alkali, turned a milky color. The water they drew to make coffee stank of sulphur and was almost undrinkable, causing all of them to have diarrhea. Lisa felt as if her insides were being scoured out, leaving her weak, with no energy.

With every mile the water became more tepid and salty and alkaline. The color went from chalky white to yellowish green to a putrid brown as it seeped sluggishly into the cattail marshes and shallow, reed-filled waters of Humboldt Lake. Vincent took to digging holes two and three feet deep, some distance back from the river, but the water that filtered in to fill these makeshift wells was nearly as bad as what they drew from the river. Even the mules closed their lips and drew back from it. Finally, in desperation, after all the water in their barrels was gone, Vincent scouted the nearby foothills and found a spring of boiling hot water that seemed to be coming up from the nether regions, so hot and foul was it. Even full of minerals, it was still better than what the Humboldt offered, so Vincent filled their wooden kegs and allowed it to cool for drinking. In an effort to give the animals more nourishment and to make the water more palatable, Vincent mixed flour in their water buckets. "A good substitute for grain," he said. "And we've got plenty of flour."

They were approaching the sink of the Humboldt, Vincent told them. After more than three-hundred miles, the river just gave up, spread out into a swampy lake and alkaline flats, and sank into the ground. To prevent the mules from becoming mired in the marshy ground around Humboldt Lake, Lisa and her father waded into the stinking marshes to cut armfuls of grass for fodder. Lisa stood thigh-deep in the marsh, perspiration soaking the top half of her body and dress while insects hummed around her head. Yet she was still able to admire the hundreds of white swans that flew in flocks over the surface of the shallow lake, landing gracefully on its blue surface. If she only had the wings of one of those big birds, she might be able to fly to California, she thought. The mental picture of the snow in the mountain ranges west of them made her shiver in spite of the heat.

When she waded out and dumped the cut grass where the mules could eat, she sat down on the ground to pull off her soaked and muddy shoes. Her wet dress was up over her knees when she noticed lumps of mud clinging to her bare legs. As she started to wipe them off, she had to choke back a scream of horror and disgust as she discovered that the mud was actually some sort of gristly black parasite. She gritted her teeth and forced her fingers to take hold of them. One by one she ripped them loose and flung their bodies away with a shiver of revulsion. There were four of them, the largest nearly as long as her hand, and they left circular red marks on her light brown skin. "Daddy," she called, "check your legs! There are some kind of blood suckers in that muddy water."

The next morning they moved on past the lake, a little dirtier, a little weaker, their water barrels filled with the vilest water Lisa had ever tried to swallow. But she had slept well and dream-free, and the air of early morning was still cool.

The abandoned wagons and dead oxen and mules she had been seeing and smelling for miles failed to excite any further interest or curiosity. She turned a blind eye to them as if they didn't exist, knowing the fate of those unfortunate travelers could well become their own. Thus, she was surprised when her father pulled the mules to a halt near two wagons.

"I believe that's the Jackson wagon. And, if I'm not mistaken, that one yonder belongs to Jacob Steckinger. What are they doing, just setting there?" he wondered, stepping down.

Lisa saw the reason for his confusion. Both ox teams were yoked to the wagons, switching their tails, patiently waiting to go. But there was no sign of human life.

Just then the drawn cover of the Jackson wagon was thrown open, and a man half fell out of the back. He caught himself, then doubled over in obvious agony.

"Sam! What's wrong?" Vincent Sizemore cried, running to his aid.

The hatless man looked up with pain-filled eyes. "Stay away!" he rasped.

But Lisa's father was already there, helping ease him to the ground. "Lisa, bring some water!" he called over his shoulder.

She took the canteen from her shoulder and ran forward. Sam Jackson, a man she remembered from their train, lay ashen-faced. "No water." He waved away the canteen. "Makes it worse. Cholera. Get away before you catch it," he gasped.

Lisa felt a shock go through her at the sound of this word. Cholera—the dread disease for which there was no known cause and no known cure. She had seen many fresh graves along the valley of the Platte as a result of this illness, but the actual sight of it struck terror in her heart. After the party had reached the cooler heights of South Pass in Wyoming Territory, they all thought the danger of this fatal scourge was behind them. But here it was again.

"Carla's in the wagon," Jackson said weakly. "No! Don't go in. She's dead. I just climbed out here to die in the open air. Don't want to die in that stinking wagon."

The sickening odor of emptied bowels smote Lisa's nose. The man's pants were stained with liquid excrement, some of it already dried. She gasped at the stench and was ashamed of herself for turning away. A sob caught in her throat at the thought of the man's suffering. She had heard horrifying tales of cholera. It was a death without dignity. Before it killed, it tortured with merciless cramps, wracking the body with bloody diarrhea and vomiting, until the victim begged for release. If the disease had any saving feature, it was relatively quick—usually only a matter of hours from the onset of symptoms to death.

She turned back to see her father swabbing the man's face with a wet bandanna. "Lisa, stay back. I don't want you to catch this."

"Daddy, nobody knows what causes this. How can I catch it?"

"I don't know, but it is contagious, somehow," Vincent replied.

"I'll go look in the other wagon," she said.

"No!"

But she was already halfway there, and pretended not to hear. Her mother had beaten her to it, and was climbing up onto the open tailgate.

"What are you doing here?" a wide-eyed woman asked, looking at Lisa and Madeline.

"We came to help," Madeline replied, all business.

"Nothing you can do. Go on outta here before you get it, too."

"Well, you haven't caught it, have you?" Madeline retorted, glancing down at Mrs. Steckinger's husband, lying red-faced on a blanket in the bottom of the wagon.

"No. Even though they cut us out of the train, I'm not leaving my Henry."

"What's that you're giving him?" Lisa asked.

"I'm dosing him with laudanum mixed with pepper, camphor, musk, ammonia, and peppermint," she replied, holding up the bottle. "And I'm rubbing him with brandy and putting on mustard plaster."

"Is it helping?"

Mrs. Steckinger shook her head sadly. "His pulse is down and these stimulants aren't bringing it up."

Lisa remembered the Steckingers as a childless couple in their fifties who were intensely devoted to one another. They, like many others, wanted to start a new life in California. Henry's shop had failed in Indiana.

Madeline moved to help by loosening the drawstring that held the canvas top closed over both ends of the wagon. The air outside was hot, but not as stifling as the air inside that smelled of the medicinal concoction.

"Aren't you afraid of catching the disease?" Mrs. Steckinger asked, wiping a sleeve across her damp brow. "It really doesn't matter about me. If Henry goes, I have nothing else to live for. But you folks have your lives ahead of you. Especially you," she added, indicating Lisa. "I'm sorry for what happened back there on the trail," she said. "But, in my opinion, that Zeke Masters was nothing but white trash, and you did what was right."

Lisa gave her a quick smile of gratitude, then said: "Can I get you some water or anything? Food?"

"No, dear, I'm perfectly fine. You can say some prayers if you like, 'cause I think the Lord has chosen this place and time to call us home." There was a look of peaceful resignation on her face that Lisa had never seen on anyone before.

"Lisa, come help me unhitch these oxen," Vincent called from outside. "They need food and water."

They stayed with Sam Jackson and the Steckingers the remainder of the day, venturing near the sick ones only to set food or water close by or to pull Jackson into the shade of the wagon as the sun moved, and to wipe him off with a wet cloth. By sunset, Vincent was digging the graves for both Jacksons and Henry Steckinger. When he finished, the three were wrapped in blankets and buried by firelight. Then, with Lisa's help, Vincent dug a fourth grave for Mrs. Steckinger who had come down with fever and was cramping.

Just as the sun was tipping the eastern horizon the next morning, Mrs. Steckinger died, and Vincent lay doubled up in agony. "Just a case of the grippe from this bad water," he gasped to his wife. "Boil some water for me and give me a bite of bread."

But Lisa knew better. Two hours later, when her mother also fell ill with the first symptoms, Lisa could hardly contain her grief and fear. She staggered away among the sandy hillocks, out toward the stinking ooze that was the Humboldt Lake. When she was out of earshot, she stopped and gave vent to her rage and frustration—screaming, cursing, blaspheming, shaking her fists at the sky, blaming God in His strength for crushing them all in this hellish place. Finally, utterly spent, she fell, face down in the hot sand, great sobs wracking her body.

Eventually she had nothing left, and sat up weakly, brushing the dirt and sand from her face and hair. Everything was gone now, and a great calm came over her. She silently asked God to forgive her for her outburst. Christ had suffered for all of them, and surely she was not greater than her Master. She took a deep breath, pushed herself to her feet, and turned around to face the ordeal she knew was coming—which probably included her own death.

For the rest of the day, Lisa tried everything she could think of, but nothing helped. Heedless of her own safety, she held them when they cried out in pain, giving them spoonfuls of the laudanum she found in the Steckingers' wagon. She swabbed their sweating faces and bodies, cleaned their uncontrolled excrement, gave them sips of water which they promptly regurgitated. Powerless to cure them, she could only try to ease their suffering, and let them know she was there. She looked in vain across the stinking alkali sink for other wagons or travelers. But, even if someone else had come, there was nothing they could do.

Finally, when her parents lay on blankets in the shade of the wagon in late afternoon, she knew it was only a matter of time. They were both comatose, and she uttered a prayer of thanks that their suffering was nearly over. As dusk came on, she spread a blanket on the ground near them and lay down, exhausted, only getting up now and then to lay a finger on their throats to check for a pulse. When she lay down again, some biting red ants found her, adding the enraging lash of their stings to her misery. By the light of a small fire she built, she could see the ants crawling on her parents as well. She tried lifting Madeline's limp, emaciated body into the wagon, but hadn't the strength. Finally, she had to settle for brushing the ants off as best she could, knowing that their bites were going unfelt.

When she could no longer detect a heartbeat in either parent, she took a firebrand for light and found a bottle of brandy in the Steckinger wagon. Then she climbed to the hard wooden seat of her own wagon and began sipping straight from the bottle. The shock of grief, fatigue, and alcohol on an empty stomach had the effect of someone stunning her with a stick of cordwood.

The next thing she knew, she awoke with a burning thirst and the sun beating down on her back. She lay along the footboard of the wagon, and it was a good five minutes before she could pull herself up, take a long drink of the vile water from the barrel, and collect her wits. This was not the best of times to be hungover, and she could remember being so only one other time in her life after a wedding party.

She wrapped the stiffening bodies of her mother and father in separate blankets, carefully avoiding looking at their faces. She wanted the vague horror of yesterday to blur quickly, and she willed herself to remember her beloved parents the way they had been in the full vigor of life.

She set about digging graves in the loose soil but, in the heat and her weakness, had to pause frequently to drink great quantities of water. The polluted water lay on her stomach like curdled milk. She ignored the sickening feeling as well as her pounding head and continued digging.

Once the bodies were two feet under the ground, side by side, she fashioned a single marker for them, to show their continuing unity in death, she told herself. Actually, she was too tired to make two. Numbly she contemplated the board broken from her mother's sewing box before setting to work with a sheath knife to gouge out the words **Vincent and Madeline Sizemore**. Then she rested her aching hands. They were callused to hard work, but were also cracked and bleeding from frequent immersion in the strong alkali water. **Died** . . . What day was it, anyway? She sat, staring blankly at the distant white clouds billowing up from beyond the western mountains. **Aug. 19, 1849**. Then she took some charcoal from the fire and rubbed it into the grooves of the crude lettering to make the words more legible. Three horseshoe nails hammered into the wood fashioned a cross, and she planted one end firmly in the ground.

"Probably won't last a month," she muttered aloud to herself. "But it's the best I can do. And God will find you." Her eyes, dry for the last twenty-four hours, filled with tears, and the glaring wasteland beyond the wagons blurred in her vision.

She took a deep breath, turning away. It was all up to her now. Why she had been spared the disease, she didn't know, but realized it could still strike her at any time. She had been in close contact with the victims. Maybe the brandy had killed whatever caused cholera, she thought. Maybe it was a preventative. But she wasn't going to sit around thinking about it.

The oxen and mules had wandered off about a quarter mile to find some sparse vegetation. On a sudden whim, she decided not to rehitch the mules, but to leave the wagon and travel light, using one of the beasts for a pack animal and riding the other. To this end, she searched all three wagons for anything usable that was light enough to transport by mule back. She got her father's remaining gold from her wagon first of all, then filled sacks with sides of moldy bacon, bags of dried beans, dried apricots, flour, saleratus, coffee, salt, several canteens and two water buckets for the mules, a few cooking utensils, what liquor and medicine she could find. And one item in the Jackson wagon that might be more valuable than anything else—a copy of LATTER DAY SAINTS EMIGRANTS' GUIDE, published the year before. She also took her father's rifle, powder, shot, and caps. She dressed in her father's best denim pants and cotton shirt, keeping her own hat. Her one remaining frock was torn and dirty and would be left behind. Somehow she couldn't bear to take any of her mother's clothes. And the sight of her own wedding dress, still wrapped in the bottom of her trunk, seemed a cruel joke. She cut up the harness and fashioned two makeshift halters for the mules, hoping they would work. She would probably have to bank on the fatigue and malnutrition of the animals to keep them under control.

Most of the day was consumed in these chores, and she had no time to feel sorry for herself. She was startled about mid-afternoon when she looked up to see several Indians on foot, watching her from about a half mile away. They were almost naked, but their brown bodies must have been impervious to the sun, she thought. They appeared to be armed with bows and arrows, but made no move toward her. "Diggers," she muttered. "That's what the men called them. They eat bugs and rodents and fish and seeds and roots . . . whatever they can find. Or steal. They're not supposed to be aggressive," she added as if to reassure herself.

She knew they had probably seen her burying her parents, but she wondered if these people had yet been stung by white man's diseases. Did they realize the significance of these deaths, or were they just waiting a chance to slip in after dark and steal the livestock and whatever they could carry away from the wagons? It would be a fatal mistake. To prevent them from the likelihood of contracting cholera, she would set fire to the two diseased wagons just as darkness was closing in.

While the silent Indians still watched from a distance, she carefully loaded her father's rifle as he had taught her to do before this journey began. Then, walking casually, she

241

carried the weapon as she went to round up the mules. The lean, tired animals had not wandered far, and it was no problem herding them back toward the wagon where she tied them. Then she fed them a thin gruel of water liberally mixed with the wheat flour she couldn't carry.

When she looked again, the Indians were gone.

One thing that was very light and could not be left behind was the charcoal portrait Clayburn Collins had made of her. She took it out of her trunk and carefully untied the cord that bound it flat between two pieces of a stiff cardboard folder. The face of the proud, self-conscious Melungeon girl with the thick braid that he had captured so well was not the person she now saw in the mirror still attached to the wagon bow. Her cheeks were lean and drawn. The whites of her blue eyes were bloodshot from sun and wind and tears. Her lips were dry and cracked. The straight, black hair had grown an inch or so since her session with the scissors, but still barely reached her collar. It was the face of a woman who had seen much and endured even more, and bore little resemblance to the portrait. But the charcoal image would accompany her, nonetheless, if only as a relic of a happier, more innocent time.

Just before dark she sat down on the wagon tongue to read the EMIGRANTS' GUIDE and decided that she would not go south across a waterless waste to the sink of the Carson River. The only reasonable alternative would be to cross what the book called, "the forty-mile desert" from the sink of the Humboldt River almost directly west to the Truckee River. The only water on this route was exactly halfway across—a boiling hot spring. So be it.

She had piled everything aside she wanted to pack on the mule and would leave at daylight, when she was rested. She estimated the forty miles would require a day and a night to

cross and wanted to attack the hottest part first while some
of her waning strength remained. The oxen she would leave
to their own devices. They would either die in this wasteland, or the Indians could have them. She had no skills in
butchering or preserving meat, especially of one of these
huge animals.

After a generous supper, she took a blazing stick from
the fire and ignited the Jackson and Steckinger wagons. As
the flames spread and leapt up, pushing back the darkness,
she climbed into her own wagon to sleep one last night, her
father's loaded rifle beside her in case of marauding Indians. In spite of a bone-deep tiredness, she could not relax
enough to sleep, with the tensions and fears of the unknown
whirling through her mind. She sat up and took out her
diary to record the happenings of the past two days by the
wavering light of the burning wagons. She sought to capture
the sharp immediacy of the terrible events before her mind
repressed them into a blur. After covering three pages, she
paused to think of a fitting conclusion.

**And so tomorrow I start once again to escape
this Valley of the Humboldt—the valley of the
shadow of death—with only the faithful mules for
company. How cruel to have come all this way and
perish before touching the shining mountains or
the green valleys of California! If I live to reach
our goal, I'm sure it's not because I am more
worthy than my parents or any of the others who
died along the trail—only more fortunate.**

She stared out with unseeing eyes at the blazing wagons
that poured columns of smoke into the dark sky. Theo-
retically she knew everybody had to die, but dealing with it

on a practical basis was like a knife in the heart. She dipped her pen and continued writing:

> **But I'm not there yet. Even though the guide book tells me trees and green grass are to be found near the sink of the Carson River to the south, I have determined to go a more direct route toward my goal by crossing the Forty-Mile Desert west to the Truckee River. If I make it that far, I'll choose one of the trails into the mountains. I hope to God I do not meet the same fate as the Donner party who took this route three years ago. I know there are many other travelers on this trail. Maybe I will be lucky enough to encounter another wagon train and get help. How I need the comfort of human company just now! But I dare not let anyone know I have been exposed to the cholera.**

She was determined to brace up to whatever lay ahead and give it her last, best effort of intelligence, will, and physical effort. If she made it—fine. If she didn't, then she would see her parents again sooner than expected. She knew the hell she had already passed through, and doubted that what was before her could be any worse. She had only herself to rely on now, only her own wits and strength to face and conquer another hostile desert, and who knew what mountains beyond that. One mistake, one wrong decision or direction, and she could die. She might still come down with cholera and die anyway. But her "strength was as the strength of ten because her heart was pure." She smiled ruefully as the Biblical quote came to mind. She would like to think this was true of her, but erotic thoughts of Clayburn Collins came unbidden to mind. She barely knew this man, so her active imagination could make of him anything she wished. It was pure fantasy. She put down her diary, closed her eyes, and leaned back against a folded blanket inside the wagon box, hoping sleep would come. But, instead, she imagined herself with the green-eyed Collins. She was safe in his arms at the Sizemore Inn. It was early summer, and everything was green in the Tennessee hills. The sweet fragrance of honeysuckle was wafting in through the open window . . . .

The heat and stench of the Humboldt sink, with its new graves, vanished beyond the dying light of the burning wagons, beyond her closed eyelids and thoughts, as the healing balm of sleep finally rescued her.

Chapter Twenty-One

Aboard the bark, Inverness,

Near Cape Horn

"And no time came for painting or for drawing,
But all hands fought, and icy death came clawing."
John Masefield

It was now three weeks since the *Inverness* had run headlong into its first winter gale. This had been followed by a succession of southwest gales that had driven her back, and still back, until she lay, hove-to and drifting, about seventy miles southeast of Staten Island and losing more distance every hour.

"Nothing to do but stand look-out," Collins said as he and Merriman met on deck at the change of watch. He jerked a thumb at the poop. "Preventer tackle's been rigged to either side of the rudder head to keep one o' those graybeards from breaking it."

The wind kept up its mournful wail through the overhead rigging while mountainous waves rose and fell around them. But the ship rode somewhat easier, and the main deck was not continually awash when the ship was hove-to and drifting leeward, like a sea bird with its head tucked under its wing. Sheets of spray were still blown over them, and most of the watch were huddled under the protection of the weather cloth—a canvas shield rigged on the windward side near the break of the poop.

Collins paused as he started up the ladder to the poop. "How long is Malloy going to keep trying to double the Horn? We might be here forever."

Merriman shrugged. "Stark was saying that he was off this cape for eight weeks one time before the captain gave up, turned tail, and ran around the bottom of the world the other way to California."

Collins shook his head. "Well, stay warm if you can. The way she's blowing, you probably won't have any sail changes this watch." He glanced aloft where the two topsails were set, but nothing else. He climbed to the poop and headed for the stairway inside the charthouse. As he passed the chart table, he stopped to have a look. South of the jumble of islands that comprised the hook-shaped tip of the continent and below fifty degrees latitude were printed in large letters, **GREAT WEST WIND DRIFT** with arrows indicating the easterly directions of the prevailing wind and current. "Didn't need a map to tell me that," he muttered to himself. "Damn wonder *any* ship can sail westward down here."

He went below to his cabin, pulled off his boots and oilskins, then several layers of clothing underneath, and fell into his bunk for three and a half hours of blessed sleep. Since they'd reached Tierra Del Fuego, the cold wind, darkness, and heavy work had combined to make him sleep like a dead man. Even if he hadn't been required to help handle sail, climb the rigging, and wrestle the heavy wheel, he thought he'd probably have been tired just from the physical exertion of bracing himself and holding onto things as he moved. As it was, he was still bruised and battered from being thrown against stanchions, and bulkheads, and ladders.

For some reason, exhausted sleep didn't come right away as he lay there, and his restless mind brought up images of their long battle to round the Horn. When Malloy was trying to drive westward, the ship was constantly buffeted, pitched, and rolled, picked up and flung down, smashed by huge seas until she had started some of her seams and a half hour of each four-hour watch required two men at the pumps.

The main deck was constantly awash while they tried to make westing, and a trip from one end of the ship to the other could be a perilous trek, even with lifelines strung at intervals.

"Should have a metal bridge for this kind of weather," Stark had growled. "Forms a walkway from the poop to the top of the midship house to the fo'castle. Owners too damned cheap to build one, I reckon."

"This ship wasn't designed for Cape Horn," Collins replied before he thought.

Stark glared at him, but stalked away without replying.

While still in good weather, Stark had directed the crew in removing the lower ends of the braces from the rail of the ship and reattaching them to the tops of the deckhouses so the men could pivot the yardarms from a higher perch, somewhat safe from the thunderous seas that fell aboard the main deck. This move had probably saved several broken limbs and possibly a life or two so far, Collins reflected.

The sun had retreated ever northward, taking most of its heat and light. Gimbaled lamps burned all day in the after cabins of the ship to dispel the gloom of the constant storm wrack. The doors of all cabins, except the captain's, were opened to the adjoining hallways to catch the draft of warm air given off by the iron stove that roared day and night in the dining room.

Every day or two, when the weather showed signs of relenting, the mates ordered more sail set and brought the *Inverness* back on course. Collins recalled with longing the one time they had nearly three days of moderate weather, when the waves were only twelve to fifteen feet high and the southwest wind came at them at about twenty knots. The yards had been braced around at a severe angle to catch the wind, and the ship had sliced through the gray rollers toward the Horn like a lean greyhound after a rabbit. Two men grappled with the wheel to hold her to it as the *Inverness* heeled to starboard and buried her lee rail four feet deep in the foaming sea.

The sun even appeared weakly at noon long enough for Stark to get a sight and work out their exact position. Collins got a look at the chart later and saw that the fix of their position was only five miles off the dead reckoning plot the mate had been keeping. A remarkable feat of navigation, or guesswork, considering they had not seen the sun for nearly a week, and had been at the mercy of wind and current all that time.

The Strait of Magellan, which someone had penciled in on the chart, was really only a circuitous passage of narrow channels between the islands that would allow a ship to cut the corner and win out to the Pacific side quicker.

While Collins was looking at the chart, Gilbert Malloy came into the charthouse from the poop and doffed his southwester to keep from dripping water on the chart table. "Too bad we can't take that route," he said, pointing to the penciled line. "Maybe in a smaller craft with a fore-and-aft rig we could do it."

"Looks like there's room," Collins had remarked.

"With a fair wind, yes," he said. "But you can count on contrary winds, and there's not really enough room to tack a square-rigger in some of those channels. Many a shipmaster has tried it, because it looks so inviting on paper, but their bones are at the bottom."

Collins nodded, studying the zigzag line.

"But the worst thing in that strait, if you don't mind the Fuegians . . . the wild natives who attack any ship that comes near or goes aground . . . is the williwaws."

"The what?"

"Williwaws. Tremendous winds that're deflected from those steep cliffs and can hit you without warning from any direction. Wreck a ship just like that!" He snapped his fingers.

As Malloy leaned close, Collins had caught a whiff of rum on his breath. Collins took a closer look and decided the captain's eyes were irritated with more than just salt spray.

Collins had made a cursory remark and then ducked away to go below, feeling nervous around the new captain. Even though Malloy didn't show any obvious signs of intoxication, Collins didn't want to be near this man with the dual personality any longer than necessary. Abel Stark had not yet discovered that the killer he sought was serving aboard the same vessel with him. And Collins didn't want to be close when, or if, that discovery was made.

These thoughts went through his mind as he lay in his bunk, willing himself to go to sleep. Maybe he had it too easy here in this warm cabin, he thought. The rest of the sailors, except the mates and Merriman, were bunking in the forecastle that had been washed out several times by big seas. Collins had taken a quick look into their quarters two days before and was shocked at the unheated room with its sopping bunks in which the men fell, exhausted, fully clothed and wet to the skin, to catch some sleep between watches, or the frequent calls for all hands. No wonder some of the crew resented him. Collins had even managed to stay dry enough in his quarters to prevent the severe chaffing at his wrists and collar where painful salt-water boils formed. The others, who were constantly wet, were not so fortunate. But Collins was just as worn and gaunt and hollow-eyed as the rest from the everlasting strain and lack of sleep and hot food. The wildest headland in the world was taking its toll on the few men of the *Inverness* who dared oppose it, he reflected.

Just as he was drifting off to sleep, he was roused up by the roar of Abel Stark's voice through the speaking trumpet: "All hands! On deck to make sail!"

Two days later they had gained the sea miles lost, and more, and were actually west of the Diego Ramirez Rocks.

"This time I think we're going to make it," Collins remarked to Merriman in the dog watch as they sat on their bunks, snatching a cold, hasty meal. The cook had scalded himself trying to prepare soup. So, for several days, their only hot food had been coffee.

"I wouldn't be too sure. Counting your chickens . . . and all that."

"I'm teaching myself to be an optimist," Collins said. "Optimism makes for confidence, I'm discovering."

"And for deeper disappointments," Merriman said.

Collins grinned. "Next thing I know you'll be reminding me of the curse Captain Blackwell put on this ship . . . that we'd all die trying to beat around the Horn."

"We're not around yet," Merriman cautioned, draining the last of his coffee from a tin cup.

"Remember, I was the one who was superstitious when we started this voyage," Collins said. "Maybe we'll have some good luck, since you and I were ordered to switch watches."

"Doesn't seem to matter, since all hands are on deck most of the time anyhow," Merriman replied.

Just then the stern of the ship dropped into a trough, and a wave thundered against the sealed door of the after cabin. Collins heard the rush of feet on the deck overhead, and they looked at each other expectantly. And, as sure as the ship's bell struck the hours, the call for all hands came down the stairway.

"The usual Cape Horn program," Merriman sighed, standing up.

"I guess King Neptune thought we were going to sneak past him without a fight," Collins said, reaching for his oil-skins.

Only a few minutes later, Collins was standing on the footrope of a yardarm, reefing the fore topsail. He and the men on either side of him were working with both hands as they bent over the yard. There was no need to hold on since the wind gusts, which he estimated at sixty knots, pinned them against the spar. While they struggled to pull in the wind-stiffened canvas, Collins got a chance to glance up a time or two as the rays of the setting sun shot under the low clouds to illuminate a jagged coastline of snow-capped black rocks several miles to the north. Had they been closer, Collins was sure he could have seen the surf spouting along the base of those granite cliffs. The sight shot a thrill of fear through him, and he redoubled his efforts.

Then a sleet and snow squall whirled down on them and blotted out everything. Stinging particles of ice lashed the side of his face. The wind had ripped off his southwester, and he ducked his head, willing his hands to clutch and grip and pull, almost glad of the numbness that would not let him feel, until later, the pain of his burst fingertips. The yard was shaking from a loose brace somewhere, and fear lanced his stomach as the footrope began to jerk and sway. Ice water was trickling down the back of his neck as he and his mates strove to secure the sail that leapt and burst from their hands like a thing alive just when they almost had it contained. Blood from their fingers streaked the white canvas.

Collins was in torment. The wind roared through the rigging, pressing the tall ship over and down, pinning them against the reeling yard with an icy blast. Ease and comfort and art were things he had known in another life, something only half remembered, imagined, dreamed. Time had ceased, and eternity had begun in this frozen hell where they struggled endlessly far above the foam-streaked sea.

They wound up losing the sail, anyway—blown out of its bolt ropes and whirled away into the murk to leeward. Both watches toiled for more than two hours to lower and reef enough sail so the *Inverness* could be safely hove-to. Their oilskins and hair were plastered with an icy mail by the time they finished and climbed down the weather shrouds to the deck. Collins was so stiffened with cold, he could hardly move. But now it was time for his watch, so there was no going below.

Gilbert Malloy, apparently seeing their condition, ordered all hands aft to the base of the mizzenmast for a jigger of rum to thaw their blood. He stood by as Louis, the steward, ladled out the liquor in tin mugs, roughly a quarter pint per man.

While Collins was lined up for his rum, feeling numb in body and mind, Malloy and Stark were conversing several yards away. But the wind brought their voices clearly to Collins.

"This gale's breaking," Malloy said. "We'll stay snugged down until daylight. By then, our drift will bring us up under the lee of the land, and we'll be ready to sneak around if the weather moderates. If it pipes up again, we'll wear ship and heave-to on the other tack."

"What?"

Collins was jarred out of his lethargy by the mate's explosive response.

"I know it sounds risky, Mister Stark," came the formal voice of command, but with the words couched in Malloy's soothing tone, "but we've been stuck here for nearly a month. If we don't take a chance, we may never get around at all."

Collins reached for the tin cup of rum and was only half listening as Malloy went on to explain that the coastline trended away at an oblique angle just at this point, so there was really no danger.

Their voices faded as Collins walked away, gulping his ration and reflecting that he had never tasted anything so good. He was chilled to the bone, and the fiery liquid started a glow in his stomach that slowly spread outward, limbering his legs and arms as he moved. Collins thought he had worked himself into good physical condition, overcome his fear and pain, and toughened up to this hard life. But the agony of Cape Horn in winter had quickly disabused him of this notion. Opposing these overwhelming forces of wind and hail and icy sea with only the strength of arm and will, living on the edge of violent death for days and weeks at a time with little food or rest were almost more than he could endure, and he felt himself cracking.

The rum not only warmed him, but was now making him sleepy. He wished his body was as strong as his will. His eight to midnight watch was just beginning. He had to do something to stay awake, so he went forward to the galley in the midship house and helped himself to a tin cup of coffee from the pot that was kept hot on the stove, day and night.

He went to drink his coffee in the relatively protected area behind the weather cloth. Fatigue and wind noise limited conversations among the men, although in the dark a few feet away Malloy was sharing a joke of some kind with two of the sailors.

The coffee restored a little of his energy that had been drained by his ordeal on the yard, so he deserted the shelter and climbed to the poop to gauge the weather. A young man named Peterson was at the wheel, but he had little to do since the ship was tending herself. Collins was tempted to go into the charthouse and get warm, but knew sleepiness would drag him down again. He did glance into the lamplit interior through a porthole and was startled to discover Abel Stark, who was off watch and normally would have been in his cabin a half hour ago. The mate had removed his southwester, but, otherwise, was still fully dressed in his foul-weather gear. He was bent over the chart table, a pair of dividers in his hand, measuring and calculating something. Their position, maybe? But why? The old man should have been in his bunk, getting what sleep he could before his next watch. But Stark was the navigator aboard, so Collins assumed he was just taking a little extra time to calculate their position, or their progress, if any.

But what held Collins, transfixed, at the porthole was the look on the old man's face. For the very first time since he had come aboard, Collins saw fear in Stark's face. Fear and age—the deep lines and sagging chin of decades of battling the sea. Maybe it was finally getting to him, Collins thought as he backed carefully away from the window. He had never seen Stark afraid of anything before. He wondered what it could be.

He went to the far side of the poop and waited in the dark by the rail, the cold wind cutting his face, while he tucked his battered and split hands beneath his oilskins.

A few minutes later, Stark emerged from the charthouse and went down the ladder to the main deck. Curious, Collins followed at a distance, and the mate made his way forward past the midship house and climbed to the top of the forecastle. Now and then moonlight appeared through the shredding clouds. In one of those brief periods of light, Collins saw the hulking figure of the mate standing by the lookout, both of them staring off into the darkness. At what? Collins remembered the rocky coast he had seen from the height of the topsail yard just at sunset. But it was at least fifteen miles away, he estimated, trying to remember how it had appeared in the brief time he'd had to look.

Then he recalled the conversation he'd overheard while getting his tot of rum. Stark just did not trust the captain's judgment or his piloting. Even to a landsman like Collins, this seemed a risky maneuver—hove-to so that the ship was drifting toward a rocky coast in the dark on the tail end of a big blow. But Collins certainly had no way of judging whether Malloy or Stark was the better sailor. Both of these men were professionals, with years of experience. Maybe Stark was just being overly cautious.

Collins felt guilty, spying on the old mate, so he crept away aft without being seen. But, whatever his reason, Stark remained in the bow of the ship through the remainder of the watch. And Collins was certain Malloy didn't even know the mate was on deck.

Eight bells signaled the change of watch at midnight. Collins lingered for several minutes, found Merriman coming on deck, and quietly voiced his concerns. Merriman shook his head. "I don't know, but it doesn't sound good. I'll keep my eyes open."

"It's Stark's watch again until four o'clock. This'll make twelve straight hours he's been up here in this freezing wind with no sleep."

"The man's amazing," Merriman conceded.

"He wouldn't be doing it, if he didn't think the ship was in danger. Fjelde thought Stark was the best seaman aboard." He looked off into the windy darkness, wondering how fast the ship was drifting toward those black granite teeth that were bared to crush their fragile vessel. "Think I'll stay on deck for a while. I'm tired, but too wound up to sleep just now. Be back shortly."

Collins made his way along the deck by the pale light of a moon that was inking in black shadows.

"Collins, is that you?"

The voice from atop the midship house stopped him in his tracks. "Riaz?"

"It's your watch below."

"Not sleepy." He looked up, trying to pierce the gloom.

"*¡Madre de Dios!*" the Cuban exclaimed. "I could sleep for a week if I had the chance."

"What are you doing up there?" Collins asked.

"Mister Stark is with the look-out in the bow and told me to stand by here."

Collins climbed the ladder to the top of the deckhouse, and the two men conversed for a time. Collins got the impression that Riaz had no idea that the ship was in any danger. He was merely following orders without question, as he always did.

One bell was struck for the first half hour as Collins told Riaz good night and started aft to go below to a warm bunk, finally having convinced himself that the ship was in good hands.

He had just reached the base of the mizzenmast when he heard a faint shout from forward, but the wind whisked the words away. "Land on the lee bow!" Riaz shouted, passing the word back. The words chilled Collins. He looked forward, but could see nothing in the blackness as clouds obscured the moon.

A few seconds later Stark came bounding along the deck with a speed that belied his limp. "Hard up your helm! Main braces . . . slack off . . . jump to it!" he thundered as he went by Collins, and in two leaps was up the ladder to the poop. "Let go that spanker sheet."

Feet pounded on the deck as men scurried in the darkness to obey. Collins joined the rush to the top of the midship house to help with the main braces as the yards were squared, helping to ease the wind pressure on the after part of the ship. He recognized the maneuver—Stark was wearing ship, which was equivalent to tacking a smaller vessel. But, instead of the bow swinging across the wind to change direction, the square-rigger had to turn a half circle the other way, with the wind crossing its stern. Collins knew this was a time-consuming process in a big sea with very little sail set. Very slowly he felt the wind direction change as the bow paid off, and they began their turn to starboard.

Men from the off watch had rushed on deck, hatless and coatless, to join the battle. Collins could hear Malloy's voice from the top of the forecastle, directing several sailors at the foremast braces.

"Land! Dead ahead!" came the shout from the bow lookout.

Collins stepped back, panting, and looked ahead. At first

he could see nothing. Then the clouds parted, and the moon reappeared. As the stern of the *Inverness* was flung skyward on a mountainous sea, he looked again. And there it was, across those cold, moving hills of ocean—black, snow-capped rocks, the vertical cliffs of a craggy coastline. And the ship was driving straight toward them!

"What the hell you gawkin' at, Collins? Get on that brace, if you don't want to swim!" Stark snarled as he leaped up the midship house ladder to lend a hand. Even the Chinese cook and the steward were on deck, pulling and hauling. It was all hands to save ship.

With agonizing slowness, the bow continued to swing to starboard.

"What're you doing, Jacobus?" Stark yelled, sliding down the ladder and bounding across the deck toward the poop. "Ease her, ease her into the big ones! Where the hell did you learn to steer? Be ready to check her, when she comes up on the wind! That's it. A couple more spokes. Now, hold 'er, full and by."

As the ship rounded up on the starboard tack, Collins heaved a sigh, thinking they were safe as the ship was now going away from the land—at an oblique angle, to be sure, but away. Then he saw they were not out of danger. The maze of tiny islands and jutting headlands into which they had blundered still reached out for them. They had to clear one especially vicious-looking point of land that thrust out into the sea between them and the open ocean. And he could tell that the amount of sail they carried was not enough to offset the sideways push of those great gray-beards that rolled shoreward.

Stark had already seen the danger and was ordering men aloft to loose the topgallant sails. As each sail was set, the *Inverness* heeled over a little more, and her speed increased.

To leeward, Collins could see nothing as the clouds again obscured the moon.

"Set the mainsail!" Stark roared.

"She won't take it!" Malloy shouted back. "Reef it."

"To hell with the reef! No time!" Stark shouted, clearly assuming command.

The huge spread of canvas caught the wind just as the flying jib was blown out. The ship heeled over sharply to port and buried her bow in a sea. Men scrambled to get off the forecastle and retreated to the base of the mizzenmast near the break of the poop. Everything had been done that could be done, and the forward half of the ship was made unlivable by the bursting seas as the ship plunged wildly ahead, over and through the waves.

Stark stood by the helmsman, giving orders, watching. Collins saw him open his mouth at least three times to give the order to set more sail, and could almost read the mate's mind as he gauged the wind and the ship. Could she carry what sail she had without the rigging carrying away? Could she carry more?

Collins could feel the ship clawing to windward, even as her forward speed increased. Solid water foamed across her lee deck as the ship was being driven as he'd never seen her driven before.

"Land on the lee bow!" a man yelled, pointing.

Stark made no move. Collins knew the mate realized their peril, and there was no more he could do about it. For the next twenty minutes the issue was in doubt. Collins hung onto the fife rail as the ship rolled down to leeward in the gusts, nearly sweeping the sea with the ends of her lower yardarms.

The moon reappeared, and Collins caught his breath at the sight of those cruel rocks gashing the sea less than a hundred yards away. He measured the angle with his eye as they rushed closer and closer, and knew the odds were a thousand to one against their weathering that last jagged tooth of land. It could all end here. He prayed it would be over quickly when the icy sea took him. At the rate they were moving, they would smash the rock with tremendous force. The black cliff loomed up so near he could see the great fissures and the sea spouting and thundering along its base. He cringed as their reeling skysails nearly touched the face of the rock. Then the *Inverness* sank down into a last great trough between two waves, and he held his breath, waiting for the ship to strike.

Instead, they drove clear into the open ocean beyond.

After a few seconds of disbelief, the crew broke into a spontaneous cheer. Collins could have sworn the wind he felt on his face was the Angel of Death passing them by.

Malloy came springing up the ladder to the poop, coatless and with his shirt nearly ripped off. But he seemed oblivious to the cold spray. "By God, that was close!" he cried. He stopped next to the helmsman, his eyes wide, apparently still stunned by their brush with eternity.

In the light of the binnacle, Collins could see Malloy's bare torso—and the tattoo of the devil's head, the anchor and the initials, G-A-M, on the upper arm. Before Collins could do anything to distract him, Stark saw it, too. It seemed to take a few seconds to register, but suddenly Stark fell back a step, pointing at the telltale mark. "You . . . *you're* the one who killed Captain Zucker!" he roared. Stark made a jump for him, but Malloy was too quick. He dodged into the charthouse and slammed the door. But he had no time to lock it before Stark yanked his knife and rammed a shoulder against the door. Collins heard the captain's terrified yell as the chase thundered down the stairs into the after cabin.

The few men on the poop looked in wonder at this strange behavior, while Jacobus held the wheel and kept the ship clawing off the lee shore. Just then, the huge belly of a mainsail blew out with a roar, shredding away into the darkness.

Collins made a dash for the charthouse, where Merriman met him, jerking his Colt from under his oilskins. They stumbled down the canted, heaving stairway as sounds of a struggle came from the captain's quarters down the hall. Yells and curses issued from beyond the swinging cabin door, followed by the blast of a gunshot in a confined space. They reached the door and yanked it open to find Malloy gasping in a corner, blood gushing from between his fingers as he clutched feebly at a gaping wound in his abdomen. His mouth was open, and, even as they looked, his eyes were glazing.

Stark's heavy body sagged against the bunk, bloody knife in one huge fist. "You son-of-a-bitch," he breathed hoarsely. "By damn, I gave you what you gave Zucker." Then his eyes rolled back, and he slumped on the bunk, unconscious.

The small room reeked of burnt gunpowder as Collins jerked open the mate's oilskins and quickly pulled away the coat and wool shirt underneath. There, in the upper part of the hairy chest, was a small, purpling bullet hole.

"Malloy's done for," he heard Merriman say behind him. "Ripped open from navel to breastbone."

"Damn!" Collins said, feeling for Stark's pulse. "He's still alive, but I don't know for how long."

Merriman reached down and picked up Malloy's pistol as the sound of running feet came to them from overhead.

"We'll have company shortly," Collins said grimly. "Better get ready to let 'em know *you're* now captain of this ship."

Chapter Twenty-Two

Truckee River

Stevens-Donner Branch of

the California Trail

". . . [W]ithin 8 or 10 miles of the river I lay down several times to rest . . . but it was death to stay there . . . I would have given all I possessed for a drink of cold water. My tongue and lips was parched and furred over so it took one hour to soak it off."

Charles Tinker, 1849,
writing of the Forty Mile Desert

"There now, honey, not too much. That'll do for now."

Lisa Sizemore felt gentle hands pulling her back from the cold, clear water—the delicious, heavenly life-giving water she had to soak up or die.

"More . . . ," she managed to gasp through cracked lips. Her tongue was in the way. "More."

"You can have more directly. You don't want to make yourself sick. Just rest a minute or two. There, now, lie back here in the shade. You've been through a terrible ordeal."

The female voice came to her ears as soothingly as the tone of her mother. But even through the haze in her brain, Lisa knew this was not her mother. The voice and accent were different, yet this woman sounded comforting, like someone she could trust. She closed her eyes and tried to relax, listening to the gurgling of water over the gravel bed in the nearby river. Instead of being soothing, the sound made her even more conscious of her unslaked thirst. A folded blanket protected her from the hard ground. And she seemed to need the padding; her bones felt as if they were poking out everywhere. And she was so weak, she had a hard time just sitting up. She would rest a minute and try again, she thought. She heard voices nearby. One of them was the woman.

"We'll have to rest here for a day or so," she said. "She's in no condition to travel."

"We can't be wastin' any more time. The snow in those mountains won't wait for us," a man's voice answered.

"One day won't hurt. We're ahead of schedule."

The man growled something Lisa couldn't hear.

"If she's an Indian woman, she's probably a lot tougher than you give her credit for. She'll come around in a few hours," the woman said.

"Hell, she's no Indian. Did you see those blue eyes? And her nose? She may have straight black hair and dark skin, but she's some kind of 'breed. And she's dressed in white man's clothes," the man answered. "She ain't spoke but one word . . . water . . . since we picked her up, so we don't know if she even talks English."

"If you felt like that about it, why didn't you just leave her on the desert to die?" the woman said disgustedly, "instead of dragging her twenty miles to water, revivin' her, only to finish killin' her by joltin' her in a wagon afore she's able to stand it."

"Did you go through the stuff on her mule? She might've stole it."

"Of course, I didn't. That poor animal was about done in, too. I just took off its pack and gave it some water."

"Well, if you think she's in that bad a shape, I'll see if I can talk the others into layin' over a bit. I reckon we could all use a breather," the man said, caving in.

The voices faded in Lisa's hearing as she lay on her back with her eyes closed. Her limbs felt as heavy as logs. A cooling breeze blew over her, drying the water she'd splashed on her clothes. The sound of the stream and the rustling of the wind in the leaves of the cottonwoods overhead gradually lulled her into a doze.

Call it a miracle, call it luck, call it Divine Providence. Whatever it was, Lisa thought, she was grateful for it—her rescue and quick recovery. "Youthful good health."—was what the woman attributed it to. One full day of rest and loving attention and water and a little food, and she'd not only regained her senses, but was on her feet and moving around. By the time they started again about thirty-six hours later, she was still very weak and tired easily, but she was definitely on the mend.

Lisa discovered that she literally owed her life to Ruth and Abner Pickering, a forty-year old couple who were emigrating from a Kentucky hill farm to cast themselves into an uncertain future in California. The Pickerings had joined a company of five small wagons, with the object of traveling light and fast, unburdened by oxen or beef herds. Their rations were as slim as the travelers themselves, containing such things as jerked beef, dried beans, dried fruit, the only bulky items being barrels of water and flour. One of the five wagons had broken two of its wheels and had to be abandoned, while its two occupants had put their possessions in another wagon and fashioned saddle pads to ride their mules. Lisa found that she and Mrs. Pickering made up two-thirds of the females in the company, the other being the young wife of one of the Argonauts.

As Lisa and Ruth Pickering rode in the back of the jolting wagon along the Truckee River, the older woman filled in the blank spaces in Lisa's recent memory. The party had come across the Forty Mile Desert the day after Lisa had started her ill-fated trek. They had found her, nearly dead from thirst and exposure, not far from the boiling spring that marked the desert's halfway point.

Lisa nodded, having only vague recollections of black volcanic rock and, later, endless hummocks of white sand with clumps of scrub growth. The whole thing was overlaid with a memory of a terrible blanket of oppressive heat. That's when her memory ceased until she woke up beside the cool, flowing waters of the Truckee River.

"The mule you'd been ridin' was so far gone, Abner had to shoot him," Ruth Pickering told her. "The pack mule was tougher, and, if he doesn't have to carry nothin' for a while, he'll make it. His feet are still in good shape."

"We had them reshod at Fort Laramie," Lisa said, looking fondly at her thin mule who was tethered on a long lead to the back of the wagon.

"Now, tell me how you happened to be out there all by yourself."

Lisa related the story of her own journey from Tennessee, including the accidental killing of Zeke Masters. Ruth Pickering's alert brown eyes, looking out from the tunnel of her sunbonnet, never wavered as Lisa told her tale of suffering and the deaths of her parents from cholera.

" 'Tain't likely you're gonna come down with the cholera now, since it's been several days, but don't say nothin' about that in front of my husband." She glanced at Abner's back on the wagon box where he was urging the team of mules around some boulders. "He's mighty skittish about things like that. We saw a heap o 'folks die along the Platte with the bloody flux."

Day by day, Lisa grew stronger, and the hollows of her body began to fill in somewhat as she absorbed nourishment and rested. Within a week she was able to help with some of the camp chores as the trail into the mountains grew rougher and more tiring. The river was swifter now as it dropped down from the mountains, rushing over boulders and forming quiet, deep pools, here and there, where they caught delicious trout to vary their plain fare.

"Sure a sight better than bush fish," Abner remarked as they ate their fried trout and beans one evening."

"Bush fish?" Lisa asked.

"Rattlesnake," Ruth interpreted. "Actually, snake's not too bad, if you can get over the idea of what you're eating."

"Prairie dog was pretty good eatin'," her husband added. "You could work up a good appetite trying to catch one o' those critters, though."

The hard, rocky trail and steep ascent was offset by the beauty of pine and fir trees, no dust, and sparkling clear air and water. To Lisa, it seemed as if they were gradually ascending to heaven, compared to what she had endured for weeks past. She had come through a fiery trial and had somehow survived it. She slept under a blanket these cold nights, and could feel her strength returning rapidly as the days wore on and they crossed ridges and mountain valleys, seeing the snow-covered peaks of the mighty Sierras still in the distance. As difficult and muscle fatiguing as it was, she knew as the early September days rolled by that she was going to make her goal of reaching California as long as she had the help of these hardy, taciturn Kentuckians.

She slid off the back of her mule for a nooning stop one day, and breathed deeply of the pine-scented air and gazed fondly at the vast mountain meadow they were about to cross. She was a mountain woman, born and reared. Not these steep, sharp mountains, but the uplands, nonetheless.

A half hour later she wrote in her diary: **If one can have forebodings of disaster, then I believe one can also have a sense of good things to come. And today I have the latter. Good health and vigor have something to do with this feeling, but it is there. There are many good people in this world, as well as bad ones. And, thanks to the Pickerings, I know I will see California before many more weeks have passed.**

Chapter Twenty-Three

Aboard the bark, Inverness,

Pacific Ocean

Just as he had discovered a pattern in the apparently aimless ebb and flow of ocean waves, Clayburn Collins also sensed a pattern in the random fortunes of men. He couldn't really define it; it was only a feeling. Yet, things continued to happen at critical moments that, in spite of all their efforts, were beyond anyone's control. As he stood by the fife rail and looked out on a sparkling blue sea, a fortunate occurrence was taking place that was not a direct result of their vague navigation. A heavy fog bank was blowing inland on a westerly breeze and dissipating in the bright October sunshine, revealing a headland that appeared to be the entrance to San Francisco Bay. He studied the chart in his hands and compared it to the shape of the notch in the high coastline before him. "That's got to be it," he said to Rob Merriman, who had strode over to stand next to him.

Merriman wore his Colt holstered conspicuously outside his jacket in case any of the crew started to doubt that he was the acting captain of the *Inverness*. "Sure looks like it," Merriman agreed. "Let's give it a try. The breeze is light and fair. Don't know how the tide is running, but it probably sucks in and out of that bay pretty strong." He turned to Verdugo who was at the wheel. "Bring her to starboard and point 'er at that notch in the hills. I believe we've made it."

"Jacobus, have the men square the yards," he ordered.

Ferret Jacobus looked sullen, but passed the word to the five men of the watch, and they moved to obey. Jacobus, his left eye still black from Merriman's fist two days earlier, was now working with a will, apparently as happy as everyone else that this voyage was almost over.

"There were times I never thought we'd make it," Collins said softly, staring at the brown coastline. His mind went back to the terrible night when the two mates attacked each other just after Stark had saved them from disaster. The foul weather had broken long enough for them to make westing. Steering only by the sun and stars, Merriman had doubled the Cape, and they started up the west coast of South America.

Abel Stark, drifting in and out of consciousness, gave them instructions on how to navigate, taking advantage of the cold, north-flowing Humboldt Current for a time. Most of the crew had accepted Merriman as the new captain, as long as he exhibited the strength and force of command without bullying them. Ferret Jacobus had been the only one inclined to test him, and Merriman had handled the insubordination quickly and firmly.

They later put in at the island of Juan Fernandez to replenish their drinking water, since they had been reduced to subsisting on rainwater tainted with salt spray. This island, famous for being Robinson Crusoe's home, also furnished them some welcome fresh fruit of strawberries, melons, and apples. The poorly-clad Chilean soldiers who manned a small post on the island never questioned who they were or where they had come from. They were only interested in trading for tobacco and pocket knives and such items they could not get. The *Inverness* was there just over one day, then hove up anchor and sailed away at the approach of another ship. It would not do to be detained now, just short of their goal, Merriman had said. Off the coast of California, they had been frustrated by light, contrary winds for several days, but now they were nearly at their destination.

"We've got to stand firm on our story about what happened," Merriman said. "Those port authorities are going to be mighty inquisitive about us. Since they're liable to be tried for piracy, there's no telling what the crew will testify to."

Collins nodded thoughtfully. "How's Stark?"

"Unconscious since early yesterday. If he doesn't come out of it soon, he'll likely die of thirst or hunger. He's lost a lot of weight."

"He's a tough old bird. I didn't think anything could put him down, even a bullet."

"That slug is still inside his chest somewhere," Merriman said. "Festering in a lung, most likely, since he's been feverish off and on ever since. I think it's going to kill him before much longer."

"I suppose we should be thankful he was alert enough to give us a rough course in navigation."

Merriman nodded. "That rum has been food and drink and pain-killer for him. Probably the only thing that's kept him going this long."

"Speaking of food, we'd better hustle up the cook to get some food ready early. We'll be too busy to eat about noon, when we hit the coast."

With their continued run of good luck, the tide was setting in when they passed through the Golden Gate. Both watches were on deck.

Collins was astonished at the forest of masts that jammed the waterfront. He guessed at least two or three hundred ships of all kinds lay at anchor just off the former village of Yerba Buena, now the burgeoning American town of San Francisco. Stretching up the sand hills from the waterfront were wooden buildings and shacks and tents of all shapes and sizes.

But he had no time to contemplate the spectacle, until they got the ship to anchor. The men worked quickly, dousing the sails. At Merriman's command, Verdugo spun the wheel, rounding the vessel up into the wind, just as the anchor was let go forward. The anchor rumbled down to the cries of gulls sweeping low overhead. The hook bit into the bottom, and the *Inverness* came to rest at the end of her long tether, pointing her sprung bowsprit proudly out to sea. She was rust-streaked, leaking, and scarred from her long, rough passage, but had brought them safely to their destination. They paid out enough chain so the bark could swing clear of any other vessels. It would mean a good five hundred yards of rowing through the jumbled mass of vessels to reach the beach, but it was as close as they could safely come.

Diaz slipped beckets over two of the wheel's spokes, and went forward. Just then Jacobus, Jack Morrison, Peterson, and Stenson began hauling boxes of foodstuffs out of the forecastle and loading them into one of the two longboats.

"Where do you think you're going?" Merriman demanded.

"Ashore," Jacobus retorted. "We're in California now. You're not in command any more."

"What about Stark?"

"What about him? Let the old scutter die," Jacobus sneered. "He's 'way past due."

A couple of the crew who'd fared hardest at the mate's hands, grinned as they continued throwing salvageable items into the boat.

"You're taking the ship's stores with you?"

"Just part of our pay for working this ship."

"Your pay will come in the diggings," Collins said, watching the crew rig the longboat to the falls.

"Don't try to stop us," Jacobus warned. "We've taken our last orders from you or anyone else aboard this ship."

Collins was glad when Merriman didn't reply. He, for one, was happy to see them go.

Diaz and Verdugo came over to Collins. "*Vaya con Dios,* my friend," Verdugo said, taking him firmly by the hand.

"Both of you are going, too?"

"*Sí,* but only as far as the shore with them." He jerked his head at the other crewmen behind him. "We were caught up in this mutiny, but we won't take the blame and go to jail. We must get ashore quickly and disappear."

"Good luck!" Collins said with heartfelt thanks.

The boat was swung over the side and lowered a few feet to the water. All but the Chinese cook and Louis, the steward, climbed in. With no word of farewell, they shoved off, and six oarsmen rowed the boatload of men and provisions quickly away and disappeared behind a nearby ship.

"Well, that didn't take long." Merriman pointed at a lighter being rowed with sweeps toward the *Inverness.*

The two Chinese men were conferring privately on the poop. As the lighter, manned by three men, swung alongside, Louis came up to Collins. "We talk for you," he said. "All same bad men take ship. Maybe so you need us." He indicated the cook.

"Thanks, Louis. We might just need someone to back up our story, at that," Collins smiled, as the four of them went down to the waist of the ship to meet the visitors.

"Ahoy, the *Inverness*," a burly man at the steering oar cried. "If you're the captain, we're here to off-load your cargo!"

"No cargo," Merriman replied.

"Then we'll ferry your passengers ashore for ten dollars a head," the man offered.

Collins thought the outrageous charge must be only the beginning point for haggling. "No passengers," he answered. "Just the four of us."

The lighterman looked confused, but pressed ahead. "Same price for the crew."

"We've got our own longboat," Merriman said. "When does the port authority come aboard to clear us to land?"

One of the other boatmen waved his hand. "Nobody bothers with that now. They're so overwhelmed with ships coming in, there'll never get around to you. You're on your own."

"How do they know we're not bringing fever ashore?" Collins asked.

"You're not, are you?" the steering man asked cautiously.

"No."

"Then don't worry about it."

"We've got a wounded man below."

"Wounded?"

"Shot in the chest a few weeks ago. He's been hanging on, but I'm not sure he'll make it much longer," Merriman said.

"I don't want to hear any more about it. Take him ashore, if you've a mind. Good luck finding a doctor. If there are any about, they're probably gone to the diggings." With that, they shoved away from the side of the ship and rowed away toward a steamer that was slowly churning toward the anchorage.

"I can't believe we were that lucky," Collins said when they were out of earshot.

"Yeah. Let's get Stark and be gone from this ship before some official shows up to stop us."

The four of them hacked away the caulking from the sealed door to the main deck, carried Stark up on a hatch cover and placed him in the one remaining boat. Collins estimated the mate had lost at least a third of his body weight.

"From the looks of that town, there may not be any decent drinking water," Collins said as he and Louis wrestled a small keg into the boat. They also brought up the remaining half-keg of rum from Merriman's cabin. "Judging from the prices those ferrymen wanted, we better take everything we can use or sell that the crew didn't abscond with."

The Chinese cook ran back and forth, retrieving some small food items from the galley, along with all the pots and pans and utensils he could fit into a canvas sack. "Maybeso get job as cook in town," he smiled.

Lastly, Collins dropped in a bag containing the powder, shot, and caps that Louis had stolen for him. He'd been carrying Malloy's pistol, loaded, since Cape Horn.

"That's about it," Merriman said, taking one last look around.

They hoisted the boat by the double blocks, swung it outboard on the davits, and lowered it. Merriman and Collins took the oars and pulled away, weaving their way among the jumble of anchored craft. Tattered sails still hung from some of the masts, as if the crews had abandoned them in a great hurry.

Collins looked back at the stout bark that had carried them so far and through so many perils. He had formed an attachment for the ship that had been his home for the past six months. There were times when he'd cursed it and feared it and been completely baffled by its incomprehensible rigging. But he had come to know it intimately and to appreciate the beauty of its design—a design that gave it life-sustaining qualities. It was the latest point in many generations of seafaring evolution. He was glad he'd managed to capture several dozen sketches of the bark in her working environment. Yet it was like taking final leave of an old friend.

They beached the boat on the sand, next to a long, narrow wharf, covered their belongings with a sail, and stepped out. Both of them staggered like drunken men as the earth seemed to heave up and down under them. They quickly sat down on the ground until their land legs returned.

The two Chinese men were afflicted the same way but burst into laughter, chattering in their native tongue as they staggered up against the bow of the boat for several minutes. Then, with much bowing and hand-shaking, Louis and the cook took their leave, each bent under two large sacks as they disappeared into the crowds of men on the waterfront.

Collins and Merriman hoisted Stark on the hatch cover and set off up the hill, attracting little attention. After a few inquiries of the passersby, only one man offered vague directions to a hospital tent set up at the top of a hill. It turned out to be a large, wooden platform with a roof and canvas sides that could be rolled up or down. Cots were arranged in rows. Collins saw no walking patients being treated. Apparently, only the seriously ill or injured need apply.

They set their burden down and waited to get the attention of a woman at a small table who was apparently doing the paperwork for two men who appeared to be doctoring. She took their names and that of Abel Stark, and twenty minutes later she got the attention of one of the doctors. "Gunshot wound, upper left chest," she said, handing him a slip of paper. "Several weeks ago," she added.

The doctor looked up sharply, then squatted and opened Stark's coat, shirt, and peeled off the cotton bandage to reveal the bullet hole that had begun to heal shut. The wound was red and angry-looking where it had mortified. The doctor put a hand to Stark's throat, then pressed open an eyelid.

"You could have saved yourselves the trouble," he said in a weary voice. "This man's dead." He stood up. "There's a hardware and undertaker at the foot of the hill, if you want a box to bury him in," he said, turning away.

"I never saw such a place," Collins said as they looked at each other.

"Like any other place that's crammed with humanity, life's cheap here," Merriman said.

"Yeah, but apparently nothing else is," Collins said as they picked up each end of the hatch cover with Stark's body. "Look at some o' these prices . . . eggs, four dollars a dozen . . . ale, eight dollars a bottle. These people are out of their minds. Who's going to pay that?"

"Whoever wants or needs them bad enough. The law of supply and demand. None of that stuff is produced here. It has to be hauled about as far as we came."

They carried the body back to the waterfront. Hundreds of men were swarming up and down the sandy streets, scurrying around like ants on huge, sandy ant hills. The whole town was in a building frenzy. The staccato rapping of hammers sounded everywhere. Workmen slid sections of prefabricated walls off the backs of wagons and stood them in place while others nailed them. Barkers in front of brick or tent gambling halls and saloons were adding their raucous calls to the general din.

"Where you going?" Merriman asked as Collins passed the hardware.

"To the boat. Stark spent all his life at sea. You don't suppose he'd want to be buried ashore, do you? Besides, why buy a coffin and try to find a spot to put him? Wait till tonight, and we'll bury him in the Bay."

"Good idea."

As they worked through a crowd of workmen toward the boat, Collins abruptly set his end of the pallet down and drew his pistol. "Get away from that boat!"

Two men jumped back, dropping the half keg of rum as they sprinted away.

"Going to be a problem securing this boat," Collins said, shoving the gun under his belt.

"Let's sell it, as is."

"We may have to use it to get upriver to Sacramento, if steamer passage is as dear as everything else."

"Yeah. I've still got some money from home, but, at these prices, it won't last long."

While they'd been gone, a fast-ebbing tide had set the boat down on a mud flat.

Later that day, the tide returned and refloated the boat, and, just before sunset, they rowed a half mile beyond the last anchored ship.

"You reckon Stark had any kin we should try to notify?" Merriman asked as they rested on their oars.

"Never heard him mention any," Collins said. "It's a shame. A man like Stark deserves to be remembered by someone."

"Live hard, die hard," Merriman said. "He asked for no quarter and gave none."

"You and I will remember him. We owe him our lives," Collins said. "Hadn't been for his seamanship, we'd all be at the bottom right now."

"He was one helluva man."

By mutual consent, they tapped the half-empty rum keg and poured two tin cups full.

"I doubt the sea will know his like again."

"To Abel Stark, an extraordinary sailor!"

They tapped their cups together and drank as the westering sun turned to a red disk in the haze.

Then, tying the boat's thirty-pound anchor to Stark's ankles, they tipped the hatch cover and the body splashed into the Bay.

"Sleep well."

They sat silently for a moment with their own thoughts; Collins musing on all that had gone before and what might yet be ahead for them.

"Well, that's it. Let's get back before it gets dark."

They pulled the boat up to shore under the protection of a long wharf to spend the night. Each of them took one end of the twenty-foot boat and slept under the sail in their clothes. Having spent several months in a comfortable bunk, Collins slept poorly. But they'd determined this was the best way to save money and protect what they now considered their property, since they'd scraped the name *Inverness* off the gunwale. Collins realized quickly that here, where the booming population had quickly outrun any external law, it was every man for himself to take what he wanted and defend what he had.

During the following week, they discovered that the new town's main businesses, besides putting up new buildings, were hotels, restaurants, saloons, gambling and dance halls, and brothels. Between eating, drinking, and whoring, at least three-fourths of the male population was trying to get out of town to the mines, many of them swindling each other in the process.

In the heat of mining fever, one merchant, who found himself overstocked with metal pans, salted the dirt in front of his store with gold dust. Then, making a public display of trying his luck at panning in the street, he used a tub of water to wash out a pan of rich dust. Before the hour was out, he'd sold three-hundred pans at $2 each, a slight mark-up from the ten cents they normally cost, and the street looked like a colony of prairie dogs had been at work.

Jobs at both skilled and unskilled labor paying $10, $20, and even $30 a day went begging as everyone fled to the interior rivers and creeks to pick up a fortune.

Collins and Merriman watched all of this in amazement. As more ships arrived from the East Coast, the lightermen were kept busy ferrying cargoes ashore to be stored in a large customs house where the merchants to whom the goods were consigned had to pay a duty to claim them. This was the main source of income for the growing city, Collins discovered. They watched draymen haul goods of all kinds up from the waterfront—barrels of flour and pork, boxes of needles, woolen clothing, thousands of yards of canvas, bundles of shovels, axes, and picks, wheels of cheese, canned oysters, boots, blankets, mirrors, furniture. The list seemed endless, as if they were trying to build and furnish an entire new civilization overnight.

Drunken shouts, singing, and gunfire punctuated the night hours as the saloons and gambling halls never closed their doors to the newly rich, the fresh arrivals, and those returning poor from the diggings to drown their sorrows.

Steamers had just begun to run upriver to Sacramento a few weeks earlier. The one-way ticket for the approximately one hundred miles was $300, and the boats were jammed every trip. Many Argonauts were buying mules to pack their gear and were tramping overland with only vague directions, or hand-drawn maps hastily printed and sold for $10 each.

They finally decided to sail across the Bay, then row their boat through the tules upriver, camping along the way. It would be hard, wet, mosquito-ridden work, Collins knew. But their voyage around the Horn had tempered them to such hardship.

Chapter Twenty-Four

Trevor Sloan scanned the latest issue of *Shipping News*, the thrice-weekly sheet that was printed in a valiant attempt to keep up with the volume of ships, passengers, and cargo that came flooding into San Francisco Bay on every incoming tide.

From the time of his arrival four weeks before, he'd wondered how he would know Collins and Merriman in this seething population of strangers. All he had were their names and a vague description—Merriman, lean and muscular, about thirty, and six feet tall; Collins, several inches shorter, dark-skinned, and green-eyed. Hardly a precise guide.

Three times a week for a month Sloan had shown up early at the shipping office to snatch a copy of the paper before the ink was even dry. But the name *Inverness* had not appeared. To see if it had already arrived in port, he'd rented a skiff and rowed out among the many anchored vessels he couldn't see from the hastily constructed docks. There were all types of craft, many of them hardly seaworthy, but none that bore the rig or the name he sought.

He tossed the paper onto the counter with a sigh and stepped to the door of the shipping office and looked once again toward the Bay where masts and spars crowded the waterfront as thickly as a forest of leafless trees. By his calculations, the bark would have had ample time to arrive here since that day he'd read about the mutiny in the *Charleston Courier*. But a journey around the Horn was a very risky venture—not a sure thing at all. His quarry might be somewhere at the bottom of the sea at this moment, making his long quest moot. Then, again, a pirated ship might very well be sailing under a different name. Of course. Why hadn't he thought of that possibility before? An outlaw crew would certainly not report the correct name of their vessel when they anchored. He could not recall seeing any lettering that had been removed or painted over. But the *Inverness* might be here by now, reported under some other name.

He resolved to make another inspection. It was only nine-thirty in the morning—several hours before he had to report to work. Since his arrival, destitute and hungry, riding on a stolen ticket, he'd been working as a bartender at the Argonaut Hotel. There was no shortage of jobs or money in this town, but the prices of everything were inflated, so his generous salary, plus many tips, was barely adequate to provide him with a room and meals, with only a little left over. But as soon as he could save enough, he had purchased a used Colt .44 with holster and ammunition. He carried the gun wherever he went, both for his own protection in this horde of wild-living transients, but mainly to be ready when he encountered the killers of his son.

Under a pier he found a twelve-foot boat with a splintered gunwale that appeared to be washed up from somewhere. After bailing out the rainwater, he took command and rowed the light hull out to make a systematic sweep of all the anchored ships. The tide was ebbing, and all the vessels had swung around on their cables and were pointing at the new city. Just over an hour later his breath caught in his throat as the name *Inverness* appeared. He stopped rowing and gaped at the large lettering arcing across the transom just above his head. Beneath the name, in smaller letters, Boston was shown as the home port. There had been no attempt to hide her name at all, even though she'd never shown up in the *Shipping News*. Perhaps she had just arrived. He rowed carefully around her, looking up for signs of life. But it appeared as deserted as most of the other vessels in the harbor.

"Ahoy, the *Inverness!*"

No answer. He hallooed twice more with the same result.

Satisfied that no one was aboard, he pulled alongside and struggled up over the rail, banging his shin painfully in the process. He tied off his boat, then with one hand on his gun, explored the ship fore and aft. Except for the galley, which appeared to have been plundered, he found everything just as he imagined it had been when the crew was aboard, even to the furled sails. The longboats were missing, so he strongly suspected the outlaw crew had abandoned the vessel with no intention of returning.

He rummaged through the captain's cabin, finding at first only the usual personal items. Then he opened a drawer and caught his breath at the sight of the big logbook. He held it to the light and leafed through its pages. The early notations were in a neat, flowing script, but those were followed by entries in two distinctly different hands, one after the other. Reading the brief entries, he quickly found out why as his imagination filled in the details of the turmoil the log recorded. He could visualize the transportation and delivery of the captured slaves, the bloodless mutiny, the deaths of two sailors, one by violence, the weeks of storms off the Horn, the clash of the two mates, resulting in one death and one severe wounding. Finally he found the name he sought. Rob Merriman had taken command of the ship. The dated entries stopped abruptly three days previously.

He closed the book and stared at its water-stained cover. So they were here. Where had they gone? They must have at least a three-day head start. Maybe they hadn't started for the gold fields yet. He tried to put himself in their position. As a member of a mutinous crew who would be jailed and tried for piracy, if caught, what would he have done? He would have brought the ship into port just before dark, and abandoned it with all haste, disappearing somewhere ashore. No wonder the *Inverness* had not been reported in the *Shipping News*. No one knew she was here.

He was about two hundred yards away when a portion of the *Inverness* again came into view among the anchored vessels. He suddenly backed water at the sight of two figures moving about on deck. He swiveled the little rowboat around and dug in his oars. If it was Merriman and Collins, here was a perfect, isolated place to confront them.

But he was too late. By the time he wove through the obstacles and reached the bark, the longboat with the two men was thirty yards away and heading toward shore. Sloan rested on his oars, gasping for breath. There was no way he could catch them, but he got a good look at their faces. The man rowing was facing him, and the shorter one, with black hair and dark skin, turned back to look at the *Inverness*. Sloan fixed their features in his mind; they fit the descriptions of the two he wanted. Were they living aboard? Not if they were wanted by the law. Likely they'd only returned for something forgotten. The logbook? His chest still heaving from exertion, he swung the boat around with the oars. He would pursue them ashore. In order to kill them both, he would have to take them by surprise, and he would have to be quick. But to make his revenge complete, he had to let them know, at the moment they were to die, who he was and why they were being shot. It would have to be carefully timed. And, if any witnesses were present, he would have somehow to claim self-defense. He suspected that murder, even in this lawless town, would have unpleasant consequences.

He rammed the damaged rowboat ashore and hurried up the hill after the two leisurely moving figures, trying to keep them in sight in the milling foot traffic. They entered an eating place, and Sloan, trying to calm his excitement, waited patiently on the street for them, a plan formulating in his mind.

A half hour later they emerged. Immediately assuming a brisk walk, he approached them. "Here ya go, gents," he said, holding out two of several brass tokens he carried in his pocket. "Each good for one free drink at the barroom of the Argonaut Hotel."

"Oh, thanks," Merriman said, reaching out for them.

"Here are two more for you," Sloan added, extending his hand toward Collins.

"What's the catch?" Collins asked suspiciously.

"Just a promotion to stir up business and edge out the competition. Lots of saloons in this town. The Argonaut had these made up when I started as a bartender there a few weeks ago. But I'll let you in on a little secret. . . ." He glanced around and lowered his voice conspiratorially. "Better use these tokens tonight, because the bosses are going to stop honoring them tomorrow. We've got about all the business we can handle. We're packing them in every night now."

Sloan affected his most jovial manner as he moved away. "I'll be tending bar tonight. Hope to see you there."

"Thanks, mister. We'll take you up on this," Collins said.

Sloan moved off down the street, ostensibly seeking other customers. He turned a corner and stopped, his heart pounding. He had been so close. What if they didn't show up tonight? He should have gunned them down then and there. But, no. It was broad daylight on the open street. And they were both armed and sober. He'd ply them with free drinks tonight, and, when they left the hotel bar, he'd follow and surprise them in the dark when their reactions were slowed. They were practically in his grasp. He could almost taste the revenge that would be his.

Sloan's anticipation was fearful. His stomach allowed for no lunch, and, at three o'clock that afternoon, he gave up an attempt to nap. He sat in the Argonaut's barroom and sipped a beer, hoping to calm his nerves as he eyed the few early customers who drifted in and out.

A sudden thought struck him, and he cursed himself for a fool. Why hadn't he been here, watching, at eleven this morning when the barroom opened? The pair might have been here already, cashed in their tokens, and left. No! The gods that control men's destinies could not have been so cruel as to allow that!

He went on duty at four o'clock, just in time to begin catching some of the early supper crowd. It was good to have a little work temporarily to distract his mind.

The Regulator on the back-bar shelf was striking six when a tall, lean man sidled up to the bar and doffed his beaver hat. "A large whisky, suh." He threw back a traveling cape to reveal a black vest and clean white shirt.

Sloan poured the drink and slid the glass toward him, thinking he detected a slight southern dialect.

As the man slipped a five-dollar gold piece from his vest pocket and placed it on the bar, Sloan noted silver cuff links and clean fingernails.

Before Sloan could turn away toward the cash drawer to make change, the man spoke again: "Suh, I believe I know you."

Sloan peered closer at the face. Yellow light from the hanging harp lamp accentuated the long nose and pouches under the eyes. Dark hair was smoothed down over the head and curled a bit long around the ears and high collar. There was a slightly familiar look to the sad, Basset-hound features. "Your name, sir?"

"J. B. Cosworth from Charleston," he replied. "And, if I'm not mistaken, you are Trevor Sloan, master of Lone Oak Plantation."

Sloan looked around quickly, but no one was within earshot. "Yes, I'm Trevor Sloan."

"May I shake your hand, suh? I was a guest at a garden party at your home once. It's good to see a neighbor so far from home."

Sloan gripped Cosworth's lean fingers.

"I was a member of your son's club for a year or so before I decided to follow my destiny to the gold fields," Cosworth continued. "I won't ask why you're here. We all have our reasons, although I would think your . . . uh . . . holdings would have kept a man of your position well occupied."

"You knew my son, Alex?" Sloan asked abruptly.

"Quite well, suh. Even though he was much younger than myself, I'm proud to say I counted him as a true friend." He sipped his whisky while Sloan hesitated, holding the gold piece between his fingers.

"Were you there when . . . at the . . . ?" Sloan couldn't seem to get the words out as he felt his neck and face suffusing with blood.

Cosworth nodded, looking sadder than ever. "Yes, suh, I was a witness to that unfortunate occurrence. In fact, I acted as his second."

Sloan could hardly get his breath. "Tell me . . . exactly

what happened!" He focused hard on the man across the bar.

Cosworth backed up a step, a sudden look of alarm on his lean face. "You didn't . . . you weren't told the whole story?" With a slightly trembling hand he raised the whisky glass to his lips, never taking his eyes from Sloan.

"Tell me every detail of that night!" The barroom had shrunk to the size of Cosworth. Sloan neither heard nor saw anything else.

"I'll start at the beginning," Cosworth said, clearing his throat. Then he proceeded to recreate the fateful night, from the time Merriman saved the octoroon, April, from being run down by the team and wagon, through the long hours of drinking, the fist fight over the girl, the challenge, the duel itself, and finally the chasing of Collins and Merriman into the river.

"You tried to stop it after they both fired and missed?"

"Yes, suh, just as the code requires. But Alexander insisted that he draw blood."

"Was my son . . . intoxicated?"

"Alexander could hold his liquor, suh. It might have affected his judgment, but never his hand or his nerve."

"I asked you if he was drunk!"

"No more than usual, suh."

"You're saying that Alex provoked the duel, and that it was fair in every respect?"

"It's true this Merriman fellow did not want to fight. But I've been a second at several affairs of honor, and I've never seen one that was conducted any better, except perhaps for the shameful attack on the two strangers afterward."

Sloan felt as if someone had kicked him in the stomach. He shook his head negatively, dropping the five-dollar gold piece back on the bar in front of Cosworth who scooped it up, downed his drink, and left, obviously uncomfortable.

Sloan thought he was going to be sick as he stumbled to the end of the bar and leaned weakly on the polished mahogany. All his worst fears had been confirmed. Cosworth had no reason to lie. As much as Sloan hated to admit it, he knew, deep down, what kind of man Alex had grown up to be. In spite of all his and Emily's efforts at rearing the boy, his son had turned out to be an embarrassment to the Sloan name—a drunken, whoring, arrogant hothead. It was a hurt that would never go away because Alex was now forever beyond reform.

He straightened up and took a deep breath. What should he do now? He'd come so far and endured so much on this quest that he could not back down. He had to finish what he'd set out to do, regardless. A Sloan would never be known as a quitter.

He turned his back to the half-dozen customers in the room, drew his pistol, and checked the loads and the action. In spite of the body blow he'd just been dealt, he steeled his resolve. Merriman and Collins would pay for what they'd put him and his family through.

Chapter Twenty-Five

With nothing else to hold them, and their money dwindling quickly, Merriman and Collins planned to leave the hurly-burly of San Francisco the next morning. Shovels, pans, saws, blankets, boots, rope, tent canvas, sacks of beans and corn meal, powder, balls, and caps for their pistols, overalls—everything they could afford and anticipated needing in the diggings was stowed in their longboat under cover of a sail. It was nearly ten o'clock that night before all preparations were complete, and they were just finishing a late supper.

"There's plenty of money circulating in this town . . . mostly dust and nuggets. Not much specie," Merriman remarked as they paid for their supper with a five-dollar gold piece—to the delight of the restaurant owner.

Collins nodded. "And, if we're going to add to that amount of dust, we'll have to get started pretty quick. A Mexican I was talking to yesterday said the rainy season sets in about December."

"We'll have our own share before then," Merriman replied. "And we can spend the bad weather snug in a tent and log cabin in the hills, somewhere near our claim."

"With a good fire going and some good books to read," Collins added, envisioning the virtual paradise to come. He was in a euphoric mood and proposed they adjourn to the barroom of the Argonaut Hotel. "Can't let these go to waste," he added, holding up the brass tokens. "Just a couple of farewell drinks before we head out for the diggings in the morning."

"Remember what happened in Charleston the last time somebody offered us free drinks," Merriman cautioned as they entered the big, crowded saloon on the ground floor of the wooden Argonaut Hotel.

"I know," Collins agreed, shuddering inwardly at the thought of that terrible night. The duel and all that followed to change their lives forever was a result of his having had too much to drink.

"We collect our free drinks, and then we go back to the boat for a good night's sleep," Merriman insisted. "Tomorrow will be a long day."

The room was crowded with customers, and the low rumble of conversation and laughter was punctuated by clinking glassware and the sound of a hurdy-gurdy somewhere in the background. They edged their way to the bar, signaled the middle-aged barkeep. It was the man who'd given them the brass tokens.

"What'll it be, gents?"

Collins ordered a large brandy and Merriman a beer.

Collins knew that good intentions have a way of evaporating like morning fog, but, after his second large brandy, he didn't really care. He raised his glass for a refill, but the bartender was being chided by a customer several feet away. "Gaw dammit, I ordered a Queen Charlotte!" the man bawled. "What's this swill you gave me? Hell, don't you even know how to mix claret and raspberry syrup?" the tipsy voice demanded.

The red-faced bartender took back the drink and poured it out, then set about mixing another, with the drunk giving directions.

Collins reflected that the bartender had probably never worked behind a bar in his life. But a job was a job, and apparently help was extremely hard to get or keep. The barman finally got around to pouring him another brandy.

A minute or two later he was suddenly aware of a stirring in the adjacent gambling hall. Voices were raised, and Collins thought a fight had broken out. But then he heard someone yell: "Fire!" The shout was taken up by others, and a wave of panic began to wash over the crowd as men swept toward the doors.

Collins didn't move as he sipped his drink. "Hell, I don't see anything," he remarked, feeling the calm courage provided by the liquor.

Just then a burly man fought his way through the mass of bodies and reached the bar. "The whole block's ablaze!" he yelled. "Everybody out! The roof's already burning, and the wind is really whipping it!"

Collins turned back to the bar to finish his brandy, ignoring Merriman's tug at his arm and the general stampede around them as everyone vacated the bar, except one drunk who was gulping all the abandoned drinks. As he tipped up his glass, he saw the gray-haired barkeep standing there with a big Colt leveled across the bar at them. "I'm Trevor Sloan of Charleston," he said, his voice trembling. "You murdered my son, Alexander, in a duel."

Collins was stunned, and nobody spoke for the space of a long breath.

"Before you die, I wanted you to know who sent you to hell."

In the second it took Sloan to ear back the hammer on the big gun, Collins was already moving. His shoulder slammed into Merriman. Before they even hit the floor the blast of the Colt's discharge was ringing in his ears.

Collins rolled away, yanking his pistol as he did so. Sloan leaned across the bar to get a clear shot, but Collins fired first from his back—and missed. Sloan yelled and jumped back behind the bar, firing as he went. A slug splintered the wood of the floor perilously close to Collins's head as he and Merriman scrambled to their feet. They raced around the end of the bar, but Sloan was nowhere to be seen. A shot lanced out from behind a stack of whisky barrels, and the two men hit the floor.

The shooting had accelerated the exodus, and the last few men were staggering out as smoke boiled in through the open doors and windows.

They scuttled for cover as another shot nicked the end of the bar. Sloan was firing blindly, not exposing himself. Collins reached over the bar and fired without aiming. His slug ricocheted off a brass beer tap and shattered the mirror behind the bar. Bottles and shards of glass came crashing down.

Collins crawled around the end of the bar, hoping to get a clear shot. Smoke and flame lanced out from between the barrels, and he felt a bullet tug at his loose shirt. He fired two quick shots at the barrels, but only succeeded in seeing two jets of amber liquid come pouring from the punctured kegs.

Merriman fired twice, with no better results.

The room was filling with smoke from the rapidly spreading fire. The ceiling was blazing, and a burning piece of débris ignited the spilled liquor. Flame ran across the floor and behind the bar, engulfing the whisky barrels with a *whoosh*. They heard Sloan scrabbling through the broken glass to an open door behind the bar. Merriman fired two quick shots and started after him, but Collins grabbed his arm. "Let him go. Let's get out of here!" Sweat was bursting from every pore as the room became an oven.

But a last look showed the bartender, face-down on the floor in the open doorway, blood running from his neck or head. "You got him!" Collins yelled.

Merriman hesitated. "He may still be alive. We can't leave him to burn up!"

Collins followed as Merriman vaulted over the bar. Broken glass crunched under their feet. Collins kicked the gun out of the unconscious man's hand. Each of them grabbed an arm. On hands and knees, they began dragging Sloan toward the nearest door at least a hundred feet away. It looked more like a hundred yards, Collins thought, as he gasped for air close to the floor. Sloan's limp weight felt like a two-hundred pound sack of wet sand. They paused every few feet to rest. Collins could only suck in super-heated air as he tried to ease his searing lungs and aching muscles. Small pieces of ceiling rained fire on them, scorching holes in their clothes. Merriman batted at his singed hair.

They started again. Seconds became eternity. *Hell could not be worse,* Collins thought. *We can't make it. We've got to give up and save ourselves.* He felt a strong tug at his boot, and looked with irritated eyes through the smoke to see four men in a human chain, pulling them the last fifteen feet to the door.

Outside, they were helped to a grassy place about a block downhill from the flames. Panting, grimy, and sweating, Collins watched the fearful conflagration lighting up the night as it roared, unchecked, up the hill, consuming everything before it. He wiped the grimy sweat from his face with a shirt sleeve and coughed. "Saving a man who's trying to kill us may not be the smartest thing we ever did."

Merriman was facing the stiff sea breeze, sucking in clean air "We'll deal with him later, if he survives," he replied.

The hillside was teeming with men and a few women, milling about in a distracted manner, some talking, others nursing minor burns and injuries or just staring in apparent stupefaction at the hell that had broken loose to devour their growing town.

Several buckets of water still rested on the ground nearby, as if someone had given up the fight to quench the fire as it grew. Collins tipped up one of the buckets and drank deeply, coughing and choking as the water went up his nose and down his shirt front. He passed the bucket to Merriman, and then sloshed the remainder over their unconscious assailant.

Sloan came to, sputtering, and attempted to sit up. Blood was oozing from the wet, matted hair. Collins watched him warily for any sign of a hostile move. But the fight had gone out of the man, and, in the wavering firelight, he looked much older. Sloan's eyes began to focus, and he looked around, then put a hand tentatively to his head.

"Damned lucky you're not dead," Collins said with little sympathy.

Sloan stared at him.

"I think a bullet grooved the side of your head. Merriman's not a very good shot," Collins said coldly.

"You two killed my Alex." Water was trickling down Sloan's face, and Collins couldn't tell from the sound of his voice if tears might have been mingled with it.

"I didn't mean to kill him," Merriman said with what seemed to Collins unexpected civility. "Your son was forcing the duel. I tried to apologize, but he just kept pressing."

"Where . . . ? How did I get . . . here?" Sloan asked in a tremulous voice, looking around, as if realizing for the first time where he was.

"The two o' them dragged you out, or you'd have been nothing but a hunk o' charred meat by now," a man standing nearby answered, holding out a partially full bottle of whisky to Sloan who still sat on the grass. Sloan took a long swallow, coughed, then struggled to his feet. He moaned and put both hands to his head for several seconds.

Collins was fairly certain Sloan was unarmed, but watched him carefully, nonetheless. He wasn't about to be surprised a second time.

Nothing could be heard for the space of a minute but the murmuring of the spectators around them and the crashing of distant buildings as the voracious flames licked on up the hill, looking for more fuel.

"You saved my life," Sloan said quietly. "And I was trying to kill you."

"I'm sorry about your son," Merriman said. "If I had it to do over, I would have stopped it somehow. It'll haunt me the rest of my life."

"No man who saves an enemy is a murderer," Sloan said.

Collins heard the voice as calm and sane.

"Thank you." Sloan thrust out his hand. Merriman looked surprised but, after a second or two, gripped it.

"My . . . pride got in the way of my reason," Sloan continued haltingly, painfully. "I knew Alexander was wild and reckless. I should have expected it, sooner or later. I. . . ."

"You don't have to say any more," Merriman broke in.

"Yes . . . this is something I have to get out. Maybe that bullet of yours knocked some sense into me. I . . . disguised my frustration and hate as family honor," he muttered hoarsely, struggling to get the words out. "I threw all the blame on two innocent men I didn't even know. Alexander got what he asked for. Maybe it's partially my fault for the way I raised him. . . ." His voice broke, and Collins saw Merriman's pained expression.

"Life is strange," Merriman said, pointing at Sloan's

297

head. "An inch to the right and that bullet would have killed you." He pulled back his blackened shirt collar to reveal the white scar on his neck. "An inch to the left and Alexander's bullet would have killed me."

As if to emphasize his words, stored barrels of blasting powder began to explode in the distance with measured booms like the thunder of cannon.

Chapter Twenty-Six

"Do you realize that we're making the equivalent of an ounce and a half of gold a day?" Collins asked as he and Merriman paused to drink from the dipper of a water bucket being passed along the line of workmen. "Twenty-five dollars!" He shook his head in disbelief at the exorbitant wages being paid by merchants to clean up and start rebuilding.

Most of the town, including numerous brick buildings, had been destroyed in the fire. But those merchants and residents directly affected by the disaster seemed more interested in quickly rebuilding than in bemoaning their losses.

"If wages are this high, then you can imagine what men in the digs are finding," Merriman replied. "We need to be on our way tomorrow. Why settle for crumbs, when a whole loaf is out there, waiting to be picked up? You've got to start thinking on a higher level."

The autumn breeze off the Bay was chilling the sweat on his back as Collins pulled on his gloves and turned back to removing the stinking, blackened timbers from the remains of a building. As he did so, his eyes fastened on the slim figure of a woman at the edge of a small group of spectators. He paused to look. Women here were outnumbered at least ten to one, he figured, so he was finding it a rare treat just to look at one. Especially one this attractive. She was dark, maybe Mexican he guessed.

He paused in his work to smile at her. She nodded. "This is where I used to work," she said, indicating the pile of blackened rubble. "I was a cook." She looked squarely at him, and their eyes locked. He was startled to see she had blue eyes. She looked somehow familiar. Something about those eyes and the shape of the nose.

"Clay Collins?" Her mouth fell open as she stared at him.

He was jarred at the sound of his name. "Who . . . ?" Then the face clicked into his memory with a rush of pleasure. "Lisa? Lisa Sizemore!"

"Yes."

Instinctively, he opened his arms, and they embraced warmly.

"God, it's good to see you," she breathed in his ear.

He backed away, suddenly embarrassed. "I . . . I'm all sweaty and dirty," he stammered.

"I don't care. It's so good to see someone from home all this way out here."

"I can't believe it's you," he said. "I didn't think I'd ever see you again. That night we spent at your inn during the snowstorm . . . it seems like years ago, instead of only ten months."

"I've still got that charcoal sketch you drew of me," she said proudly. "The thought of seeing you again was the only thing that kept me going through a lot of trouble since then," she added, reddening slightly.

She was dressed in a white blouse and a full skirt, and her hair was cut differently than Collins remembered it. And she looked thinner, older. Maybe it was because he hadn't seen many women in nearly a year, but she looked beautiful.

"You remember my friend, Rob Merriman?"

"Oh, yes." She offered her hand.

"Where can we talk? We've got a lot of catching up to do.

Rob, tell the boss I'm off the job for a while," he added as he pulled off his gloves and tucked them under his belt.

"Come to the gold fields with us," Collins urged the next day as the three of them sat in a makeshift tent restaurant. The afternoon wind gusted off the Bay, billowing the top of the big tent. "After all, you were burned out of your job as a cook."

"I could do something else. Sewing. Taking in washing. The pay is so good here, I hate to leave it. After all, I'm alone in the world now and have to make as much money as I can while this boom lasts," she answered, looking at him with those penetrating blue eyes.

"I hate to see you as a washerwoman. You'll develop big muscles, and your hands will be all coarse and red."

"How can you even think of trying to protect me, after hearing what all I've already been through?" she laughed.

"That's exactly why," he retorted.

"From what I hear these miners saying, it must be even harder in the gold fields. And there is no assurance of finding enough to even pay expenses," she added with indisputable logic.

"You surely didn't come all this way to work for someone else for wages, did you?" Collins asked. He threw up his hands in mock exasperation. "Woman, you've already seen the elephant. Go for the whole circus! See it out to the end. We're only a few miles from the nearest diggings. Let's go before all the creeks and rivers are staked."

"What would they think of a woman in the gold fields with all those men?" she mused, obviously bending in his direction.

"This is a new society. The old rules of behavior don't apply here. Nobody cares what anyone else does, unless there's some harm in it. I'd bet my unfound gold that your parents would be out there, panning, if they were here. Why do you think they started on this trek? They weren't content with the way things were at home. They'd want you to finish their dream."

He stopped talking and noticed Merriman sitting back, sipping his coffee and eyeing the two of them in silence, obviously not wanting to add his opinion.

She was silent for several seconds, first regarding him frankly, then dropping her eyes. Collins thought he'd never seen a woman as lovely. But she wasn't just a delicate mountain flower. She apparently had the toughness and resiliency of an India rubber ball.

"Let me get my things," she finally consented, then smiled. "I guess living along the creeks couldn't be much worse than being in that rat-infested boarding house."

"We'll pick you up about sunrise."

Epilogue

The trio tried four different locations before staking a claim on a remote creek that showed consistently good color. After several weeks of ten-hour days wading in icy water and shoveling sand and gravel into their rocker, it became apparent they wouldn't get rich on the gold dust they washed out. But it was more than they'd found anywhere else, and was sufficient to pay expenses.

A few months later, in April of 1850, all fifty-seven inhabitants of the mining camp of Knock 'em Stiff turned out to witness the joining in Holy Matrimony of two dark-skinned people from the hills of Tennessee. Everyone agreed that Clayburn Collins and Lisa Sizemore made a handsome couple. A sometime preacher shed his miner's overalls and donned a tail coat and top hat to perform the brief ceremony. He then led the way out of a drizzling rain to the refreshments in a large tent where he proceeded to get roaring drunk. Old-timers who'd been there for more than six months were unanimous in stating they'd never seen a party like the one that followed.

As soon as the weather faired up, the happy couple left their partner, Rob Merriman, to work the claim, and departed on two mules for San Francisco. There, the groom secured a lucrative job as an engraver for Baldwin & Company, a private firm that was about to begin minting gold coins.

Several weeks later, Trevor Sloan stood on the San Francisco wharf, waiting for a boat to take him to the steam packet in the Bay. He clutched a letter in his hand from his beloved wife, Emily, in Charleston, begging him to come home. His memory of recent events was rather spotty, and he sometimes had trouble pulling up the mental image of her face. But it was with a deep sense of satisfaction and happiness that he read how she had recently recovered from her long illness, and was working with Jason Biggers to manage his estate.

Time seemed slightly out of joint since his head injury, but several months had passed rather quickly, and yesterday this letter had arrived on a mail packet, recalling to mind many of the details of his life in South Carolina and the plantation he owned.

He put his fingers to the healed wound on his scalp. The scar was still sensitive to the touch where a bullet had plowed a furrow. But all that was behind him now—all the destructive hatred that he'd allowed to eat away at his insides. It had burned itself out just as the old San Francisco had burned away. He longed to turn his back on the noise and commotion of this new booming town and get some peace and quiet. Perhaps time and rest would put his life back into a familiar, comfortable pattern once again.

"You ready to shove off, mister?" the boatman asked, holding the boat next to the wharf.

Trevor Sloan nodded, slipped the letter into his pocket, and stepped down the ladder to begin his long journey home.

Author's Note

Nearly everyone loves a mystery. This may partially explain why books and articles continue to be written about an obscure group of racially mixed people whose origins are lost in the mists of the southern Appalachian mountains.

This group, known as Melungeons, exhibit characteristics of both Caucasian and Indian. Beyond this obvious fact, hardly anyone seems to agree on who they are or where they came from. Even the name, *Melungeon,* is of uncertain origin. It could derive from a French term meaning "mixture," or a Greek word meaning "dark," or possibly from some other language altogether.

French explorers first encountered these dark-skinned people in the 1690s, living in the mountains of what is now east Tennessee. Although they had Caucasian features, their skin color ranged from brown to bronze to olive to nearly white. And some of them had blue eyes and reddish hair. But, more amazingly, they spoke outdated Elizabethan English, practiced a form of Christianity, and all had British surnames such as Collins, Gibson, Goins, Nash, Sexton, Mullins, Bowling, Sizemore, Hale, Minor, and numerous others.

What do the Melungeons, themselves, say? They have no early written records of their own, because they were mostly illiterate until the late 19th and early 20th Centuries. Their only oral tradition indicates they are of Portuguese descent. Many of them have physical features consistent with Mediterranean people, yet how to account for the English names and language?

Articles have been written about them since at least the 1890s, and serious studies have been conducted from the early 1970s. Recently, anthropologists, historians, archaeologists, linguists, and scholars of various disciplines, some of them of Melungeon descent, have undertaken the task of unraveling the tangled threads of the Melungeon past. Since there is so little hard evidence, most of the researchers' efforts to date have resulted in tantalizing speculation.

Far-out theories that they are descendants of a lost tribe of Israel, or of ancient sea-faring Phoenicians, or Romanian Gypsies have pretty well been discounted by serious scholars, even though they admit that the much-diluted blood of these ancient peoples could still flow in the veins of modern Melungeons.

One of the most popular theories is that they are descendants of the lost colony of Roanoke who gradually mixed with one or more of the small East Coast Indian tribes such as the Croatan, Lumbee, Powhatan, Hatteras, Pamunkey, Catawba, Chickahominy, or even the more numerous Creek and Cherokee. Some of these tribes have become extinct or lost their tribal identities through epidemic diseases and intermarriage.

More than one hundred men, women, and children mysteriously vanished from an English colony on Roanoke Island, along the North Carolina coast between 1588 and 1590. A supply ship, returning many months later than expected from England, found the colonists gone, and their cabins and part of their log stockade torn down. If a massacre had occurred, evidence of it, such as bones or bodies, were not found. Some discarded possessions were scattered around. The word "Croatoan" was carved on a post. The ship's captain took this to mean that they had taken refuge with a friendly Indian tribe of that name on an island some fifty miles south. Severe storms prevented him from sailing to the island, and he quickly abandoned the search and sailed away to the Caribbean on other business. No trace of the colonists was ever discovered. Many think they intermarried with the Indians and gradually migrated inland over time.

During the 1500s, the English, Spanish, and French were all competing fiercely for a foothold in the New World. Today, much of the detail of this period in American history is overlooked or generally forgotten. But expeditions sent out from all three countries raided and burned each other's settlements, killing and enslaving the inhabitants, sometimes with the reluctant help of treacherous native tribes. The three powers fought each other for decades from Florida to the Chesapeake Bay. In 1566, Pedro Menendez de Aviles planted a settlement named Santa Elena, on what is now Parris Island, South Carolina. From here he ordered Juan (or Joao) Pardo, possibly a Portuguese in Spanish employ, to lead a force of soldiers inland on a march of exploration. They eventually reached the area around present-day Knoxville, Tennessee before turning back. During this march of several months, Pardo planted a series of four or five forts between eastern Tennessee and coastal South Carolina. Almost immediately the soldiers who manned these forts clashed with local Indian tribes. Within a few short years all the forts were abandoned. In addition, the three hundred settlers in Santa Elena, under attack by the French and their Indian allies, withdrew to Saint Augustine, Florida in 1576.

Current theory has it that an unknown number of Spanish soldiers or colonists mingled their blood with that of the Indians during this period. The Spanish and the Portuguese themselves are the product of considerable cultural and racial mixing (Moors, Jews, Turks, Basques) for centuries, stretching back at least to the time of the Roman Empire. A number of modern Melungeons are predisposed to particular medical conditions that are common among Mediterranean people, adding to the strong circumstantial case that the Melungeons have roots in that part of the world.

Vastly oversimplified, then, Melungeons are probably the *product* of English, Indian, and Spanish/Portuguese (with the racial mixtures each of these broad groups brought with them).

Instead of being a "racial island" as some historians dubbed them early on, the people called Melungeons are really only one stage in the more or less continuous blending of the various types of the human species since the beginning of time. It is a mixing that is still going on as Melungeons are slowly being assimilated into the general population.

Scots-Irish and English immigrants began settling the region in numbers in the late 1700s and early 1800s, and quickly outnumbered the Melungeons who were noticeably different from themselves. These later arrivals coveted the land occupied by Melungeons, and the Tennessee Constitutional Convention of 1834 took up the question of these racially mixed people, declaring them "free persons of color," lumping them with all other dark-skinned people, other than Negro slaves. Census-takers identified them as "mulattos" or "free persons of color", abbreviating this as "fc" or "fpc" after their names. This designation meant that they were deprived of the right to vote, barred from public education, could not testify in court against a Caucasian and, most importantly of all, could not own land. This allowed the newer settlers to move onto Melungeon land, and the

Melungeons were gradually forced to retreat from the more fertile valleys and coves to the mountains. Most were very poor, keeping to themselves and living off the mountains by hunting, gathering wild fruits and roots, growing and preserving food, occasionally moonshining or counterfeiting. Some of the men took outside jobs for wages, such as boatmen on the rivers, herdsmen, or lumbermen.

The Melungeon characters—Clayburn Collins, and the family of Lisa, Vincent and Madeline Sizemore—I have created for this novel are purely my own invention, and are not based on any historical persons.

Tim Champlin, born John Michael Champlin in Fargo, North Dakota, graduated from Middle Tennessee State University and earned a Master's degree from Peabody College in Nashville, Tennessee. Beginning his career as an author of the Western story with *Summer of the Sioux* in 1982, the American West represents for him "a huge, ever-changing block of space and time in which an individual had more freedom than the average person has today . . . For those brave, and sometimes desperate souls who ventured West looking for a better life, it must have been an exciting time to be alive." Champlin has achieved a notable stature in being able to capture that time in complex, often exciting, and historically accurate fictional narratives. He is the author of two series of Western novels, that concerned Matt Tierney who comes of age in *Summer of the Sioux* and who begins his professional career as a reporter for the Chicago *Times-Herald* covering an expeditionary force venturing into the Big Horn country and the Yellowstone, and Jay McGraw, a callow youth who is plunged into outlawry at the beginning of *Colt Lightning*. There are six books in the Matt Tierney series and with *Deadly Season* a fifth featuring Jay McGraw. In all of Champlin's stories there are always unconventional plot ingredients, striking historical details, vivid characterizations of the multitude of ethnic and cultural diversity found on the frontier, and narratives rich and original and surprising. His exuberant tapestries include lumber schooners sailing the West Coast, early-day wet-plate photography, daredevils who thrill crowds with gas balloons and the first parachutes, Tong Wars in San Francisco's Chinatown, Basque sheepherders, and the Penitentes of the Southwest, and are always highly entertaining. *Swift Thunder* is his latest title.